Palmetto Boy

D.A. Jobe

TIMBER GHOST PRESS

Palmetto Boy

Palmetto Boy is a work of fiction. Names, places, and incidents either are products of the author's imagination or are used fictitiously. Any resemblance to actual events, locales, or persons, living or dead, is entirely coincidental.

All rights reserved. No part of this book may be reproduced in any form or by any electronic or mechanical means, including information storage and retrieval systems, without permission in writing from the publisher, except by reviewers, who may quote brief passages in a review.

Copyright © 2026

Published by Timber Ghost Press

Printed in the United States of America

Edited by: Beverly Bernard

Cover Art and Design by: Greg Chapman

Interior Design: Timber Ghost Press

Print ISBN: 979-8-9925767-3-3

www.TimberGhostPress.com

CONTENTS

To Steve.

1

SCENE OF THE CRIME

1982

Lady's saddle was on backwards, her legs tangled up with Phantom's. Horses were lined up on the living room carpet, toppled over like dominoes. Obi Wan Kenobi lay beside them with his legs in a split, like he'd been made to ride, but his legs didn't bend that way. No horses on Tatooine.

Eleven-year-old Alane Jannell stood frozen in the doorway, A/C from inside the house escaping into the humid September afternoon.

"Move!" Her little brother, Philip, shoved past her and she grabbed for him. He stopped short when he saw the toys on the living room floor, which used to have furniture but didn't anymore, and had been empty when they'd left for school that morning. Now it looked like a playroom. Puzzle pieces dumped out of the box, Matchbox cars crashed into the wall, crisscrossing tracks in the beige carpet showing they'd been rolled into each other. Stuffed animals, action figures, books. A toy debris field.

"It wasn't me," Philip said, sweat dripping down his pale, freckled face.

"Shh." A jittery feeling started in Alane's stomach. Someone had been in here. Played with their toys.

Might still be inside!

She listened hard over the blood pounding in her ears and heard scratching at the back door; Blackie wanting in. There was a sharp tang of cat box odor in the air.

Philip breathed wetly beside her.

"Come on," she whispered, pulling her brother as she backed out of the house, quietly closing the door.

They raced down the sidewalk to the Gomez's house two doors down, book bags smacking their sides. The sun blazed; thunderclouds bunched in the distance.

"There's someone's in our house!" Alane blurted when Mrs. Gomez opened the door.

The woman's brow creased as she guided them inside. "Are you okay?"

Alane caught her breath, nodded. "Can I call my mom?"

"In here," Mrs. Gomez said, leading the kids to the kitchen. From the caved set of Philip's shoulders, she could tell he was about to cry.

Alane had never been inside the Gomez's house, even though she and Mora, the youngest daughter, played together.

"My mom doesn't like people to come in," Mora told her once, with an *I know it's weird* eye roll.

Now a gust of warm cooking smells hit Alane's nose. Her stomach rumbled. Something bubbled and released steam from a large pot on the stove. The Gomez's countertops were bare and tidy, the table set for three.

Mrs. Gomez handed Alane a handset from a yellow wall phone. Her fingers shook as she dialed. As the phone rang, she braced herself for her mom's exasperated, *WHAT IS IT*?

"Someone broke in the house!" Alane said when her mother picked up. She rushed to describe what she and Philip had seen.

"Was anything taken?" Mom asked.

"I don't know. There were toys *everywhere*." Alane saw movement behind Mrs. Gomez in the kitchen doorway. Mora. The girls looked at each other. Mora's eyes were questioning.

"Let me talk to Mrs. Gomez," Mom said.

"Of course," Mrs. Gomez said into the phone, smiling reassuringly at Alane. "They can stay until you get home."

Mrs. Gomez replaced the receiver. "Your mom is on her way. You can wait in Mora's room."

Alane and Philip followed Mora down a dim hallway. The Gomez house was laid out like Alane's, with a bathroom and three bedrooms. Mora's bedroom was airy and pink and smelled like new clothes. A white canopy bed was neatly made. A fancy doll in a lacy white dress nested between lavender ruffled pillows. Next to the wall was a doll-sized crib, highchair, and dresser. A long shelf high on the wall held a row of dolls with fine, frilly dresses and shiny black shoes.

Alane stared at the dolls, and Philip wandered over to the window to look outside. He pushed past the ruffled curtains to part the blinds. The light outside was fading as the storm moved in.

Alane turned to see her friend pushing the doll from the bed at her. "You can hold her," Mora said.

The doll's body was hard and rigid, and it stared at the ceiling with wide blue eyes framed by spidery lashes. Alane held it stiffly, afraid to drop it. "What's her name?"

"Linda." Mora pointed at a doll at one end of the shelf and named them all down the line. "Odalys, Cindy, Molly..."

Philip walked over to study the doll in Alane's arms, reached to touch the delicate dress. Mora blocked him. "Don't. You'll get her dirty."

Mora took the doll from Alane and turned her over, pulled a plastic ring in her back.

I like to be picked up, the doll said, the *up* more of a wheezy creak as the string rewound.

Mora placed Linda gently in the cradle, tucking a little quilt around her. "I'm only allowed to play with one at a time," she said.

Odalys, Cindy, and Molly's shiny eyes seemed sad now to Alane. What if she could only pick one of her model horses to play with at a time? That would be hard.

Alane toed off her sneakers and crawled on top of the bed with Mora, sinking into the comforter, like into a fluffy cloud. Philip explored the room, a girl's habitat of breakable, mirrored, ceramic things, then he went back over to the window.

"What happened?" Mora said.

"Somebody broke in our house," Alane said, her voice speeding up as she described the toys scattered around. *Her living room was a* crime *scene now*.

"I see a police car," Philip shouted.

The girls hurried over to look, then ran to the living room, leaping on the couch to see out the window behind it. The squad car pulled into the Jannell's driveway, lights flashing. Up and down the street, neighbors came to their windows. Luis and his mother, neighbors from across the street, peered out their screen door. The two houses next to them were unpainted gray stucco. No windows and doors yet; just open rectangles, dark eyes watching. No sod had been laid yet. The lots were littered with construction rubble, pink puffs of insulation, and crushed coral rock.

Headlights appeared down the street, Mom coming in her beige Datsun.

"Come on," Alane said.

The kids rushed out to the Gomez's front step, watching as Alane's mother in her work outfit with her Jewelcor name badge got out of her car and met the policeman at the door. The adults were too far away for the kids to hear their conversation. Mom let the officer in the house and followed him inside. A light clicked on behind the drapes. By now, nosy Luis was standing in his yard watching; Alane glared at him.

Philip grabbed her hand and she squeezed it. "What if the robber's still in there?" Philip whispered.

"The policeman has a gun if he is," Alane said, a buzzing thrill in her stomach.

The minutes ticked by, and her hand in Philip's grip got sweaty and itchy. The squad car's lights spun lazily.

When their mother emerged from the house, Philip broke away and ran across the yard to meet her. She took his hand and walked him back over to Alane. "Are you all right? The policeman checked everywhere in the house and there's no one inside. He wants to ask you some questions."

Alane and Mora exchanged a look. *Ask you some questions* was what cops said before they took you to a mirrored room with a hot light bulb hanging down.

Mom smiled tiredly at Mrs. Gomez who stood on the other side of the screen door. "Thank you."

The officer stood just inside the Jannell's door, pen and notebook out, when the children and their mother walked in. Blackie barked out back.

Alane had seen a real policeman before, in school. Officer Friendly. He hadn't had an actual gun. This policeman did. He didn't look as "friendly" either.

"It looks to me like some kids broke in," he said, gesturing around with his pen. "The back door was unlocked. If I had to guess, I'd say it was probably neighborhood kids who knew your dog and weren't scared. Your mom didn't see any valuables missing," he said, giving the room one last sweeping look. "You folks just move in?"

Alane's gaze slid to her mother, who tucked ash brown hair behind her ears and glanced away. "No," Mom said.

The policeman didn't know there used to be a couch over there by the window. A lamp table. Coffee table. All gone. Just bowls in the carpet where their feet used to be, that mom couldn't vacuum flat.

Somehow without being told, Alane knew not to ask why.

Philip, surrounded by toys, reached down for cardboard 3-D glasses and put them on. He gazed around through the red and blue eye holes. Probably because he didn't want the policeman to see him crying.

Mom said, "Go check your rooms to see if anything's missing." When Philip hesitated, she said, "It's okay."

Even though the overhead light was on, the hallway seemed tunnel-like and shadowy. Alane pushed her door open. Everything that had been in her closet was now outside of it. Board game pieces, stuffed animals, Sunshine family dolls. Otherwise, her room looked like it had this morning. Cluttered, dark, with dirty clothes on the floor, smelling of crayons, Love's Baby Soft, and stale cigarette smoke like the rest of the house.

Most of her model horses were still on the shelf. Just a few gaps from the ones taken to the living room. The choice of horses seemed random; they'd left her favorite ones alone. She turned in a circle. Her gaze caught on the bed, covered with a rose-gray coverlet, and her throat tightened. Blaze was gone.

She'd seen the stuffed brown horse with a white face in a restaurant gift shop last year. Her parents had surprised her with it once they got in the car after eating. Mom had stuffed it inside her purse.

Alane stepped over the toys on the floor and searched under the bed pillows. No Blaze. What else was gone? Fear shot through her. Grandma's ring!

She went to the jewelry box on the dresser. A tiny one-armed plastic ballet dancer sprung up when she opened the lid, twirling in front of an oval mirror as notes from *Somewhere My Love* plinked.

Be here! *Please be here*! Alane dug through costume necklaces, Avon perfume pins, and mood rings for the ring box.

Philip screamed down the hall outside her room. Alane ran to the living room, wide-eyed, afraid the robber had popped out and taken her little brother hostage.

Still in his 3-D glasses, Philip was in their mother's arms, his Little Professor calculator swinging from the strap on his knobby wrist. "My race cars are gone!"

"What?" Mom said, looking upset now instead of just tired.

Philip burst into tears. His two cars ran on an electric track. Their mother held him tight, as if just realizing they'd been robbed.

"Blaze is gone too," Alane said. "And Grandma's ring." She held up the blue velvety box, the little empty slit like a flat mouth, watching her mother's face.

It seemed to sag. Her mom closed her eyes, like her head hurt.

Alane looked at the officer who'd been scribbling in his pad. "They went through my room. Can you dust it for prints?" She'd seen it done on TV.

"I really don't think that's necessary," her mother said.

Not Officer Friendly threw Mom a *kids-ya-gotta-love-'em* smile she didn't return.

He looked down at his pad again. "I'll file a report for your insurance, but I'll be honest, it looks like a bunch of kids got in and were just messing around."

As he let himself out, Mom sighed. "What a mess." She rubbed Philip's back. "Let's pick this stuff up."

Alane put the empty ring box back in the jewelry box and then went around the living room picking up her horses, carefully placing them back on the shelf in her room. Kneeling down to put the toys back in her closet, she wondered who had broken in. She and Philip knew every kid in this neighborhood. Even if they didn't play with them, they knew their faces on the bus. Which of them did this? Could it have been one of her friends? She clutched a saucer from an old tea set to her chest. Tears spilled from her eyes and down her cheeks.

She heard sniffling in the doorway and turned to see Philip, his face red and splotchy.

He whispered, "Palmetto Boy did it."

She shook her head and stared at the Little Professor calculator hanging from his wrist. Her belly tickled.

"There's no Palmetto Boy."

2

HOME ALONE RULES

37 YEARS LATER

Alane joined the checkout line, cart filled with bags of small animal bedding, food, treats, and a plastic cage in a box. Her son Ray held a small cardboard pet carrier and looked through a hole in the side. She couldn't help imagining how that giant blue eyeball must appear to the terrified mouse inside.

Dogs barked from the kennel attached to the pet store and a playroom behind a glass viewing wall. Synthetic lawn turf, tennis balls, dogs running around. In line, the woman in front of her struggled to untangle the leashes of two pugs wrapped around her legs.

The place smelled of mealy pet food, pee, and cleaning solution. They inched slowly through the line.

"You know how I feel about this," Alane said to Ray.

"I'm using my own money."

"That's not the point. I thought we said no pets."

"*You* said that. Papa Wessel said fine."

"Papa Wessel doesn't have to live with it." Their elderly landlord and his wife couldn't refuse Ray anything.

Ray scowled at her. "You can't change your mind now! We're in line!"

He lifted the box and peered in a hole again, and the thick bandage around his elbow bunched under his sleeve, demolishing Alane's resolve. His expression softened. "BeBe already thinks she's coming home with us."

BeBe? Shaking her head in defeat, Alane loaded the cage and supplies on the conveyor belt. It didn't seem right to put the mouse's box down too. *I didn't know pet shops could still sell animals*. When she was a child, pets just showed up. Strays Dad rescued. One time, a skinny puppy, black lab-mix—weren't they all lab-mixes back then?—followed her and her brother, Philip, home from the Mound, a pile of construction debris where they played, and despite Mom's angry, *"No more animals!"* he stayed on. Alane and Philip weren't the most creative at pet names, simply calling him Blackie.

Small animals like BeBe. *Did the store order them on the internet*? She didn't want to think about what this poor mouse had already been through just to get to this store.

A *fancy* mouse, though none of the mice in that glass tank looked any different than the ones in the regular tank to her. This one had white fur and red eyes. Was that the fancy part? BeBe cost $7.99. A bargain for fancy.

As the cashier rang up their items, Alane had a feeling they'd just rescued this mouse from winding up as snake food.

What Ray had *really* wanted was a hamster. But the cage and supplies were more than the boy had budgeted for, so he'd had to scale back on the actual pet. This was one purchase Alane wasn't going to subsidize. She did not approve. Not at all.

The box in Ray's hand shook, and she heard, and almost felt down her spine, the mouse's tiny claws skittering around inside.

Finished at the checkout, they headed toward the exit.

"Wait!" Ray veered off to stop at the Cat Adoption Center by the front door.

"Ray, we don't have time." Alane groaned and trailed reluctantly after him.

A dozen wire cages backed up to a glass window, most of the cats curled up asleep in their sherpa beds. Little cards were tacked on the cages with a Fancy Cat logo. Was every damned animal *fancy* in this place? Where were the Plain cats? The Shabby cats?

BeBe's box dangling from his hand, Ray gazed through the glass at a fluffy black kitten named *Toby*, from what it said on the card. The kitten tracked his finger with intense green eyes before batting clumsily at the glass. "Isn't he cute?"

That little upraised paw and the pink bean pads caused an uncomfortable pressure in Alane's chest, and her gaze dropped to the newspaper lining the cage floor, the words ISLANDS TURNED PINK the only text in focus so that it looked slightly bolded, hovering above the page. She blinked and the newsprint was gone, the cage bottom covered with a faded blue towel.

"Adorable," Alane said, legs unsteady as she turned the cart. "I bet he'd gobble up BeBe with no problem. Come on."

It started raining on the way home, and Alane turned on the wipers, noticing a big mosquito-looking thing—a crane fly, she thought it was called—over the defrost vent, wings down, legs curled like a tiny tumbleweed. It didn't matter how hard you tried to keep the bugs out in South Florida, they always found a way in. This one had probably flown around the windows all night, banging into them, until it died. Good thing she didn't turn on the defrost. It would have blown the thing back at her. She opened the center console for a fast-food napkin but found only straws.

The woman who'd caught BeBe with a fishnet and put her in the box had suggested, unironically, that they keep quiet on the way home, so it would be less traumatic for the mouse. Considering BeBe must have been transported to the store somehow, like through the *mail*, the little thing was probably bulletproof by now. Alane thought of that story she'd loved so much as a kid, *Black Beauty*, and how the horse's owner put him in a pasture next to a train track when he was young so the noise wouldn't spook him after a while.

Did BeBe feel alone after being with all the other mice in the pet store tank? Maybe Ray should have gotten a pair. *No*! *God, no.*

He'd bugged her and her ex-husband, Brad, for years for a pet. She'd originally suggested a fish, but Ray looked at her like that was the equivalent of a pet rock. "You can't play with a fish!"

Alane turned down their street. "I don't want the mouse out of its cage," she warned. "I don't want it running around on the floor. You agreed."

The rain came down harder as they pulled into the driveway behind the Wessel's home, a split level with a detached garage and second-floor apartment where she and Ray lived.

Alane reminded Ray, "I have a catering job tonight. You can have a snack later, and I'll bring dinner home for us."

Nothing from the passenger seat. Ray looked at his phone, pet box on his lap.

"Did you hear me?" she said.

Still no reply.

Shutting off the car she turned to look at him. "You know, it's customary when someone is talking to you to answer back. Even just a grunt of acknowledgement is good."

He grunted.

She gathered her purse and popped the trunk latch. "Home alone rules tonight while I'm gone. Go get Papa Wessel if you can't reach me."

"Okay."

He's twelve. He'll be fine, she thought, grabbing the cage box out of the trunk. She'd been a latchkey kid at his age. She'd been responsible for her little brother every day after school. *It's good for him to be independent.*

But independence could be dangerous. She knew that. She glanced again at Ray's bandaged arm.

They pounded up the wooden stairs, Ray shielding BeBe's box from the rain with his body. Alane propped the cage on her hip to unlock the door. Rain pattered the saw palmetto plants in the rock garden below. Mrs. Wessel's landscaping was neat and minimal with hibiscus bushes and aloe plants. The yard had the green preciseness of a golf course. Both the Wessels were retired and, in their own words, *putterers*. Mrs. Wessel gardened while her husband, who went by Papa, was always working on some project around the property.

The door swung open on a small galley kitchen with a 70s-era Formica dinette table, vinyl floor, a window over the sink. Alane dumped the box and bags on the kitchen counter. She put the teakettle on while Ray took the mouse back to his room. He was soon back to open the box and assemble the cage. Blue, orange, and red tubes stuck out the sides and straight up into a little lookout bubble. No way was that tiny mouse ever going to be able to reach the opening of that tube, let alone climb up it. Alane said nothing. Ray would figure it out.

The clean, grassy smell of shavings filled the air as Ray poured a layer on the bottom of the cage, fluffing it into the corners. He placed a little green see-through plastic igloo in the center and stepped past

Alane to fill the water bottle. Alane smiled at Ray's excitement even as slight unease filtered through her.

"Remember our deal," she said, bringing down a mug and putting a tea bag inside. "You're responsible for cleaning her cage. Every week. Otherwise, it's going to get nasty and that's not good for her or us. I'll watch her on the weekends you're with your dad, but otherwise you need to feed and water her."

"I know."

He needs this, she thought.

The last few months hadn't been easy on either of them. The separation, a new apartment, a new school. Then the accident on Thursday night, when she was working a catering job. Ray burned his arm on the oven door when it sprang back as he was pulling out chicken nuggets.

That never would have happened if I'd been home.

This thought, like others—*what if the separation screws Ray up forever*—she accepted and let pass from her mind like dark, ion-charged storm clouds. Mom meditation.

She reminded herself that BeBe was just a small pet. Confined to a cage.

Ray had taken the cage to his room. Alane could hear him murmuring to the mouse.

"Be careful handling her," Alane called. "She'll bite."

The kettle whistled and she poured her tea, took the mug with her down the hall. The apartment was small but cozy, perfect for her and Ray. The Wessels—the kindest people, parents of a teacher friend—had offered it to her this past June when she and Brad separated. She could just afford it on her long-term substitute teaching salary, with child support and catering jobs when she could get them.

"Coming in," she called out before parting the SpongeBob curtain covering the door. *Past time to switch this out to something for a teen.*

Ray was sitting on his bed, watching BeBe as the mouse explored her new home. She dug in the shavings. Nose lifting to sniff. Movements quick and jittery. Little pink ears trembling. The cage looked enormous.

Alane leaned against the door jam. "How's she settling in?"

"Good, I think," Ray said, his eyes never leaving his pet.

He looked so sweet, so young, she had the urge to hug him. But in the last year he'd taken to evading her full embrace, smiling and giving her a half-hug instead. Keeping her at arm's length.

She glanced around his room, the contents frozen in time, like her boy, between child and teenager. Stuffed animals he wasn't ready to get rid of (dust sponges with accusing eyes, Alane thought of them) next to a game console and monitor on a desk, his baseball team duffle bag, Star Wars collectibles. His room had that musty teenage boy smell—dirty socks, dust, sun-warmed mud.

Tucked in the corner by his bed was The Bunker, the refrigerator box she'd learned long ago not to call a playhouse. How old was this one now? She and Brad must have replaced it a year ago; Ray had insisted they bring it in the move. Not to his father's place, of course. Her mouth flattened.

Ray had cut a crooked door in it, reinforced it with camo duct tape, and finagled a locking mechanism on the door, which mostly hung open. He'd painted it black, adding KEEP OUT and a biohazard symbol. He'd been into zombies then. One window with a little fabric flap for him to peek out. It was looking worn now, accordioned on one corner.

"It's for privacy," he'd said when he'd dragged the first of the Bunkers into his room, what, four years ago now, nobody bringing attention to the open doorway to his room, the exposed hinges where a door had once hung.

Alane had taken it down. Had taken them all down.

She'd peeked inside his Bunker recently. A blanket from when he was small was on the floor, some pillows, a battery-operated lantern, books, a handheld video game, and a box of fruit snacks. He'd ingeniously cut a hole in the wall to feed his phone charger through.

"Don't leave any open packages," she often reminded him. "We'll get bugs."

Now she looked at the empty pet carrier box on Ray's dresser and wondered if he'd decorate BeBe's box, too, so they'd both have their own Bunkers. Like nesting boxes.

Late that night, Alane lay awake. She couldn't hear BeBe in her cage. It was easy to imagine nothing had changed about their lives, but Alane felt the animal's presence, felt an uneasy shift in the balance. Her bedroom's ceiling seemed far, far above her, murky and dark in the distance, her bedroom seeming to stretch to the size of a great cathedral, an airplane hangar, she in her bed in the vastness, small. Like BeBe in her cage. A blunt heaviness pressed down on her chest.

Eventually, she drifted to sleep, jolting awake hours later, drenched in sweat, a child's scream reverberating in her head. A hoarse, shredded scream like glass fragments rattling in a jar.

This child had been screaming for a long time.

3

A THING ABOUT DOORS

The garage echoed with the sound of tapping as Ray pulled up on his bike after school. Inside, Papa Wessel worked to loosen a rusted bolt on the supports of an old park bench. The stooped man wore stained jeans—dungarees, Papa called them—a plaid shirt, and black shoes with Velcro fasteners like Ray used to wear when he was little. Fine, wispy white hair poked out from the sides of a Miami Marlins ball cap. A portable radio played the local news station.

"New project?" Ray said, leaning his bike against the wall inside. He hung his helmet on the handlebars. Papa's garage workshop smelled of oil, fertilizer, and sawdust.

"Picked it up at the ReStore for the garden," Papa Wessel said, wiping his forehead with his sleeve. "Gotta get it apart to clean it up. I could use a hand."

"Sure." Better than doing homework.

Ray dropped his backpack on the cement floor, took the wrench and the can of WD40 Papa handed him, and began working on removing the rest of the bolts.

The bench was slatted with weathered, cracked wood. One of the slats was missing, leaving a gap that reminded Ray of the lounge chairs at their old neighborhood pool with missing straps, the ones the last people to arrive ended up with. The arms of the bench were curly and metal.

"How was school?" Papa Wessel asked. This was always his first question for Ray.

"Fine." This was always Ray's answer.

School sucked. Ray didn't know anybody here, and the kids all had their friends already. They didn't need a new one. His hand slid into his pocket for the padlock there and he rubbed the ridges on the metal casing.

"You got that pet like you wanted?" Papa asked.

The man must have seen the cage box in the recycling bin. Papa Wessel wasn't a nosy man, now. He'd made that clear to Ray's mom when he'd given her an envelope from a lawyer a delivery guy had left for her. He just *liked to keep an eye on things.*

"Yeah. I didn't have enough money to get a hamster, so I got a mouse. I promise not to let her free in the apartment," he rushed to add, because maybe Papa Wessel didn't like the idea of mice loose in his place.

"I know you're responsible." Papa Code for *so don't let the varmint out of the cage.*

After removing all the bolts and putting them in a bowl of some kind of smelly rust-removal stuff, Ray and Papa sat on foldable camp chairs, an ancient metal cooler between them. The old man handed Ray an off-brand cola that had a chemical taste.

"Your mother working late?"

"She has a catering job."

Papa Wessel grunted. He had that grunt down that his mom mentioned. "She works hard." Ray could tell this was something Papa Wessel valued. It maybe made up for Mom's weird door thing.

Talk about cringe. Ray was home when Papa Wessel came in to repair the toilet a few days after they'd moved in. The old man had looked around at the open doorways and bare hinges, hands on his hips, bushy gray eyebrows bunched together. "What's this?"

"Oh, I'm sorry," Mom had said with a breezy air. "I know I should have asked first. They just make me feel closed in. It's how it was in my old place. I guess I'm just used to it."

Papa Wessel grunted that time too, but it was disapproving. "I'll store them downstairs."

And that's where the doors had been since, leaning against the back wall of Papa Wessel's garage under moving quilts.

Ray knew Papa Wessel well enough to know that he'd not liked Mom taking down his doors. But he was also the kind of guy, maybe like Ray's dad had been in the beginning, that gave Mom some leeway because she was pretty and had an honest face.

Until Mom started taking Ray to playdates when he was small, he didn't realize other families had doors inside their homes. Doors for the bedrooms, doors for the bathrooms. In the Ranew house there were no doors. There had never been doors. When he'd grown old enough to realize it was *not normal*, he'd asked his dad about it.

"Your mom has a thing about doors," was all he'd said. Dad had seemed to accept it as one of Mom's quirks. Like how obsessive she was about cleanliness. And making sure there was a stockpile of food in the cabinets. She wasn't a prepper, not like the people on those reality shows Ray used to enjoy watching. She just explained that she liked knowing it was in the house.

Dad had told him once when they were at a field messing around with a drone during Dad's drone phase that Mom had grown up poor. "She wants to make sure there's always something to eat."

Mom herself never talked about any of that. She wasn't one to tell lots of childhood stories. There was a whole life before Ray that was a mystery. He knew his grandmother was dead, and he'd never even met his grandfather. Mom's brother, Philip, lived on the panhandle. Ray had seen him a handful of times. A big, burly, quiet kind of guy whose wife, Genevieve, was nice.

Uncle Philip had doors.

When Ray was a kid and didn't know any different, he'd invited friends over. Nobody had said anything. There might have been one or two who commented on whatever fabric he had over the door, usually a cartoon or, as he grew older, something sci-fi or LEGO. Whatever show he was into. Mom liked to change them up, make a big deal out of it. He hadn't really made any friends yet at this new school that he'd felt like he wanted to hang out with here. Even if he did, he'd feel strange now about bringing a friend home. Maybe he could just say there hadn't been any doors when they moved in. They'd probably tell everyone at school how weird he was.

It was normal for a kid his age to want some *privacy*. There was a drape covering the doorway, but a piece of fabric didn't have any soundproofing. This hadn't been as much of a problem at their old house because his room had been on the other side of the second floor, but here, his room was *right nex*t to his mom's.

So yeah. He had his Bunker. If kids thought he was weird for not having doors, he could imagine what they'd say if they found out he chilled out in a refrigerator box. Pun intended. It was the only place he could go to be totally alone. Where he could shut everything out. When he put his earbuds in, it was like he was in a closed little cell. The cardboard was thin, but it was thicker than the drape and an added barrier between him and his mother.

Ray swallowed the last of his soda and crushed the can in his fist before taking it and Papa's empty to the recycling bin around the side of the workshop. Papa had his hat in his hand and was scratching his head, listening to the weather on the radio, when Ray returned. The meteorologist was saying, "We've been watching closely a pretty significant tropical wave working its way off the coast of Africa. A number of computer models have been picking up on this wave, and as we continue through the week and into next week, we could see some development there, so we'll keep an eye on it."

"Another one?" Ray asked, and Papa gave his usual affirmative grunt. It seemed like this year there was a new potential hurricane swirling somewhere every day, but most of them had fizzled out, swerved away from Florida, or just dumped a bunch of rain.

Papa put his hat back on. "Now don't you worry," he said, apparently mishearing Ray's sarcasm for anxiety. "This whole building and the house are made of solid concrete blocks. Mrs. W and I've ridden out every hurricane the last thirty years, even Andrew, so any storm comes you'll be fine." He nodded at Ray with upraised brows; Ray nodded back.

After Ray helped Papa Wessel stack the bench slats and metal parts, Papa said, "Good place to stop."

Ray hung the tools on the wall pegboard. There was a hook for everything. Papa Wessel had said he could borrow any tool he wanted. "But you have to ask first."

Ray grabbed a broom and swept up the rust flakes and wood splinters and threw them in the bin. As he swept near a wastebasket, he smelled something rotten and thought it was coming from the bin. But the source of the odor was a small white box behind it. He picked it up and dropped it when he saw a lizard inside.

Papa Wessel peered over his shoulder. He bent past Ray for the box, not without some creaking of his bones, and tossed it in the trash.

Ray couldn't tear his eyes from the tapered green tail sticking out. "Is it dead?"

"Seems to be," Papa Wessel didn't sound happy about it. He pulled the trash bag drawstrings closed and walked it to the garage door, setting it outside. "The traps are for roaches and crickets, but sometimes lizards and snakes get stuck in 'em."

Ray returned to sweeping so Papa Wessel wouldn't see the horrified tears that had sprung to his eyes. *Come on, it's just a lizard*. But he kept thinking about BeBe's little pink feet stuck in glue as she slowly starved to death.

"You saw what happened at the Robinsons' down the road," Papa Wessel said, as if picking up on his feelings. "Whole house had to be fumigated."

Ray remembered. One day he'd come home to see the neighbor's whole house covered in what looked like a red and white-striped circus tent. Mom had said they were setting off bug bombs inside to kill roaches that made him picture soldiers in camo with gas masks tossing RAID grenades into the rooms.

Papa Wessel had complained about the tent bringing down home values, so he'd started going around the property every few weeks with a tank sprayer. *Not going to pay for something I can damn well do myself*, he'd said.

He kept the bug poison, respirators, wicked sharp garden shears, and a machete inside a cabinet locked with just a vintage #5 Master lock.

Ray hung the broom on its hook. "I'd better get started on my homework," he said. The sky was growing dark.

"Appreciate your help, son," Papa Wessel said. "We'll start stripping her tomorrow."

The apartment was dark inside with just a night light illuminating the hallway. Ray snagged a cracker pack from the pantry and went into his room. His mom and he had lived in this place three months now, moving in right after school ended, and there were still unopened boxes in the corner. Mostly picture books, school papers, and toys he didn't play with anymore but wasn't ready to let go of.

Chewing crackers, he checked on BeBe. She must have finally explored the blue tube, which stretched out from the side of the cage, because the treats he'd planted there were gone.

"Good job," he said, spraying cracker crumbs.

She was currently sleeping in her igloo under a mound of shavings. He checked the clear lookout bubble on top of the cage; the treats were still there. BeBe was too small to climb the yellow tube straight up. He wondered if there was a way to reconfigure the tubes so the lookout bubble could stick out the side of the cage.

The air around the cage smelled of mouse poo. A petting zoo smell. He sprinkled fresh shavings on the floor of the cage. BeBe poked her nose out of the pile of shavings, watching nervously. With a fingertip, Ray moved slowly to pet her, but she scurried to the back of the igloo. *I'll have to get her to trust me*. Maybe he would take her inside his Bunker with him sometime, so she could run around and get used to him.

He flopped on the bed with his phone and watched a lock picking video, a dude with two-million subscribers opening a 14-pin padlock. He wasn't allowed to have his own channel yet, but he'd started to film himself picking locks. Mom didn't even really like him having a phone. But with the catering jobs, she worried about him being alone for hours at a time after school.

He watched more videos, finished his crackers, and dropped some crumbs in BeBe's cage. The mouse eyed them suspiciously, nose wiggling, before covering herself up in shavings again.

When Mom texted a reminder, Ray got started on his homework. He grabbed another cracker pack and a juice box and sat at his desk working on math problems, twirling the straight brown hair over his forehead.

Plink. He lifted his head and looked toward the drape. The strange tinny sound seemed to have come from the direction of the hallway, dark now but for the nightlight. He heard BeBe rustling in the shavings. He returned to his worksheet, finished another problem. Then again, a single *plink*.

He knew what the sound reminded him of—the toy xylophone he'd had when he was little. A light hammer tap would send a note vibrating before it slowly dissipated.

Maybe it was a neighbor's wind chime. Mrs. Wessel didn't like them; said they were *obnoxious* and scared the birds. Except it had sounded like it came from inside the apartment.

Ray got up from his desk. Night had fallen, and it was dark outside his window. The glow of the hall night light outlined the drape. He pushed it aside, eager to track down the source, to leave the math problems. He started in the kitchen, pausing to listen, hearing the faucet drip. But that wasn't the sound. Moved to the hallway, poked his head in the bathroom. Paused on the other side of the drape over Mom's bedroom doorway, listening hard. Nothing.

The fabric was patterned with pastel flowers that looked gray and faded, like the dried, brittle rose Mom had once shown him that had been pressed in an old book. He held there, holding his breath, heartbeat speeding up a little, the silence a muted static in his ears. A floorboard creaked, and something made a dragging sound, and he got the sudden feeling that he wasn't alone in the apartment. Fear compressed his chest. His fast breath fluttered the fabric by his mouth. He imagined sticking his finger into the fabric and feeling the other side, his fingertip poking a hard skeletal, half-decayed chest, maybe pushing into the flesh. A zombie standing there, swaying back and forth, with cloudy eyes and peeling flesh.

You're just freaking yourself out. But Ray didn't care what the sound was now. He wanted his mother to walk through the door.

Something metal crashed below him, making him jump. Papa Wessel must be down there messing with his tools. That was what the *plink* was.

Ray yanked the drape aside. Mom's room was empty. Light from the pole outside filtered in on the unmade bed. Ray flicked the hall light on and returned to his room, leaving his bedroom drape open. *It's all those zombie movies you watch*, his mother would say.

He took his laptop and papers into the living room and turned on the TV to a cartoon, the kind where all the characters seemed to be yelling. Their voices filled the apartment, making him feel not so alone.

4

7734 FOR HELL

Children's voices filled the classroom along with the sounds of pencil sharpeners, laughter, and chairs scraping the floor. Alane moved around the room, stopping at each of the low tables.

"How are you doing, Courtney? Looks good, Ethan. Remember to show your work...

Ari, good job."

Her fifth graders worked in groups to complete a set of math problems. The room smelled of markers, after-recess B.O., baby wipes, and hand sanitizer. Alane had been with this class since the beginning of the school year. Kay, their regular teacher, was out on maternity leave, but the kids knew Alane from last year. She'd been a regular sub at Edgewater Elementary; Kay had requested her multiple times. She always provided detailed and clear instructions for what Alane had to cover. Today, Alane wished she had requested her own sub so she could have stayed in bed.

The catering job the night before had stretched late into the evening, with guests lingering well after the event was scheduled to end. The staff had to stay and wait to clear the tables, food, and beverage service. Alane had worked the bar, and toward the end of the evening a guest had just come up and grabbed a couple of bottles of wine for his table of five. Not sure if that was even allowed, but she didn't stop him.

Alane disliked leaving Ray at home that long at night, but it couldn't be helped. She'd furtively texted him several times to check on him, even though she knew it annoyed him. His *K*, when she reminded him to brush his teeth, and his thumbs up emoji when she asked how his homework was coming, were all the evidence she needed.

Tomorrow she'd have "office hours," something she'd started a couple years before, to sit with him after dinner at the kitchen table, working on her own projects, paying bills, grading papers, or meal planning. Basically, just being available, while he worked across from her. Ray seemed to like it, liked to be able to depend on their time together.

She liked the flexibility of substitute teaching. She could be off summers with Ray, and her day ended just an hour after his. He could have walked to the middle school in their old neighborhood, but now they lived in a different town, and the school was three miles away, so he rode the bus.

Alane stood in the center of the classroom, her gaze sweeping the room as her mind went to her son. She knew Ray missed his friends. It had been a difficult adjustment for him. There weren't many kids in the new neighborhood to play with. The amount of time he spent by himself worried her. In the beginning of the school year, he'd complained a lot about stomach aches and asked to stay home from school. The school counselor felt the pains were the result of anxiety. Was there such a thing as an *un-anxious* kid these days? Alane didn't think so. She had been an anxious child. More than one report card came home with *cries easily* in the comment section. She didn't remember anyone ever asking her why that was.

Ray got annoyed with her for being so involved, for talking through things endlessly, for the pros and cons lists they made, but these were skills he'd need. That was her job, guiding him through these things.

She reminded herself to ask him what classes he wanted to take next year when it was time. Growing up, she couldn't remember her parents ever being involved in that process. She'd been on her own. Which was why she'd ended up in regular gen ed English class when she could have taken honors. Sometimes she wondered where she'd be if her parents had actually taken an interest.

She moved to her desk to take a swig of the soda concealed in an insulated aluminum water bottle, hoping the caffeine could give her a jolt. Subbing was great when it came to flexibility, but it didn't pay much. At the time of the separation, she had a decent amount in savings, but now, even though she held to a strict budget, it was dwindling. The catering jobs kept them afloat, but it was exhausting. Her ex's car sales job provided inconsistent money, so she'd been almost obsessive with budgeting over the years to have savings for lean months, but now, as a single mom, all months were lean. She really should find something that paid more, but what would she do with Ray in the summer or on teacher workdays? She had no family close enough to help. She couldn't ask the Wessels to watch him, even though they'd probably say yes. They were elderly, and he was a teenage boy. That was the age kids got into trouble. Or got hurt.

These fifth graders were advanced academic program kids, so if anyone looked in the window, they'd probably just see chaos and disorganization. They were free to move around, use resources in the classroom, and work in groups, but the noise volume was eleven. Even still, she noticed when it edged higher. Her gaze narrowed on four laughing boys huddled together at the corner table, and she headed in that direction. At this age, they were so involved with whatever silly thing they were doing, they didn't notice until she was already standing over them.

"What are you guys doing?" she asked. They immediately straightened. That's when Alane saw the upside-down calculator in Vincent's hand, the numbers on the screen: 5318008. She kept her expression stern while inside she snort-laughed.

BOOBIES.

She didn't say anything, just held out her hand and the boys handed over their calculators.

She remembered as a kid doing the same thing, and 7734 for hell. Giggling with her friends. How did these things get passed down? The kids always acted like they'd invented it.

"Get back to work," she said and took the four devices over to the teacher's desk. The calculators were cheap with a solar panel, oversized buttons, and no OFF switch. She cleared the display that the boys had been laughing about, but instead of clearing, the display began to cycle through numbers, figures flickering in and out. A worn-out solar cell.

She went to drop it in the waste bin beside her desk when the calculator display lit up brightly with numbers that came in quick bursts with spaces in between, slipping off the display as more formed behind, a run-on sentence of numbers. Voices in the room grew distant, and the calculator trembled in her fingers as numbers flickered and scrolled across the display, faster and faster, as if an invisible toddler banged on the buttons. Her skin turned cold.

No, no, no. She held it away from her at arm's length.

Her gaze shot to the boys, but they weren't furtively watching for her reaction to a prank. But that's what this had to be. A trick. Or a glitch. Like on Philip's Little Professor calculator years ago, when words appeared in the display, messages that he told her came from Palmetto Boy.

It was a trick, she told herself now, eyes glued to the blinking numbers. *None of it was real.*

The numbers danced so fast they became a blur. An *A* formed, an *L*... another *A*. Impossible.

Alane thrust the calculator away and it clattered to the floor. The room went instantly quiet, as the students turned to look at her, bug-eyed.

"Oops," she said, trying to sound breezy, but even she could hear the shake in her voice.

For heaven's sake, it's just a broken calculator.

She picked up the waste bin and walked it over to the calculator. It lay face down on the floor. Idiotically, she wished she had something like a paper towel to pick it up with. Instead, she put the rim of the bin on the floor and kicked the thing in with her foot. She had one of the boys collect the rest of the calculators and put them away.

You're just tired, she told herself at her desk after the kids had gone to the cafeteria, close to crying when she thought of how many hours were left in the day.

Alane arrived home that afternoon with grocery bags to find Ray in the garage with Papa Wessel.

"What are you working on?" she asked, leaning against the garage door frame, feeling the heavy bags pull on her shoulder muscles.

Ray pinched the paper respirator mask off his face so it hung around his neck. "A park bench for the garden."

An old timey bench, she saw, currently in pieces, with iron filigree arm rests and legs.

"He's been a big help," Papa Wessel told her, wiping his hands with a rag.

Surprising tears sprung to Alane's eyes. She was so grateful to him for taking Ray under his wing, showing him how to build and fix things. He was a gruff old guy. She'd thanked him before, and he'd become noticeably uncomfortable. He seemed to enjoy Ray's company. On weekends when Ray was gone to his dad's, she'd noticed Papa Wessel moved slower, quieter. Everything was quieter without Ray. Brad was a good father, a fun father, she had to give him that, but he wasn't what she'd call *handy*.

She left the two working on the bench and climbed the steps to the apartment. It was dark inside. She flicked on the lights. An empty cup was on the counter, a cereal bowl with a film of milk on the bottom, and an empty fruit snack package. She sighed. *Can you not put your trash in the garbage?*

She kept cut-up veggies and cheese sticks in the fridge for Ray to eat after school, but she usually ended up eating them. Cereal was his usual go-to. She took dish liquid, milk, and bread out of the bag and put them away, then took the rest of the groceries to the linen closet she'd converted to a pantry outside the bathroom. She frowned when she opened the door and a soup can rolled into her foot.

The bottom shelf was a mess. Cans and pasta boxes had been knocked over. Annoyed, she restacked the cans of vegetables, dry spaghetti, and soup, adding the chicken broth she'd gotten on sale today.

Straightening, she surveyed her *stockpile*, as Ray called it. There'd been more food in here when they first moved in, before things got tight. When Ray was just a baby, Alane had gotten into couponing, and for the next two years she'd amassed an enormous supply of shampoo, dried pasta, toothbrushes, canned food, cereal, and ramen that she'd kept on shelves in the garage. It had been a source of pride for her, walking out of the store with a full cart of groceries for $20. Brad liked to tease her, said she actually spent more because she was buying things she didn't need. But it had given her purpose, made her feel better, safer. She'd spent hours planning, clipping coupons, searching online for deals, organizing her shelves. Whenever they ran out of something, there was a replacement.

It eventually became too much, the couponing, after she returned to work. She'd scaled way back, buying just one Sunday paper, following a couple of blogs, and going for a few deals. Now she was down to three shelves in the hall closet, and it gave her an edgy, unsettled feeling. Ray liked to say they were prepared for the zombie apocalypse. His teasing didn't hurt like Brad's because he was almost sincere. And they never ran out of cereal.

After dinner, Alane had office hours, and Ray sat with her at the table, working on an English essay while she planned out the meals for next week and painted her toenails. Ray read his piece on light and dark in *Romeo and Juliet* out loud, like she suggested, and afterward they checked off the rubric to make sure he'd done everything he was supposed to. Being a sub had its benefits. When he was done, he shifted in his seat and asked, "Mom? What happened to my old xylophone? Is it somewhere here?"

Alane could picture the toy instrument in her mind. "I think we donated it. Why?"

"Just wondering."

He gathered up his school supplies and shoved everything in his backpack, then headed for his room.

"Hey, can you try not to make a mess in the pantry next time you're in there?" she called after him. "A bunch of stuff was knocked over."

"It wasn't me," he said.

"Who was it then? There's only two of us." But he'd already disappeared behind the drape of his door.

5

LORD OF THE LOCKS

Ray wiggled the metal pick and heard the first *snick*.

Yes! Three to go. Hunched over the lock, finger light on the tension wrench, he felt for the second pin.

Snick.

Then a few minutes later...

snick....

snick.

The shackle sprung. He pushed it back in, started over again. The scuffed #5 Master was his first legit lock, a present from his dad for his tenth birthday. Ray had learned on it. *Conquered* it. Now he could pick it with his eyes closed.

He leaned against the pile of blankets inside his Bunker, headlamp on, beam shining on the metal housing as his fingers worked, the picking kit beside him. BeBe explored the floor around him. Breaking The Rules. But the Bunker was reinforced with duct tape at the seams. There was no escape.

Inside, the box was outfitted with a string of LED lights that weren't on now, a speaker, and an overhead net where he kept comic books, snacks, and an extra blanket. His earbuds and a paper respirator that he'd kept after helping Papa Wessel spray paint a plant stand hung on adhesive hooks high on the cardboard wall. He also kept his locks in here, inside a plastic toolbox locked with the #7 Master.

He was too big for his Bunker now, to be honest. The walls bowed when he leaned on them. The cardboard around the door had been torn and repaired so often it was almost all duct tape now. A flap he used to be able to open for a peephole had torn off, the little opening now covered with a square of black fabric secured with more duct tape. As flimsy as his Bunker was, though, Ray felt safe inside. It was solid concrete around him.

Tonight, Ray had piled some diced apple by his knee to entice BeBe closer, but even though she eyed the fruit, starting toward it several times, whiskers twitching, she wouldn't come any nearer. One day she would. Ray was patient. He would gain her trust so that she'd eventually let him hold and pet her. Let him keep her in his shirt pocket.

"Ray!" Mom shouted from the kitchen. "Dammit, I need to get in here!"

Nice! She must have discovered the C. R. L. he'd placed there this afternoon.

Cabinet Restraint Lock.

Gently, he herded BeBe into a corner so he could scoop her up, feeling bad for scaring her. One day, he'd signal and BeBe would hop right into his hand.

"RAY!"

He lowered the mouse into her cage, secured the lid, grabbed his lock picking kit, and went to the kitchen. His mom stood with her hands on her hips, scowling.

"One of these days I'm just going to use a bolt cutter." She sounded more tired than angry.

Kneeling by the double doors of the pots and pans cabinet, Ray opened his kit and started picking the #3 Master on a chain he'd wrapped around the door pulls. The tools glinted in the dull overhead light. In minutes, he unlocked it, grinning when the shackle sprung free. He threaded the chain out.

"There you go!" he said, as if he'd done her a favor.

Lord of the Locks.

"You're getting good at that," she granted. "I need you to set the table for dinner. Put your locks away."

He grabbed plates from the cabinet above the counter. "Mom, I was wondering..."

He saw her tense, already suspicious of what he was going to ask. A *no* in her mouth. "I was thinking it would be cool if I could have a channel. You know, where I could post my lock picking videos."

She sighed like his words weighed a thousand pounds. "I don't think so, Ray."

"But why?" His fingers tightened on the plates. "Other kids have their own channels."

"We've been over this. I'm not comfortable with you sharing videos with strangers on the Internet."

"There's a way to make it private so nobody can see it."

"I said no."

Ray banged the plates down in front of their seats at the table. She was always treating him like one of her fifth graders. It was worse since his burn. It hadn't even hurt at first, just the bang of the oven door on his arm. He'd held the red patch by his elbow under cold running water, sucking in through his teeth from the sting. By the time Mom had gotten home, the skin had blistered and hurt a lot.

"Why didn't you call me?" she had said.

Ray had been quiet on the drive to urgent care, eyes watering from the pain, holding a cold washcloth to his burn.

"You have to be *careful*, buddy," she'd told him. 'No more using the oven, okay, from now on."

Then, to herself, the words softer, cracking in half, "I've got to figure something out. This isn't working."

He was only allowed to use the microwave now.

Ray sulked through dinner then went to his room to do homework. It was dark outside, and he saw his pale reflection in the window over his desk. He slipped the #3 Master out of his pocket and stuck the tension wrench and pick inside and jiggled it around for the pins.

Snick.

For as long as Ray could remember, he'd been into locks. Specifically *picking* them. From what Dad said, it all started with a cheap plastic treasure chest Ray got as a gift. The chest had come with one of those mini luggage padlocks. Like so many small things, he'd lost the key or forgotten where he'd hid it. In tears, he'd taken the box to Dad, who'd unwound a paper clip and worked it around inside the keyhole to pop the lock.

Ray had looked up at his dad in amazement, like it was magic. And it sort of was. Until that moment, Ray had always thought a lock meant you couldn't open whatever it was unless you had the key, but now any door, any treasure box, could be opened without one, if he knew how. He'd asked his dad to show him again and then spent the whole afternoon trying it himself, feeling a rush every time it popped open. After that, if there was a lock in the house (front door, back door, file cabinet, desk drawer) he picked it, working on it for hours sometimes, until he succeeded. Dad encouraged it, becoming interested himself in the beginning, watching online tutorials with Ray, buying new locks to play with.

"Is it even legal?" his mother had asked the year dad gave him a lock picking kit for his sixth birthday.

"He's not going to be a criminal," Dad shot back. "He likes it, and it keeps him busy. What's the harm? It's a good skill to have."

Especially in case of a zombie apocalypse. Or *any* apocalypse. Watch any end-of-the-world movie. Lock picking was essential for scavenging. Which door would the provisions be behind? Think about it. The one with a big padlock. A bolt cutter could work, sure. But not on a deadbolt. And anyway, there was no skill, no *artistry* in using a bolt cutter.

Now, Ray had a collection of nine locks that he kept lined up on the bottom of his toolbox, each increasingly harder to pick. Four—including the #5 Master—he could open in less than a minute: eleven seconds for the #5. Two locks he could open after a lot of fiddling. Three had so far defeated him. Lock picking for Ray was like solving a puzzle. He always had one with him for when he was bored. When he first got into it, he'd mess around with his locks while he was riding the school bus, or in the cafeteria, sometimes even in class if he could get away with it, though kids started looking at him strangely, and he imagined them thinking *is that against the law?*, so he cut back at school, waiting until he was alone to pick. An afternoon could fly by while he picked. He wouldn't even hear his mother come in his room until he heard the smack on the top of his Bunker. It was kind of funny how he liked to pick locks in a house with no doors.

"It's a beautiful day," she'd say. "Go outside and ride your bike or play basketball! The kids across the street are out."

What she didn't seem to get was that those kids were in *elementary school*. Nobody his age was outside; they were inside playing video games or goofing off on their phones. He'd seen them get off the bus, go into their houses, and *poof*, reappear the next morning at the bus stop. Ray never said this to Mom, but she really had no *right* to bug him about going outside. Not after moving them away from their old neighborhood where he had *actual* friends and plopping him down in Hallandale where he didn't know anybody. There were a couple of okay kids in his classes, but none of them lived in this neighborhood. Anyway, no way in hell was he inviting anyone into a house with no *doors*. People probably thought he was weird as it was.

Nobody other than Mom and Dad knew about the lock thing. Not even Papa Wessel. Ray wanted to show him so badly, but not everyone thought it was okay for people to pick locks. Ray got the feeling Papa Wessel wouldn't think it was okay.

Now, Ray released the final pin on the lock he was picking. *Snick*. The shackle popped up. Clicking it back, he set it aside, opened his history notebook.

He'd been working for a while when something caught his eye, a glint in the air, a dust mote in the lamplight, but when he looked directly where he thought he'd seen it, there was nothing there. It was then that he noticed a dusting of white powder on the corner of his desk that rose up into a tiny peak, spreading out, like someone had dumped the contents of a sugar packet there.

He touched it, feeling fine grains. Put it to his nose, like a TV detective. No smell. He didn't touch it to his tongue though. Could be poison. Brow furrowed slightly, he looked behind him, as if the answer were there, and then around, up. His gaze narrowed on a tiny irregular hole in the ceiling above him.

Ray moved his books and laptop to the bed, then climbed on top of his desk. The window reflected his outline as he cautiously straightened. His room looked different from this height. The ceiling above him was shadowed, the light blocked by his body. He heard voices from the TV in the living room. Hesitatingly, he reached up to touch the hole, which was smaller around than his fingertip. Felt the edges. They were rough, stained brown, tiny bits of drywall shredded. Like... tiny sharp teeth had chewed it. He snatched his hand back.

The desk wobbled under his feet. He rubbed his hand against his pants, now imagining that he'd felt a puff of damp hot air from up there blow on his finger before he'd taken it away. Like something alive up there. Something watching him. Something holding very, very still.

The fine hairs on the back of his neck lifted.

Bruh. He climbed down. *It's just a hole*.

Papa Wessel probably drilled it for wires for something and didn't clean up the dust. Or a mouse or squirrel was up there. It smelled BeBe's food. Maybe, if it was a mouse, he could catch it and put it in the cage with BeBe as a friend. Ray walked out to the living room where Alane was watching the weather on TV. A white circular cloud swirling over a blue map. The tropical wave the radio weather guy had been talking about. It had a name now: Rose.

"Mom, was Papa Wessel in my room today messing around?"

"No," she said, not taking her eyes off the screen. "Why?"

"Nothing."

Ray rummaged for tape in a drawer. But before he returned to his room, after a quick glance at the living room, he went to the end of the hall.

Today the drape over his mom's doorway was open. The bed was unmade, covers all in a pile. Going to the closet, he pulled the fabric there aside, aiming his phone flashlight inside the dark interior. Clothes, boxes, shoes. The panel on the ceiling that opened to the attic was in place.

Papa Wessel had brought in a ladder once to show Ray what was up there: beams and pink insulation and trapped Florida heat. Ray swept his phone light beam over the ceiling. Then checked Mom's bedroom ceiling and the hallway's. No holes.

Back in his room, Ray climbed back on the dresser, ripped off a small piece of tape, and sealed the hole. Then he returned to his homework, occasionally glancing up, a prickly sensation at the base of his neck, a feeling like eyes were watching him.

6

THROUGH HER TEETH

Alane woke to a silhouette standing over her bed.

"Ray?" she said. His face was half in shadow from the streetlamp shining outside her window. "Baby, what's wrong?"

"You were making funny noises." A voice younger than his twelve years.

"I must have been dreaming." She sat up, holding her sheet to her chest, rubbing her face. Her fingers came away wet.

He edged closer, leaned against the bed. "What were you dreaming about?"

Her brow knitted. "I don't remember."

"It sounded like you were crying."

She touched his arm. "I'm sorry for scaring you. Everything's okay."

He lingered for a moment, clearly unsure. If he'd been younger, she would have patted the bed beside her. But he was past that age now. Why did it seem like at twelve they needed cuddling more than ever but cringed away from it too? He said good night and went back to his room.

She grabbed her phone from the bedside table, 3:12 a.m., and lay back down, feeling disoriented. She had no recollection of the dream, only a fading sense of grief, for what loss she didn't know. The separation probably. That's what a psychologist would say. She'd been to enough of them. "Your loss over the relationship is manifesting in nightmares."

She stared up at the ceiling, listening to the creaking of the apartment. The air conditioning kicked on, ruffling the drape over the doorway.

The next day at school, she limped toward dismissal with the grim persistence of a marathon runner with the finish-line garland of flags in the distance. After locking her classroom door for the day, she headed toward the front doors, passing Angie in the hall.

"See you at Jen's birthday happy hour!" the other teacher called out.

Fuck. Alane opened her mouth to make some excuse. *Actually, I forgot I have this thing. I'm not feeling well.*

But she'd already said she'd go. Weeks ago, when the invite went out. She'd been excited about it at the time. How come the day it was supposed to happen, she felt like she'd rather do anything else?

"I'll meet you over there," she said over her shoulder.

Alane sat in her car, staring out the windshield, thoughts swinging wildly between *you should go* and *just text Angie and say Ray called and he needs me for something. It's an emergency, sorry, something's come up...* dreading the whole awkward contortions over settling the bill. She always tried to keep it cheap at these things, but they ended up splitting and then it cost her more than she was expecting, or could afford.

The parking lot emptied around her. The crane fly's wing, crinkled now, shone dully in the sun. She'd forgotten to get the dead bug out of there. Wasn't that just like every other thing she couldn't get to? If she had any courage, she'd just grab it by its twig leg like Ray would and toss it out the window.

Resigned, she drove the couple miles to Petals Bar and Grill, parked, and texted Ray. *I'll be a little late. Office Hours when I get home.*

The teachers shouted and raised their glasses when they saw Alane coming toward their table. She didn't deserve it. She forced a smile and hung her jacket on the back of the chair Angie had saved for her. A server came around and took orders for appetizers. Alane ordered a glass of chardonnay. The conversation centered, like it usually did at these things, around school, the administration, training, burdens put on teachers, kids, all punctuated by toasts to however many days left until break or to Jen.

Alane knew these women, liked them, they were friends. Tonight, she couldn't bear them.

The teachers' voices were thunderous in the nearly empty restaurant, one of those Applebee's-type places with retro decor, plastic menus with too many choices, and a bar that always had one or two guys sitting at it.

That would be me, she thought. *Trying to hook up with someone at Petals*. The idea was exhausting.

When the platters of potato skins, loaded fries, and mozzarella sticks arrived, Alane gulped down the rest of her wine and put a ten on the table.

She spoke close to Angie's ear. "I have to go."

"You okay?"

Alane bobbed her head. "Yeah, yeah. Just tired."

She waved at Jen, dredging up the last ounce of energy she had for a bright, exuberant "Happy birthday, girl! Have fun!"

Later, at home, fried food smells from Petals still clinging to her hair, she heated up leftover chili for her and Ray. She poured a glass of wine from the half bottle in the fridge.

During *Office Hours*, Ray watched videos for science class and Alane drank wine. She really should work on her resume. For months now she'd told herself she needed to look for work that paid better. She hated to leave subbing. It was perfect as far as flexibility so she could be home with Ray on school breaks. *Theoretically*. She was having to take on extra work at night and on the weekends to make ends meet, which meant she had to leave Ray alone anyway. She told herself it was okay. He was getting older now.

On her phone, she emailed the catering company manager to let her know she could work this weekend. Just the anticipation of serving for several hours made her shoulders feel weighed down. She pulled out the ironing board and pressed her catering outfit. The Wessels would be around; Papa Wessel would keep Ray busy. Alane wasn't the only teacher with side hustles to add income, whether it was selling fancy leggings, essential oils, or dildos, or grocery shopping for an app, dog walking, or Ubering. The gig economy was supposed to be freeing and flexible, so why was it so damn tiring? At least with catering there was usually leftover food she could bring home. Many times, she and Ray had made a meal of finger foods and heavy appetizers.

Alane finished the bottle, setting her glass by the sink, noticing for the first time a gleaming new curved faucet replacing the old one that dripped.

"Ray?" she asked, staring at the fixture, then turning around when he didn't answer. "*Ray*."

He looked up, pulling the earbuds out of his ears.

"Was Papa Wessel in here when you got home from school?"

He shook his head no and put the earbuds back in.

Alane felt a hot rush of anger followed by guilt. *You should be grateful.* If it weren't for the Wessels, she wouldn't have been able to leave Brad. Here her landlord was, replacing a leaky faucet for free, without her even complaining about it.

If only he'd let her know first. The man was a little too free about entering the apartment when she wasn't home for whatever maintenance he thought the place needed, leaving a note in his block handwriting. And now she saw the scrap of paper on the floor, which must have blown off the counter when the door had opened.

Shouldn't leak anymore now—P.W.

Sitting on the couch later that night, the sense that she should be *doing* something pressed on Alane. She watched the news, feeling mildly concerned about Rose being upgraded to a tropical storm. Projections had her coming for the South Florida coast. But every year there were hurricanes, some stronger than others. She scrolled through Facebook, looking at what everyone else had done last weekend—wineries, quick trips to the beach, kickboxing, museums. She should do more with Ray. She added *plan day trip with Ray* to the list she kept on her phone that seemed to get longer and longer with nothing ever getting checked off. She saw she was tagged in Jen's birthday happy hour post. She swiped through the pictures of her friends having a good time. She wasn't in any of them.

Alane was asleep even before her head hit the pillow that night, but sometime in the early hours of the morning, while it was still dark, her eyes blinked open. *Ray*?

The room was empty. Mouth dry, she sat up, the oversized T-shirt falling down her shoulder. A flash lit the room through the window. But when she didn't hear thunder, she laid back down again. Just heat lightning.

The room lit up again, and this time she thought she saw movement by the door. Her breath caught as the bottom of the drape gently billowed out at the bottom. Like someone had walked past on the other side.

"Ray?" she said, aloud this time.

She pushed herself to a sitting position, listening. The A/C wasn't on. She heard the cicadas outside.

Quietly, she pushed the covers off and stood. The floor was cold under her feet. The room lit up again, then plunged back into darkness. Her eyes focused on the closed drape, and for a second, she was overcome with an irrational wave of fear, an urge to jump back into bed and cover her head with the blanket. Instead, in a sort of compromise, she turned on the lamp. She shoved aside the drape over her doorway and the rings rattled on the rod. The hallway was empty. She tiptoed down the hall, looking in on Ray. He was turned away from her, sleeping soundly. It *must* have been the A/C kicking on that caused the drape to move; she just hadn't heard it.

Soft rustling from the mouse cage brought her close; she bent down to look at BeBe, digging in the shavings. Ray's room lit up with another flash of lightning, and the mouse bolted into her igloo. A whiff of mouse poop hit Alane's nose, light and not unpleasant. Ray had done a good job of keeping the cage clean.

Pulse slowing down, she walked to the kitchen for a glass of water. The microwave clock said 4:52. She rubbed her gritty eyes. Another night's sleep interrupted. She debated if she should just stay up, but no. She could still get an hour of rest. She went back to bed. Even after months sleeping alone, it still felt decadent to have the whole bed to herself.

Two excruciating years. That's how long it took for Brad and her to come around to the decision to separate. He was already seeing someone and had just opened his own location in the family business. *Ranew*'s, of the locally famous used car dealerships. The one with the stupid jingle that stayed in people's heads. *Cars for less, Just Like Ranew.*

People instantly thought of it when they heard Alane's last name. "Oh, like that car dealership!"

Yes. Through her teeth.

That annoying jingle burrowed in deep.

Alane intended to change her last name the first chance she got, to something just for her. She'd shed her maiden name when she got married; she didn't want it back.

She heard the first faint titters of birds outside. Thinking again of her friends' smiling Facebook posts, she decided *I'll take Ray to the beach this weekend*, then dragged herself out of bed for the day.

7

IN THE GRIP OF A DARK IMPULSE

"RAY!"

Ray stirred in his bed. A violent groan out in the hall jarred him fully awake. He heard the sound of cans being stacked.

"Can you not just grab things out of here without making a mess?" Mom said.

He dragged himself out of bed and ventured into the hall, tripping over a can of soup that spun away. "Jesus!"

Mom grabbed the can before it careened down the hall. "Watch your mouth." She stacked it on top of the other cans so roughly he was surprised the whole tower didn't fall down.

He surveyed the mess in front of the pantry, struggling to understand what he was looking at. A box of spaghetti had been opened and seemingly upended on the floor, like pick-up sticks. With a huff, his mom got up and pushed past him to get the broom and dustbin. Back again, she shoved the dustbin at him, and he grabbed it loosely, confused.

"Help me," she snapped.

"But it wasn't me!"

"Ray, just be quiet and help."

He held the dustbin against the floor while she swept up the spaghetti, grumbling, "I really don't have time for this."

"I didn't—," he started. Then, he gave up. She was too pissed for it to register. He'd just tick her off more. Right then, he felt like snaking his arm behind everything on the shelf and sweeping all of it off onto the floor.

How'd you like that?

Mom snatched the dustbin from him and stalked into the kitchen, then brushed past him to the bathroom, disappearing behind the curtain. All these curtains; sorry, *portiéres*. Her attempt to make it seem like this was how the kings and queens lived. He studied what was left of Mom's stockpile and yanked the drape closed. One of her stupid cans probably wasn't stacked right and fell over, knocking over the other ones. He rolled his eyes. *You need to chill, Mother*. His shoulders loosened when he heard her start the water for her shower. It wasn't his fault she was so stressed out. Shouldn't have broken up with Dad then.

Things weren't great at the end between his parents, but at least Ray had had friends in the neighborhood to hang out with when the vibe got too weird at home. Elijah and Caleb, who barely texted back anymore. Now, his time was split between here and his dad's new condo in Lauderdale, and he didn't belong to either place. It was all the same furniture from the old house, so it should have seemed familiar, but none of it was in the right spot anymore and looked wrong.

It wasn't fair. He was doing okay in school, dealing with the mess his parents created. Mom needed to back off. She didn't understand what he was going through.

Fuck her stupid cans.

He and Dad used to joke about Mom's obsession with hoarding food. Dad used to say it was a quirk. Now he called them *Issues*.

It was too early for Ray to leave for school, but he couldn't stand to be in the apartment with her, so he showered when she was through, dressed, slipped the #5 in his pocket and his picking tools in his backpack, went out the door without saying goodbye, and headed downstairs. He sat on the bottom step to wait for the bus, picking open the #5, closing it, opening it again. His gaze drifted to the deadbolt on the garage workshop.

Dad's voice warned in his head. *What is the first rule of lock picking? Don't pick anything belonging to someone else without their consent.*

He glanced around; he was alone in the yard, his mom still upstairs.

I won't go in. I just want to see if I can do it.

Seven minutes. He had that long until the bus came. Ray went to the door and looked through the darkened window. Cabinets, bench parts, license plates screwed to the wall, the old cooler. Taking his pick set out of his backpack, positioning his body to hide what he was doing if Papa Wessel were to come out of his house, Ray inserted a tension wrench into the keyhole, inserted the rake tool, and started scrubbing it back and forth. His bandage bulged under his long sleeve.

The rumble of the approaching school bus broke his focus. Stepping away from the door felt like being peeled off, like a strip of Velcro. His shoulders and jaw ached from being hunched over, concentrating.

He zipped the picks in his backpack and hoisted it over his shoulder. He hadn't actually broken the code, right? What he'd done was no different than jiggling the knob to see if it was open.

At the bus stop, kids in shorts and T-shirts clustered in quiet groups, most of them looking at their phones. He stood apart, eyes on his feet, rubbing the #5 in his pocket. His long-sleeved shirt stuck to his back from sweat. He felt a twinge of guilt again about trying to open Papa Wessel's workshop door.

It's not a big deal, a voice inside insisted. *I was just playing around.*

The school day passed as it usually did with whole hours he would not be able to recall at the end of the day. It wasn't him just dodging the question when people asked him how school was. His favorite class, which wasn't a total yawn, was fifth period science. Today, Mr. Sowder stood behind his desk with a wide grin, like he couldn't wait to show them what he was going to light up with the Bunsen burner on his desk.

Mr. Sowder was Ray's youngest teacher, a Black man in his twenties with curly hair, a beard, and glasses, who cracked jokes and could shoot a bored *come-on-man* look at anyone screwing off in class—usually Braden Walsh who thought he was *so* cool—and get instant silence. Nobody wanted to be called out by Mr. Sowder.

Ray went to his seat next to Allie Singer, who wasn't popular but was *popular adjacent*, from what he'd overheard the girls in P.E. say. On the first day of school, when Ray had found out he had an assigned seat in this class, he'd been relieved, because he didn't have to wander around looking for an empty chair. Allie Singer probably thought *ew* when she saw Ray sitting at her table. He'd noticed the way her gaze strayed to Braden Walsh. Why did girls always go for those dudes?

The bell rang, and Mr. Sowder didn't say anything, just stood at his desk until everyone's attention was on him. Without saying a word, he lit the Bunsen burner, put on an oven mitt, and picked up what looked like a one-inch piece of aluminum foil with a pair of tongs.

"Don't stare directly at the light," he said, stepping back and holding the material at arm's length over the flame. It instantly ignited in a white flash that left spots in Ray's vision even though he tried not to look.

Ooooohs and *cools* erupted in the room. After that, Mr. Sowder walked around the room with a piece of the silver ribbon that he said was magnesium, along with some ashy residue from the demonstration, so everyone could see up close, and then told them to work with their lab partners to answer questions on a worksheet. Everyone started talking at once.

"What evidence indicates a chemical change has taken place?" Allie said beside him. She twirled long brown hair in her fingers.

Her pink-polished fingernails mesmerized Ray, like the magnesium ribbon incinerating. "Um, the powder?" he said, cringing as the words left his mouth.

Nice job genius.

"Yeah. The fire made it into a new substance." Her brown eyes tracked to Ray's elbow and the noticeable bulk under his sleeve, but she didn't say anything. He felt his ears grow red and hot.

The rest of the exercise was excruciating, with Allie filling in the worksheet with her big curlicue writing and him stammering ideas that sounded clear in his head but came out of his mouth jumbled and stupid.

When Allie Singer smiled at him, it made him feel funny inside.

Stepping off the bus after school, Ray saw the driveway was empty, the garage door shut. He knocked on the Wessel's door, silently rehearsing what he'd say. *Are we working on the bench today*? Nobody answered.

Ignoring the voice inside warning him not to break the locksport code, he took the pick set out of his backpack and set it down on the bottom set. Took one last look around. *Just one more try.* When he put the wrench in the keyhole, something that had been tensed all day loosened.

...this kid came out of nowhere to be in this competition, the announcer said in his head, *the youngest in history...*

He didn't know how long he'd been at it before he felt a satisfying click, and the deadbolt turned. *Yes*! He punched the air as his imaginary audience burst into applause and cheers. He swung the door open in triumph. He was just about to close and lock it again when he hesitated.

After a quick glance at the driveway for any approaching cars, he went inside. Cooler than outside. As if drawn by some unseen force, an illicit desire as powerful as any taboo thing he shouldn't look at, he walked to the corner where the glue trap with the lizard had been. Papa Wessel had replaced it with another one. Ray bent over to pick it up and peeked in the end at a cricket stuck inside. The insect leaned on its side, legs splayed. He carried the trap over to the worktable and set it on the scored plywood. He took a flat screwdriver down from the peg board.

Holding the trap up, in the grip of a dark impulse, in a moment that would stay with him for life, he wedged the tip of the screwdriver under the crickets rear and carefully pried it up. The top of the bug's body separated from the bottom, and greenish-white fluid oozed out. The cricket struggled, and Ray dropped the trap with a gasp. Regret immediately filled his stomach like acid.

I'm sorry. I'm sorry. He looked around through a sheen of tears. Not knowing what to do, finally, he picked up the trap with trembling fingers. The cricket was still. Gently, almost reverently, he replaced the trap back where he'd found it then backed out of the garage door and locked it again.

At 3 a.m. that night, he was awakened by a sound like someone scratching a nail quickly back and forth on a hard surface. BeBe must be gnawing something in her cage. The edges of the little igloo were already frayed from her teeth. Except, as he listened, the sound wasn't coming from the direction of the cage. It was coming from above.

Ray climbed blearily out of bed. The sound abruptly stopped. Dim light from the outside light pole filtered in through the slit in his curtains. He bent down and peered into the mouse's cage. BeBe was curled up inside her igloo, asleep.

He flinched upright when the sound started again: light, intermittent, louder for a frightening second, light again. Rotating his head like a satellite dish, listening, he followed the sound to the corner of his room and stared up, even though he couldn't see anything. It was too dark.

Was there a rat up there? A bug? The cricket flashed in his mind with a full-body shiver. The sound stopped again. Whatever was making it was *alive* and it knew he was down here. Ray didn't know how he knew that; he just *did*. He held his breath and imagined whatever it was holding its breath too. Again, almost tentatively, the chewing started again. Heart in his throat, Ray backed toward the light switch and flicked it on. His eyes watered in the bright overhead light. The sound stopped. He crept to the corner but couldn't tell if the hole was any bigger. The tiny size of it eased his fear. Nothing could fit through that.

Leaving the light on, he climbed back into bed, lay there stiff and listening, but the sound didn't resume, and he fell asleep. But later that night, while Ray slept, the little mouse BeBe froze, flattened inside the hut, pink eyes gleaming in the dark, breathing fast, the soft little ears alert, body trembling as the gnawing went on.

8

SPACES BETWEEN THE BUSY SIGNAL

The cart's front left wheel spun in a grinding squeak as Alane pushed it down the grocery store aisles, lost in thought. Even though she swore to herself each Sunday grocery shopping trip to get enough so that she wouldn't have to make any trips during the rest of the week, she always found herself here. *I'll just run in.* Always for one or two items, and then next thing she knew she had ten, fifteen things in her cart. This had been a sore spot in her marriage. A flash point. Because even though she was strict about budgeting, almost to the extreme, and even though she had all the intentions, she never stuck to the grocery budget, even with the couponing. It got to the point where she'd hide the bags in the trunk until she was sure she could get them in the house without her ex catching her. She had the stores' circular in her hand and a couple of coupons. Crackers were on sale, and she had a coupon making them free. She always got a thrill when she got a deal like that, and there were times she missed the couponing, but it had become too time consuming, almost like a second job. She loved seeing the abundance, here at the store and at home. She knew what empty shelves looked like, cabinets dark and hollow as her stomach had been as a girl. Just a jar of beef bouillon cubes, salt, some spice jars. That ache, looking inside so hopefully. Some days hopelessly. She promised herself when she was old enough to work, she'd never see the backend of a cabinet again.

She dropped a box of Ray's favorite cookies in the cart. He expected it now, a treat from the store. She knew it was a bad habit. She joked with him about how she was rewarding him with food. Was that so bad? Bringing him these things, it was the fulfilment of her promise to him. To herself. There were worse parenting failures.

The fatigue of the school day caught up with her in the frozen food aisle, and she suddenly felt like simply walking away from the cart, leaving it behind, but she didn't, because the employees would have to put it all back. She put a frozen pizza in the cart for tonight, headed for checkout. Only one lane was open—she just couldn't deal with self-checkout tonight—and stood behind an older man who unloaded his cart onto the belt.

Her phone rang. She looked at the number on her screen expecting Ray's name and sucked in a breath. A number she hadn't thought of in years but recognized instantly. Helpless to stop herself, she swiped to answer and brought the phone to her ear.

"Hello?" Breathless. Shallow.

As soon as she heard the repeating busy signal, she knew answering had been a terrible mistake, but now her ear was frozen to the phone.

Beep ... beep... beep. That sharp, ear-piercing tone you'd get when, years ago, the person you called was on the phone.

Or you called your own number. To get the Party Line.

Beep ... beep... beep.

And now, between the beeps, she heard the voices. Faint and crack-ly. Like old recordings. A small, tinny voice.

"What's."

Beep.

"Your."

Beep.

"Name."

Alane nearly dropped the phone, punched END, stared at the phone in her hand with eyes that felt too wide for their sockets. That voice.

She knew that voice.

"Excuse me?"

Alane looked up. The cashier was waving her forward. She blurted, "Sorry!"

She loaded the conveyor belt abstractly. *You just imagined it.* Calls went to voicemail now; you didn't get a busy signal when you called your own number.

But just to be sure, she called her own phone number when she got in her car.

"Main menu," the robotic female voice said. "To listen to your messages, press one."

Alane checked recent calls and saw a call from a number she didn't recognize. Not the number she thought she'd seen.

What's up with you lately? She laughed uneasily, remembering the calculator earlier in the week. Must be the lack of sleep.

She hadn't thought of the party line in years. A memory came to her of hanging out in one of the houses under construction in her neighborhood when she was a girl. There were about two hundred homes in Princetonian, all brand new or being built, with stucco walls and humble facades, a style part Mediterranean, part military housing. Alane could smell the warm, clean scent of freshly cut lumber. There was a dusting of sawdust on the concrete slab, gritty under her sneakers. The drywall hadn't been hung yet, just the wood framing, exposed pipes. A breeze blew through the open interior, with no glass in the windows. *Keep Out* signs were posted everywhere on the houses under construction in their neighborhood; that didn't keep the kids out.

Mora and Luis were in one of the bedrooms, trying to toss a frayed rope over a beam in the exposed roof.

"What are you doing?" eleven-year-old Alane said.

Mora said, "Making a swing."

The yellow plastic cord they'd found, like something you'd use to tie a mattress to the roof of your car, was thin and light, and kept fluttering down. As Mora and Luis worked, Alane went to the window and leaned out of it. She pretended this was her own house. She looked at her house across the street. 25413. It looked still and empty. Mom wouldn't be home for a while. Dad... she wasn't sure.

Mora whooped behind her. Finally, they'd gotten the rope over. Luis tied the two frayed ends together, pulling it tight. Luis was a year younger, in fifth grade. Taller, dark hair. His striped T-shirt pulled across his stomach. He stepped back so Mora could try the swing first. She sat down gingerly, the rope stretching down as the knot slipped. She got up and Luis pulled the knot tighter.

"Hey, you been on the beep-line yet?" Luis said, testing the rope with two hands. He stepped back so Mora could get on the swing again.

"What's a beep line?" she said, kicking off.

"You call your phone number and people talk in the spaces between the busy signal."

"Huh? What people?" Alane asked.

"People from school. Anyone."

Mora got off after just a few swings. "We need to put a board on here." The cord had left red dents on the backs of her bare legs.

"Let me try." Alane sat down. The cord stretched until it squeezed against her sides. She swayed a few times, but the cord dug painfully into the sides of her thighs. "Ow."

Alane wiggled out of the rope. "Let's try the beep-line."

"I don't know," Luis said, looking like he regretted telling them now. "My parents will be home soon."

"You brought it up," Alane said. "Now you have to prove it."

The truth was, Alane didn't care about this beep line thing he was talking about. Luis was always making stuff up. She wanted to get into his house so she could find out if he was one of the kids who'd broken into her house and taken her stuffed horse and Philip's toy cars. She'd sneak into his room and look around.

Luis's house was just a few degrees cooler inside than outside, and there was a box fan blowing. Alane thought the living room furniture looked like something from a palace. The couch had wooden arms that were carved in fancy designs, and the flowery cushions were covered with thick, shiny plastic. An avocado-green rotary phone sat on an ornately carved side table. Alane sat down on the couch, plastic crinkling under her and sticking to the backs of her sweaty thighs. Mora knelt on the carpet. Luis dialed, putting the receiver to his ear.

Alane could hear the steady *beep... beep... beep...*

"Hello?" he said in the short silence between them. He scrunched his face, listening. "Luis," he blurted before the next *beep*.

"What's..." *beep*

"your..." *beep*

"name?" *beep*

"There's no one there!" Mora said. "Stop lying!"

Luis held the phone out to them. "Listen!"

Alane sat next to Mora, receiver between their ears. *Beep. Beep.* Then a girl's voice, "Lizzie..."

beep "where..."

The girls' eyes met. Mora whispered, "Did you hear that?"

beep "do..."

Alane nodded. Luis's face was *I-told-you-so.*

beep "you..."

beep "...live?"

Over the next five minutes they talked between *beeps* to Lizzie, who lived in Florida City, was in the eighth grade, and liked ice cream. Luis started pacing around the room, casting worried looks out the window. Finally, he wrestled the phone out of Mora's hands.

"You have to *go*," he said.

Alane got to her feet. "Where is your room?"

The girls walked down the hallway, Luis trailing helplessly behind. The house was laid out similar to Alane's, to everyone's. Luis's room was sparsely furnished with just a bed and dresser. Alane opened his closet door, expecting him to stop her, but he didn't. Clothes hung sloppily from a rod. Shoes littered the floor alongside a football, a few toys. She crouched to tie her shoes, even though they were tied, to surreptitiously peek under the bed. Nothing. No stolen goods. Unless he'd hid the stuff somewhere else, Luis wasn't the thief.

She straightened. "Let's go," she told Mora. "Bye, Luis." He followed the girls to the door and stood on the porch as they left.

That night, while Mom and Dad were watching TV, Alane motioned for Philip to follow her into the kitchen. "I want to show you something," she whispered. "But you have to *swear* not to tell mom and dad."

"I swear."

She picked up the receiver, listened first out of habit to see if there was a dial tone, then called their own number. The busy signal blared;

she listened for movement from the living room. Then she put her ear back to the receiver:

"your..."

beep

"...number?"

She shoved the receiver at Philip. "Here. Listen." His eyes widened as he listened to what sounded like someone saying their phone number, one number at a time. Philip gave Alane a questioning look.

"It's the beep-line," she whispered. "If you dial our home number you can talk to people in between the beeps."

"Weird," he said. After a minute, already bored, he handed her back the receiver. She put it up to her ear. The people exchanging numbers must have hung up. Someone new asked, "Who's" *beep* "there?" A small child's voice. Very faint. Echoey, like it was coming from outer space.

"Me," Alane answered the next silence between the beeps.

"What's..." the child began, the voice oddly high, creaky.

Beep.

"Your..." The word came fast, ending with *rrrrrr.*

Alane knew that noise. It sounded like Linda, Mora's doll, when Mora pulled the string and it rewinded.

Someone's making a doll talk into the phone! She glanced at Philip.

"What?" he asked, grabbing at the phone.

She blocked him with her shoulder. "Hold on," she hissed.

"...name?" The child-doll finished.

Beep.

Alane blurted a word between each *beep*. "Mora is that you?"

"What's..." the child said again in the same recorded plastic voice. Alane's neck started to feel hot.

Beep.

"Your..."

Alane's fingers trembled. This voice was different. Deeper. Gruffer. Not like a doll anymore. Not like a child either. She lifted the phone away from her ear.

Beep.

"...name?" She heard a sly smile in it that made the hair on her arms stand up.

Alane was vaguely aware of Philip beside her and muffled voices from the television in the other room. She waited, still.

The silence between the *beeps* stretched out unnaturally, as if something on the other end waited too.

9

PROS AND CONS

An oily, sweetish smell, like bad cheese, hit Ray's nostrils when he ducked around the drape into his room, already half out of his shirt. He smelled his armpits, wondering if the odor was from him. Nope.

Tossing his shirt on the pile of dirty clothes in the corner, he walked over to BeBe's cage and sniffed the air. Just the warm, dusty scent of shavings and droppings. He raised his chin and sniffed again, but now he couldn't smell it anymore. His eyes narrowed as he noticed the tape he'd put over the hole in the ceiling dangling down. He walked underneath it, scratching his burn through the bandage; it had itched like crazy all day.

Shirtless, he climbed up onto his desk. Was the hole bigger? He thought it had been the size of a ball bearing before but couldn't be sure now. Standing on the desk just underneath, he caught another whiff of the odor, a trace so slight he couldn't be sure if he'd actually smelled it again or just remembered it.

He jabbed the tape back against the ceiling. It was silly but he got the sense something was right there on the other side. Something small and still, with sharp eyes and teeth. Something waiting until Ray went away before it moved again.

That's dumb.

Ray climbed down. It's just a bug or something. He almost texted Mom, who was at this minute calling her own cell number in the grocery store parking lot. But she'd just get annoyed at *One More Thing*. She was stressed out about them being on their own without Dad, and about money. Ray wasn't supposed to know about that. Mom never brought it up around him. But Ray could tell by her worried face when she checked the bank balance on her phone. Ray didn't have a word for the feeling in his chest when he saw that face.

I'll handle it myself, he decided.

He pounded downstairs to the garage and tried the door. Locked. He checked the driveway; Papa's car was there. Didn't Papa say Ray could borrow stuff if he asked?

He ran to the house and rang the doorbell. Papa opened the door looking like he had just woken up from a nap. But he seemed pleased to see Ray standing there. "What can I do for you, son?"

"I was wondering if I could borrow some bug spray," Ray said.

Papa frowned. He glanced at the apartment over Ray's head. "You all having trouble with bugs?"

Crap. Now he'd be worried their apartment was infested like the Robinson's or that Ray and his mom weren't keeping his place clean. Ray thought fast. "There's a hornet in my room."

Papa's bristly eyebrows went up. "Just smack it with a shoe, boy."

Ray must have made a disgusted face because the old man snorted. "I got a fly swatter in the garage; I'll grab the keys." He left the door open a crack as he went to find them.

Ray groaned inside. What was a *flyswatter* going to do!

Papa returned and handed Ray the keys on a worn leather fob. "Lock up and bring me the keys when you're done."

Ray unlocked the garage door. Memories of the cricket made him wince. This time, he'd get what he needed and get out. He wouldn't even look at where the trap was.

The lime green flyswatter hung on a hook. He couldn't say why he even took it, except that Papa would think it strange if he didn't. As he turned to leave, his gaze slid to the padlocked cabinet. He glanced at the keys in his hand, the small brass one that opened it. Crouching in front of the cabinet, ignoring the disapproving voice in his head and shooting glances over his shoulder, he unlocked and opened the door. Odors of warm particle board, cleaners, and solvents wafted out, tickling the inside of his nose.

Hoping for a bottle of Raid, he only found the big spray canister of pesticide. Way too big to sneak upstairs. And with his luck if he tried to use it, he'd spray poison all over himself. Images flashed of his skin dissolving where the drops hit or his eyes melting into jelly from acid.

He looked at the box of glue traps, queasy with guilt. But if the thing in the attic crawl space was a beetle or a termite, he could trap it with one of these. Opening the box, he grabbed a flat plastic wrapped package and shoved it in his waistband under his shirt. Papa wouldn't notice if he took one; the box was nearly full. He shut and locked everything up and ran back up to the apartment with the flyswatter.

In his Bunker, he watched a YouTube video about how to assemble it, noticing but actively *not* looking at thumbnails of other videos about the cruelty of glue traps and how they should be banned. He peeled off the wax paper to expose the glue, folded the cardboard over, and secured it with a tab. Both ends of the rectangle were open, like a Hot Pocket sleeve.

He placed the trap under his desk against the baseboard, where the video had suggested, thought about making a trail of bread or peanut butter, but that would just bring ants. Straightening, he heard BeBe rustling behind him and sat down beside the cage.

"You don't go near that thing," he warned her. "It's dangerous."

He'd have to be extra careful now to watch her when he took her into the Bunker with him.

"You get him?" Papa wanted to know when Ray returned his keys later. Ray's imaginary hornet.

"Yes, sir."

"Knew you would."

The praise made Ray's stomach knot.

Back in the apartment, he curled on the couch with a snack and his laptop to do his science homework. Best class ever today. Mr. Sowder had let them ignite magnesium ribbon on their own. Allie had lit the Bunsen burner. Ray was not mad about it; he was still cautious from burning himself with the oven. Mr. Sowder came around with a tray of tiny ribbon pieces. Allie took theirs and held it over the flame with tongs. They looked away when it flashed and then back at each other, wide-eyed behind their safety glasses.

"That was *awesome*," she said, grinning.

His stomach dropped into his sneakers. Allie Singer was cute as hell in safety glasses.

Why did she have to like that Braden guy? Ray and Allie could be talking, and if Braden said *anything*, she'd break off mid-sentence or stop listening to Ray and look over. Ray would be left sitting there talking to himself.

What would Allie say if she knew that in five minutes Ray could unlock any door in the school building?

An hour later, finished with his lab report homework, he checked on BeBe, refilling her water and dropping in some treats. Then he examined the ceiling hole. The smell was gone, but the drywall around the hole was stained brown. And where the edges of the hole had been fairly circular before, now there were ragged chips where it looked like little teeth had chewed. He stood still and listened but didn't hear anything up there. He also checked the glue trap, even though he knew there hadn't been enough time for it to work. He wondered if the trap would even catch whatever was up there. What if it was a squirrel or—his imagination soared—a raccoon!

An idea came to him then, and if Ray had stopped to write a pros/cons list—like Mom made him do every time he had to make a Big Decision, folding a piece of paper vertically halfway and listing each in a column—it might have looked like this:

Pros

Find out once and for all what's making the chewing sounds

Prove there's nothing scary there

See if there's something dead up there

There might be a raccoon I could maybe trap and tame

Cons

What if there is something bad up there

By the time he'd grabbed his headlamp, pulled a chair into his mother's closet, and propped a plastic bin from his room on top of it, his mind had run through all these possibilities, and the pros definitely outweighed the cons. Besides, when he really thought about it, it was silly to be so freaked out about some sounds in the ceiling when it was probably nothing.

It's probably more afraid of you than you are of it, Papa Wessel would have said. He might have even given Ray a gently disappointed look as if to say, 'Now, you aren't scared of a little mouse, are you?'

Ray clicked on the overhead dome light illuminating Mom's clothes and boxes and shoes on the floor, then climbed up on the chair and bin. He reached up to slide the ceiling panel aside, turning his face away from the dusting of drywall that came down. Invisible heat billowed down from the dark crawl space. He sniffed but didn't detect the oily smell from earlier. He just smelled baked wood.

The apartment was quiet, just the faint sounds of birds chirping outside and the Wessel's A/C unit running. The crawl space was pitch black above him. Heart beginning to race, he clicked on his headlamp, steadying his feet on the bin as he stretched to see over the lip of the opening. The headlamp beam shone on pink insulation and pine beams. With shaking knees, he panned the light around, the feeling like whatever was living up here scuttling just out of sight, causing him to breathe fast.

Plink.

The bin under Ray's feet wobbled and he nearly fell. He grabbed the ceiling frame, gasping for air.

Another faint *plink* from below. A single chime, like from a xylophone.

It must be in here!

Excited, he slid the panel back and climbed down, moving the chair and bin out of the way so he could search the closet. Nervously, knowing he was stepping over some line of privacy of his mother's—living so close together in this tiny place, could she really be mad if he'd looked through her things?—he poked behind the shoes, dragged out boxes, and rifled inside. Mostly papers, old photo albums. Then, in the back, a battered cardboard box with a lid. The handhold on the side had been reinforced with tape. ALANE in black marker, writing he didn't recognize. He dragged it out of the closet. The flaps had been folded closed. Inside, on top, was an old girl scout uniform, stiff with age and so crisply pressed he thought it might snap if he unfolded it. A smell of dust and some other scent, like a cold fireplace, filled his nose. Next a packet of what looked like old school assignments.

Then, at the bottom, he felt something hard and pulled out a yellow box decorated with flowers. It had a gold latch with a tiny keyhole, but the lid popped open when he pressed the release. A one-armed plastic ballerina in a faded pink net skirt popped upright in front of an oval mirror. In the compartment below, he found ropes of pearls, big gold earrings, a pendant in the shape of a peacock with jewels in it or places where jewels had been. These could be worth something! Getting more excited, he found a ring box that creaked and split when he opened it. Empty. Disappointed, he dropped it back in the box, closed the lid, and turned the box around to find a crank. It creaked when he twisted it, and a few notes played then ground to a halt. The ballerina made one jerky half turn before becoming still again. She might have been painted once, but she was all the same pink now, with just the impressions of eyes and lips and hair. Closing the box, a final gasping *plink* sounded. He set it aside and went back into the carton to see what else was inside. He'd never seen any of this stuff before and was curious about these artifacts from his mother's past. Digging around, he found a book. A diary. It had a clasp too, which was locked, but would be as easy to pick as his old cheap treasure chest.

Hearing tires on gravel outside, he quickly shoved the jewelry box back in the carton. Another *plink* from the music box. *Stop*! Otherwise, Mom would know he'd been digging around in there. Diary under his arm, he pushed the carton to the back of the closet where it had been before, arranging the shoes how he thought they'd been, and hurried to put the chair and bin back. He tossed the diary in his Bunker. By the time his mom looked in on him, he was on his bed, phone in his face, lungs on hold so she wouldn't see he was out of breath.

10

SOMETHING DEAD UP THERE

Laughter and conversation carried into the vestibule where Alane and the rest of the catering staff refilled appetizer trays. Alane arranged bacon-wrapped scallops on a silver tray, breathing in the savoriness, and carried it out into the ballroom, where Silver Creek Academy, an exclusive private school, was holding its annual gala and silent auction. Parents in black tie sat at round tables or stood at cocktail tables drinking wine and craft beer, eating hors d'oeuvres. A projection screen played a slideshow of images of the school and grounds, students in smart uniforms socializing on the lawn, smiling at the camera with the Eiffel tower behind them on a school trip, riding horses. The overhead lights were dimmed, and a DJ played yacht rock.

Alane weaved around the tables, catching snippets of conversation. A looming ban of the annual father/daughter dance was the main topic, with some parents for it, citing no equivalent dance for moms and sons, others against, some suggesting an alternative, like an American Ninja Warrior competition with their moms. Come to think of it, open it to girls too. It was hard to imagine any of these chic moms in heels and pointy nails doing a Tarzan swing over a tank of water. Then again, they all looked fit, so maybe they could.

Alane and Edie exchanged a smile as she slid by, carrying a tray of empty glasses, napkins, and toothpicks.

Alane held her scallop tray out to people who barely acknowledged her existence, as if the trays were floating around on their own. She felt the ache in her feet after teaching all day. But the exuberant party mood in the room was catching. She hummed along with the music. It was easy to forget all her worries.

Unlike teaching, serving was easy. She didn't have to think, just smile, offer the tray. Take the trash. It was fast paced, mindless, physical. Pick up the orphaned glasses. *Can I take that for you*?

Hours later, after the plates and tablecloths had been cleared away, she and Edie and Roslyn, who'd tended bar that evening, loaded up the carts in the catering company van to drive back to the catering company office. They spooned leftover appetizers into to-go containers. One perk of working these events was the leftovers shared among the serving staff. It supplemented hers and Ray's meals.

Roslyn popped a mushroom in her mouth. "You guys heard there's a hurricane coming?"

"You mean Rose?" Edie asked. "I thought I saw it was just a tropical storm?"

"What's that, the twentieth one this season?" Alane asked, putting her containers into a plastic bag.

"It'll go around or head out to sea like the others," Edie said.

"Let's hope it doesn't turn into anything," Roslyn said, "because the Kenton's wedding is in two weeks, and that would suck if it was cancelled. I mean, how are people supposed to live?"

This talk of hurricanes and event cancellations had Alane feeling anxious. Her savings had taken a serious hit after taking Ray to urgent care for his burn. *I need a better paying jo*b, she thought, like she did almost daily now. Long term subbing and side hustles weren't enough, but when she thought of applying somewhere, it worried her to give up the flexibility. She'd have to leave Ray for longer periods of time. *Isn't he alone all the time* now?

Not the same. The catering jobs were just sometimes. Her back and legs ached as she helped load the heavy warmers into the van. Afterwards, she stood with the others outside the venue waiting for Lisa, who was inside, making sure things had gone smoothly and the client was happy.

Edie stretched her back. "I'm getting too old for this." Old for her was twenty-six with young kids.

Lisa arrived with an envelope. "They gave me this for all of you," she said, and the group gathered around for their tips as she tore open the envelope. Inside was a thick stack of cash. Counting it, Lisa's expression turned confused.

"Huh. There's $750 in here. That would be $150 each."

The servers laughed hopefully and glanced at each other. Excitement and relief raced through Alane. *$150*! Her mind was already tucking it away in the bank. That's a whole day's teaching.

But Lisa stuffed the bills back in the envelope. "This seems like a lot. I want to make sure this isn't supposed to go toward their bill."

"They did so well on the auction, they're just passing it on to us," Roslyn said.

"Maybe," Lisa said, doubt in her voice. "They've left now, so I'll have to call them in the morning. I'll let you all know tomorrow, and if it's meant for you, you can come pick it up."

"All right, sure," Edie said, taking her car keys out of her pocket.

Everyone said sure, all of them forced to act like it didn't hurt, to hide that they really needed it now. Alane played along too, while her insides were twisted, wondering if she'd ever see any of it.

A half hour later, she opened the door to the apartment, juggling her purse and to-go containers. "Ray, I'm home."

"Hi, Mom!" he called from his room.

She spread the food on the table and went to her room to change, sticking her head around the drape at Ray's doorway. "What are you up to?" Even though he was usually lock picking. And, surprise, he was. Her nose wrinkled. "What's that?"

Ray was on his bed, hunched over the lock. "What?" he said. But she could tell from his tone he knew what she meant.

"That smell." She walked into the room as his shoulders curled in slightly, as if bracing himself. She caught the movement and hated it. That he immediately saw her as a threat. A presentiment of conflict. Like storm bands around an eye.

It didn't take her long to see the hole in the corner of the ceiling. The smell grew stronger as she moved under it, an unpleasant musty smell that was strangely familiar causing a sick feeling in her stomach. "Where did this hole come from?"

"I don't know."

She caught the nervousness in his voice and also the relief. He'd been hiding this.

He joined her under the hole. "I thought it was a bug or animal up there. But when I looked in the attic I didn't see anything. I opened the window in here, but the smell won't go away."

"There might be something dead up there. I'll ask Papa Wessel if he can take a look." She leveled him a look. "Next time just tell me."

"Okay," Ray said, his voice lighter. "I didn't want you to worry."

"Did you finish your homework?" she said, looking pointedly at the lock in his hands.

"Yeah."

"Okay. I brought some food home from the party. It's on the table."

Alane went to her room to change out of her uniform, taking a shower to clean the scent of food out of her hair and that oily smell out of her nose.

Back in the kitchen, hair in a towel, she set out containers of applesauce with their dinner of reheated appetizers. When questions about his school day fell flat, seeming to exhaust them both, she asked, "What lock are you working on now?"

Ray sat up, came to life. "I'm really close to getting the Master 140. I'll show you!"

It felt a little cheap, how easy it was to just zone out and watch Ray pick his lock. She drooped back in her chair. Arranged her face into an expression of interest as he explained the steps.

In bed later, she scrolled her phone, eyes growing heavy. Roslyn had been right about the storm; it was now officially a hurricane. A category-1, far out to sea. If it turned this way and there was no Kenton wedding, things were going to get tight real fast around here. She cut off the phone and put it on the bedstand.

The next morning broke cloudy and humid. She rolled over and sat up, swiping hair out of her eyes where it had come loose from a bun. Getting out of bed, something snapped under her foot on the floor. She bent over, blinking in confusion.

Why was there dry spaghetti all over the floor?

A dozen pieces, some broken. No box in sight. She gathered them up, bewildered, annoyed.

Ray, what the hell.

Her fingers clenched so hard a piece in her hand broke into tiny bits, which she brushed into her open palm. She walked to the hall, but when she looked in at her son, he was asleep.

Alane scanned the hallway floor. Clean. But spaghetti stuck out from under the hem of the pantry drape. She swept the fabric aside.

Another new box spilled out on the floor. She picked it up to pour in what she had in her hand and that's when she noticed the teeth marks scoring the end flap. Nibbles, tiny bites, puncture holes like someone had driven an ice pick repeatedly through it.

Something's got into the pantry, she realized, goosebumps breaking over her bare legs. Something that had carried pieces to her bedroom in the night.

Eaten there while she slept.

11

BORING-EST DIARY EVER

Mom's car was in the driveway when Ray got home from school the next day. The garage door was open, and Papa Wessel was on his knees rummaging through the locked cabinet. Adrenaline coursed through Ray's body. *Does he know*? Did he notice there was a glue trap missing? Ray thought he'd been extra careful putting everything back exactly where it had been. Papa turned around and Ray tensed.

"You're home late, ain't you?" the old man said.

Ray let out a breath. "I missed the bus, so I walked."

Papa Wessel accepted this without comment, probably because he walked four miles in knee deep snow up a mountain when he was Ray's age. The man got heavily to his feet, holding a heavy-duty flashlight.

"Your mom told me you got a pest problem."

"In the attic."

Papa pursed his lips. "Probably some critter made a nest up there. Help me with the ladder. We'll take a look."

Ray hoisted the wooden folding ladder over his shoulder and lugged it up the stairs. When he pushed open the door, Alane was standing just inside, arms crossed. He flinched.

"Where have you been?" she demanded.

"I had to stay after class to ask my teacher something. I missed the bus." He stood in the doorway, balancing the unwieldy ladder.

Her arms dropped. "You walked all the way home? Why didn't you call me?" Her eyes shifted as she noticed Papa Wessel behind him; her mouth thinned.

"It's just a few miles," Ray murmured.

"I can come back," Papa Wessel said, realizing he'd walked into something.

Alane's face relaxed. "No, no." She waved him inside. "Now's fine. I appreciate you checking it out."

Ray trailed Papa Wessel with the ladder feeling her laser eyes on his back. He knew she was not done with him yet. Ever since he'd burned himself, she'd treated him like a baby. He was almost *thirteen*. His jaw clenched. Plenty of kids walked home from school. What was the big deal?

Ray showed Papa the hole in his ceiling. The old man hummed his displeasure. Then they went to Ray's mother's room, Ray using the ladder to move the drape aside.

"Set her there." Papa Wessel pointed inside the closet and Ray unfolded the ladder. He held it as the old man carefully climbed up with little puffs and groans and slid the panel over. He looked down at Ray. "Hold her steady."

Ray nodded, tightening his grip. The rectangle just above Papa's head was pitch black. The perfect horror movie set up. A serial killer or zombie could be living up there. Waiting in the dark, mouth slavering, teeth snapping. *Wait*! Ray thought, and when he heard Papa ask "Eh?" above him, he realized he'd said it aloud.

"Nothing."

Papa took another step up, putting his head up into that portal of blackness, lifting the heavy-duty lamp and panning it around. Ray held his breath.

"Nothing up here I can see," Papa Wessel said after a minute. He slid the panel back and started down the ladder. On the ground he turned to Ray's mom, who appeared at the closet opening.

He dusted his hands. "No way to know without really poking around up there. Might be mice or squirrels. I'll pick up some traps next time I'm at the hardware store."

As Ray folded the ladder his mom said to Papa Wessel, "Thanks. Just let me know when you're going to do it so one of us can be here."

There was the tiniest edge to her request that Papa Wessel wouldn't have noticed, just Ray, because he knew she hated when their landlord entered the apartment without asking her first.

"Will do."

Ray followed him out, noticing the way he looked the place up and down all the way to the front door.

After putting the ladder back, Ray climbed the stairs back up, feeling more weighted down than he did with the ladder. Mom was standing in the same spot as before, but this time she was holding up her diary. "Do you want to explain why I found this in your Bunker?"

Ray slammed the door, liked how it made her flinch. "You're not supposed to go in there. It's *private*!"

"So is my diary."

He brushed past her. "There's nothing even in it! All you wrote was Nothing Happened on every page. Then you didn't even write that, just NH, NH, NH, NH over and over for like a year. Boring-est diary ever."

She marched after him. "It doesn't matter what I wrote. You had no business reading it. I don't go through your things."

"You just did," he fired over his shoulder as he slapped the curtain across his doorway aside and stomped into his room. He flopped on his bed, banging his burned arm but barely feeling it.

Mom didn't follow him but stayed just on the other side of the drape. "Ray, I know you're here a lot by yourself with nothing to do." The anger had drained from her voice. "But that doesn't mean you should be going into things that don't belong to you. I need to trust that you can occupy yourself and not get into trouble. Otherwise, I'm going to have to hire someone to watch you."

"I don't need a babysitter!" he shot back, even though they both knew she was bluffing.

"Then you need to respect my boundaries. And I'll respect yours." She paused. "Deal?"

He didn't answer right away; he let the silence drag out a little. Then he grumbled, "Fine."

She pushed aside the drape; he wouldn't look at her. "Ray, I'm sorry for going in your box. I heard a noise and came in to check on BeBe. I saw your blanket sticking out of the box and thought it probably needed a wash. When I pulled it out the diary came with it. By the way, there's a reason diaries have locks, but I supposed you picked it."

"It's really not much of a lock."

"I thought there was some kind of oath you took not to open locks without permission."

"It's a code," he muttered. The edge was there, and he didn't care. His stomach was twisted into knots.

Her arm dropped and she looked at him. "What?"

"It's a *code*, not an oath." A code, he had to admit he had broken in the last few days. "I'm sorry. I shouldn't have read your diary." He didn't even try to make it sound sincere.

Mom stepped into the room. "What is this about, Ray? Where is this attitude coming from?"

"I don't know." His chin rested on his chest.

She let the silence drag out, then said, wearily, "I don't want you in my things again unless you ask first. Understand?"

He stared at the wall, hearing the swish of the drape when she left.

Later that night, after he'd eaten dinner in front of the TV while doing homework, he dragged his bed comforter into his Bunker and brought BeBe in with him to work with her more on trusting him. She wasn't running from him anymore unless he made a sudden move, and when he put treats down by his leg, she'd come over and sniff and nibble them. Next, he'd try to pet her. Just lightly. Not enough to scare her. She scurried around, leaving little poops he needed to remember to pick up.

Moving slowly, quietly, he pulled out a lock he'd been working on picking out of the case and started patiently working it, his mind drifting. He thought about the reason he'd missed the bus and his stomach flip-flopped inside. *Snick*, one pin released. Straightening, he refocused his efforts.

He wasn't sure how much time had passed when a light scratching sound made his head come up. He looked for BeBe, found her in the corner, unmoving, whiskers quivering.

The sound started again, louder. *It's back*, he thought, sitting up. The thing in the attic. Mice or squirrels, Papa Wessel had said. He stuck his head outside the box to listen.

The chewing noise came from the hole. He crawled out of the Bunker door, over the worn, duct-taped strip of cardboard that served as a threshold, and stood up. Ninja quiet.

This time, when he tip-toed under the hole the chewing didn't stop. He heard it even clearer now. Teeth gnawing at the drywall or wood up there. Frenziedly, like it was trying to escape. Hair raised on the back of his neck. He slipped back to the Bunker as the gnawing went on, grabbed his phone, texted mom: *come fast. B quiet* then crept back under the hole. Now he saw tiny powdery grains of ceiling sprinkling down like dust motes.

Mom appeared beside him, and he put a finger over his lips then pointed at the hole. Opened his eyes wide at her. *Do you hear it*?

Head tilted, Mom nodded, moved closer to look up. The gnawing stopped.

They stood still for a minute in silence before Ray whispered, "What is it?"

Mom whispered back, "Some kind of animal probably."

She turned, leaving Ray standing with his head back, staring up, wishing he had x-ray vision to see what was there. He pictured a tiny mouth with yellow, needle teeth. Saliva dripping. Was it looking down at him right now with one beady eye?

He jumped when Mom screamed. "RAY!"

Spinning, he saw his mother stumble toward his Bunker. Something white darted away, vanished behind the dresser. Swift. Low to the ground.

BeBe!

The mouse had escaped his Bunker and was racing along the baseboard, toward his desk.

Right for the glue trap.

12

THE THINGS THAT EAT US

"Get her!" Alane screamed.

Ray ran to block BeBe, cupping his hands to catch her, but she veered away, a white streak.

"The trap!" Ray cried, as he slid on his knees to corral her with two hands before she scurried under the bed.

"What trap?" Alane looked around, saw a glue trap under his desk. Sprinted for it, stomped it flat with her foot. She picked up the trap by a corner, held it away from her.

Ray finally caught the mouse by the bookcase. He held her close to his chest in both hands, her pink tail dangling through his fingers. "Are you okay, girl?" he said softly into his closed hands, eyes brimming with tears. "I'm so sorry."

This is why I didn't want a fucking pet, Alane thought. "Why don't you put her back in her cage?" she suggested tightly.

Ray gently lowered the mouse into the cage and wiped his eyes with his sleeve before turning around.

Alane held up the trap. "Where did this come from?"

"The garage."

"This kind of trap is really dangerous to have around BeBe." She pictured the little creature stuck to the glue, those delicate pink feet, and shuddered.

He wouldn't meet her eyes. "I know."

"If you know, why did you bring it in here?"

He didn't answer.

"What was the mouse even doing out of her cage?" she asked, her voice rising.

"She was in the Bunker with me. I was trying to get her to trust me."

"You knew the rules." Severe. Glacial.

A good mother would have comforted her distraught child.

But the bad mother. The *effed-up* mother said, "What the hell were you thinking?"

His face crumpled.

This is how it happens, she thought, her own eyes welling now. *This is how we make the things that eat at us.*

"I'm going to get rid of this," she said, holding the trap like she would get stuck to it herself, leaving the room.

Out in the kitchen, she tossed the trap in the trash, shivered again, and then poured herself a glass of water and drained it. It had been a couple of rough days with Ray. First her diary, now this.

The diary. She reached for it on top of the fridge where she'd stashed it. Ray had never gone through her things before as far as she knew.

It's this apartment, she thought. It was so cramped they were practically running into each other. *He's here all alone after school. Bored. Of course he's going to get into things he shouldn't.*

She opened the diary decorated with pink roses and 1983 written in a child's block letters on the inside front cover and flipped through gold-edged pages.

Took a pracktec test. Past it. Tony and Philip had pertend sowrd fights. That's all.

today the air conditoner broke. It was hot.

went to school came home stayed in room all day. Regular after that.

Most of the pages were blank or marked with *nothing happened* or *NH* or just a big *N* at the end of the book. Alane wondered at the child she had been, uninterested in writing in this thing, but determined to fill every last page.

She closed the diary, latched it. Held it over the trash can for almost a minute. But when she thought of the little girl curled up on the bed writing NH over and over, she couldn't do it. Maybe eleven-year-old Alane was just trying to convince herself nothing happened. Maybe, even now, she needed to believe that.

As Alane passed Ray's room with the diary, she said through the SpongeBob drape, "I'm going to order pizza for tonight, okay?"

A muffled "okay" came back.

Inside her closet, she pushed shoes out of the way and dragged out the old box. She went through the contents, breathing through her mouth so she wouldn't have to smell the musty, dirty ashtray scent clinging to everything inside. She found her plastic Noah's ark with the animals still inside that Grandma had gotten for her, zebras and hippos and elephants, a pair for free with a fill up at a gas station. Phantom was here too; the only horse left from her collection. Next, she found the jewelry box. Ray had probably been in this too. She opened the lid, and the little ballerina sprang up. She'd been so upset when her little brother Philip accidentally broke the arm off. He'd liked to pretend it was a pirates' trove of jewels.

The chunky costume jewelry had all belonged to Grandma, whose sandals, culottes, and earrings always matched. Alane put a big, oversized ring on her finger. The faux blue stone was cloudy.

She opened the velvet ring box with a flicker of hope, but it was empty of course. The bright platinum cocktail ring gone. A lifetime ago now, but still she felt the ache.

She remembered vividly the afternoon her mother had gestured for Alane to come into her parents' bedroom and climb up onto the bed. Her mother sat cross-legged with a pink vinyl makeup bag that was discolored gray on the edges, no zipper pull. Her parents' room was sparsely furnished, a full bed with an ivory dot spread and a long dresser with frames on it. Mom loved family photographs. The hallway outside was a whole gallery of them, from when Alane and Philip were babies to now, and older black and white photos of her grandparents and parents when they were young. Grandmother had died a year before, and Alane was too young to have grieved. There had been some falling out in the years before she died; Alane didn't know what happened, only that they didn't visit grandparents anymore. But Grandma's letters arrived almost every week to her daughter, until her sudden death.

Mother opened the bag, sliding the closure to open it without the pull. She pulled out a green felt ring box. Held it in her hand and put the makeup bag aside.

"This was Grandma's wedding ring," she said, and opened the box. Gold, with tiny sparkly diamonds. "It's a special keepsake."

Mother put it in Alane's small palm and sandwiched her hands around her daughter's. "I want you to have it."

Alane looked up wide-eyed, almost alarmed. She didn't have any jewelry that had *real* diamonds.

Her mother squeezed Alane's hand hard enough to hurt. "Put it somewhere safe."

But nowhere was safe.

Now, sitting on the floor of her closet, Alane returned the ring box to the jewelry box, closed the lid, and turned the crank, but no music played. Broken. The jewelry box went back into the carton. She dusted her hands, feeling grimy.

A door slammed in the hallway. Heart in her throat, Alane scrambled to her feet and hurried into the hall.

"Ray, did you hear that?" she asked outside his drape.

"Hear what?"

"A door slamming."

A pause. "No." The *o* drawn out, a hint of sarcasm.

Okay, she reasoned. Papa Wessel was probably downstairs.

So why had it sounded right outside her bedroom? Like a door being blown open and banged back against the wall by force. Prickles of unease ran up and down her arms. She consciously slowed down her breathing. *There are no doors in this apartment*, she reminded herself. *It's that stupid keepsake box full of bad memories making you hear things.*

You should throw it out.

But that box was all she had left from when she was a kid. Even if she did toss it, even if she set fire to every last thing in there, she'd never erase the memories completely.

Alane tried the front door. Locked. She went down the steps. The garage was dark. The banging sound must have carried from a neighbor's house. When she climbed back upstairs, Ray was in the kitchen, a worried look on his face.

"It was nothing." She pulled a cold bottle of wine out of the fridge and poured a small glass. Her hands were trembling.

"I'm really sorry," he said. "About BeBe."

"It's okay," Alane said, the good mother again. "I'm sorry too." She put down her wine and pulled him into a hug. "Did you have the trap in there because of that hole? It's just a mouse or squirrel like Papa Wessel said."

"I know."

Her phone buzzed on the counter, making her jump again. *Jesus.* She patted Ray's back before letting him go and then checked the screen, expecting that spam number that kept popping up ever since the grocery store, but it was Lisa from the catering company.

"Hey!" Lisa said when Alane answered. "So, the tip last night was right. The client paid their bill in full so you can come by the office and pick it up."

"That's so nice of them," Alane said, feeling a dizzying release of tension. "I'll stop by after work tomorrow. Have you been following the weather? I hope the storm doesn't hit us."

"So far, the Kenton wedding is still on. Let's hope this thing blows over. I remember growing up my mom would have us pile all our shit on top of the beds because of the 'storm surge.'" Lisa laughed. "Not *once* did we get flooded out. This thing will swing out to sea, watch."

"I hope so," Alane said.

"Other reason I'm calling is that I'm short Friday night for that retirement party and the job's yours if you want it."

Every sore muscle and sleep deprived cell in Alane's body objected, but she said, "Sure. I'll do it."

Alane hung up. turned on the news, and ordered pizza online as the meteorologist reported on Hurricane Rose, a small red and yellow blip swirling in the Atlantic.

13

SO SCREWED

Cage the Elephant's *Ain't No Rest for the Wicked* blared from Ray's earbuds as he wiggled his fingers on the pick in the padlock.

Sweat gathered behind the bandanna over his eyes. Even though he had cut makeshift "A/C" vents in his Bunker, the air didn't circulate. *I should install a fan in here.*

He felt like he was in an isolation tank. No sight. Music drowning out sounds of the metal tools clicking. Just the lock in his hands, the trainer his dad had got him when he first got into picking with a clear panel revealing the insides.

Feathering the tensioner tool with his other hand, working the pick by feel, the pins released one after another. He felt the last *snick*. The shackle popped up.

Ripping off the blindfold, squinting from the overhead LED lights, Ray threw an *oh-yeah* grin at his phone camera on its tripod, and hit the button to stop videotaping. He watched the video for his time. Thirty-two seconds! Sweet. Next time, he'd wear gloves too, so it was harder to pick by feel.

When he closed out the camera, a notification appeared from an unknown number, text message partially visible in the bubble.

Ray Ranew is this you WTF

Feeling a tremor of unease, he fell back against the blanket and opened the message, heartbeat accelerating with every word he read, his entire body seeming to draw into itself.

Ray Ranew is this you WTF did you put this stuff in my locker?

Allie. She'd found what he'd dropped into her locker through the ventilation slits yesterday. Perspiration gathered on his forehead and between his shoulder blades.

He yanked the earbuds out. Read the text again. Of all the reactions he'd imagined her having when she saw the magnesium ribbon in her locker, *pissed* was not one he expected.

He hadn't *planned* to steal a piece of magnesium ribbon for her yesterday. It just sort of happened. He'd found himself in the empty science hallway after school, Mr. Sowder's door right there. He picked the lock, then the cabinet. Broke the lock picking code without even thinking about it. Took a tiny piece. Too small for Mr. Sowder to notice. Then, he'd locked back up. He'd laid the piece down on a piece of blank loose-leaf paper. He didn't write a note. He'd folded it up carefully and fed it through the slits into her locker.

He thought she'd be happy.

I'm sorry, he tapped out, then backspaced. He didn't know what to do. Apologize? Deny it? Ignore her? Sweat crawled over his scalp like tiny bugs. His knee joggled up and down.

His stomach lurched when he saw dots appear under her message. She was typing more.

The message pinged. *I told Mr. Sowder. Not cool. You could have gotten me in huge trouble.*

Ray felt sick inside.

Mr. Sowder would tell the principal, who would tell Mom, and she was already mad over the diary and him letting BeBe out of her cage.

He closed the screen and put his head between his knees, eyes filling with tears.

He'd be kicked out of school.

Arrested.

The Bunker suddenly felt airless. Suffocating. Leaving the phone, he crawled out. The air was almost icy on his flushed face, the tips of his ears. He saw his reflection in the dark window, as he got to his feet. Everything felt strange; the floor felt like it was tilting.

I'm so screwed.

It was just a tiny *piece of ribbon*, a voice inside countered.

He paced the room, restless, then lay back on the bed. *I'm so* stupid!

His chest felt weighted down with rocks. Allie would never talk to him again. He stared up at the ceiling, feeling hot tears leaking into his ears.

He wasn't sure how much time had passed when he heard something. On the other side of the wall, in the hallway. Mom was at another catering job. She was worried the big outdoor wedding next weekend would be canceled. "I have to take any job that comes up," she'd said.

It was a light tapping sound. One time, on his phone, he'd seen a video of hands with long pointy nails tapping on a microphone. The sound reminded him of that. He slowly got out of bed and put his ears to the wall beside his Bunker. The tapping came again. Quick and light. It moved a foot up the wall, then down, zigzagging in little bursts, as Ray followed with his ear. He felt a tingle start at the base of his neck and across his scalp. *The thing in the attic*, he thought. It had found a way out and was free in the house! He pressed his ear against the wall, eyes wide, listening to the light taps on the other side, the skittering more searching now, angling up then forward and down, forward again. Ray stepped back. If it kept moving that way, it would come to his door where there was just a flimsy drape.

He dove into his Bunker, not caring how much noise he made, pulled his legs up and pushed himself against the back wall, listening. The tapping had stopped, or he couldn't hear it over his thumping heart. After a few minutes, he quietly crawled over to the door, trying to control his breathing, but his breaths were escaping his lips in shallow bursts. What if that thing was in his room now? Was right there outside his Bunker? He held his breath and listened for light taps on the cardboard. He closed his eyes, swallowed hard. He'd never been so scared.

What finally made him look was BeBe. He'd left her out there! He crept to the door and peeked out. Let out a relieved breath. She was in her cage. He looked the other way. Nothing. But he couldn't see the whole room. Over to the peephole. He'd cut it in just that spot to be able to see if his mom was at the door of his room. He lifted the scrap of fabric. For a few breaths he didn't see anything. Then the drape moved.

A dimple appeared at the top, like a finger poking tentatively on the other side, as if whatever it was was testing the surface. Then, the dimpled deepened. More little dents appeared in the fabric, one by one, and he realized they weren't fingers, but feet. Four, he counted, with a sigh of relief. A squirrel, like Papa Wessel said. But then another foot stepped onto the drape. And another. Six. Clinging to the fabric. He pictured a giant grasshopper. With sticky, pointy feet, clinging to the drape, making it swing into his room from the weight.

Ray stared paralyzed, watching the thing make its careful way across the drape. He wasn't thinking about BeBe anymore, but if he'd looked, he would have seen the mouse huddled inside her igloo, hunched low. As the thing reached the other side of the drape, it scuttled off. Moved at impossible speed so that the curtain billowed. It raced light and quick on the other side of the wall to Mom's room. Then... silence.

Long minutes passed as Ray stared out the peephole, barely blinking. He felt a pressure in his bladder. Cold all over. His mouth was dry. His cheeks were wet. He grabbed for his phone, called Mom, but it went to voicemail. He didn't leave a message. Papa Wessel! Ray scanned the Bunker, looking for something, anything to serve as a weapon. He grabbed his biggest lock. He crept out of his Bunker, eyes fixed on the curtain. He opened a dresser drawer, silently, inch by inch, until his hand could fit inside to grab a sock. He shoved the lock inside until it hung in the toe. He grabbed BeBe's travel box, caught the mouse and put her in it, ruining weeks of work getting her to trust him. He couldn't leave her in the apartment alone, not with that thing in here.

Box in one hand, sock in the other, facing that curtain, he considered waiting for Mom, retreating with BeBe back into the Bunker. But Mom wouldn't be home for hours. And the refrigerator box never looked flimsier than it did right now. It wouldn't keep the Giant Grasshopper-thing out. He could call Dad, but Dad would just tell him he was being silly and to go out there and check it out. And he didn't want Dad to know Mom wasn't home. She hadn't told Ray to keep it a secret; he just knew he shouldn't say.

He breathed in, set his jaw, hefted his weapon, and barreled through the curtain, shouting like he'd seen in war movies when the soldiers ran towards gunfire. The sock got caught in the fabric and the rod came crashing down. He let it go, didn't stop. The hall was dark and empty. His heart was beating so fast and hard in his ears he wouldn't have been able to hear if anything *was* there. He sprinted for the door, jostling BeBe, and pounded down the steps, not looking back. Almost slipped on the wet wood. It was pouring, his clothes and shoes soaked by the time he got to the Wessels' porch under an awning. He banged on the door, breathing hard. Mrs. Wessel answered, concern wrinkling her face more than normal.

"Ray? What in the world?"

"There's something in the apartment!" He blinked rain out of his eyes.

"Bruce?" She called over her shoulder. Movement inside the house, a recliner being quickly lowered.

Papa Wessel appeared in a white undershirt with faded plaid pajama pants. "What is it son?" he looked around. "Where's your mom?"

"Working. There's something in the apartment."

"What?"

Rain spluttered from his lips. "I don't know. I didn't see it. But it's big!"

"All right, buddy, all right," Papa Wessel said kindly. His eyes went to BeBe's box in the boy's hand. "Hang on, let me get my shoes." He said something low to his wife as he passed.

Waiting, Ray started to feel stupid. The Wessels didn't need him bothering them. Forcing Papa Wessel out into the rain. He was an old man. It was probably just a dumb squirrel like the man said. *Two* squirrels. To account for all those legs.

But he and Papa Wessel went back to the apartment and searched it top to bottom, and they couldn't find anything. The old man examined the hole in the corner of Ray's room. "I'll patch that up for you tomorrow."

Before leaving, Papa said, "Whatever it was is gone now." He rubbed the back of his neck where the white hair was curly. "Are you okay by yourself? Do you want to stay at the big house and wait for your mom?"

Ray shook his head. “No. I just thought I saw something. I’m sorry to bother you.”

Papa Wessel brought his hand down on Ray’s shoulder. “I’m right down there if you need me.”

“Thanks,” Ray said, and shut the door.

He turned and looked down the hallway. Every light blazed in the apartment. He felt tired and limp. After putting BeBe back in her cage, he grabbed his lock box and went into the living room and turned on the TV. He retrieved his sock tangled in the curtain and took the padlock out and arranged it in a line with the rest of his locks on the coffee table. As he watched cartoons, he picked each one, going down the line, until they got too difficult. His phone rang an hour later. Mom, having seen that he called. She sounded tired. “Is everything okay?”

“Yeah,” he said, not wanting to tell her about Papa Wessel coming over. She felt like he pestered the old man enough. “Mom, can we talk about maybe putting the doors back up?”

“What?” she said, and he knew from her tone she’d heard what he’d said.

“The doors. Could I at least have my door put back on?”

Her sigh was long. “Ray. Please. Can we talk about this later?”

“Okay,” he said, gathering a blanket around him. “When are you coming home?” *Soon, please.*

“Ten-thirty at the latest. I’m sorry. I don’t like to leave you this long by yourself.”

“It’s okay. I’m fine.”

“I’ll bring you something to eat.”

“Okay.” He hung up.

At eleven, Mom came home with a take-out container of warmed over pizza rolls. He ate while she sat with him at the table, rubbing her eyes, asking about his day, occasionally scrolling her phone. She didn't hassle him about all the lights being on, the SpongeBob curtain rumpled on the floor by the wall (*sorry it just fell*, he'd told her), and he didn't mention the doors again. After saying good night, he walked to his room. Cautiously nudging the curtain with his toe, he noticed a snag in the fabric and a tiny hole, as if something sharp had been caught there. He lifted that part of the curtain to study it closer and something fell to the floor.

A slim black claw.

14

NIGHT TERRORS

Alane came awake, goosebumps prickling her skin, blinking, her bedroom coming into focus. She sat up, all her senses on alert.

"Ray?" she called softly and climbed out of bed. Cool air hit her bare legs under the sleepshirt. She ducked around the curtain at her door. Bright light spilled into the hallway from Ray's room. Her brow furrowed when she saw the kitchen chairs stacked in front of his doorway. "Ray?"

Edging around a chair she walked to his bedside. He was deep asleep. She tucked the blanket around him, listening to his breathing. Soft and steady. BeBe rustled around in her cage.

Alane's heartbeat settled. Something else must have woken her. Another bad dream? Another slamming door? Her shoulders unconsciously lifted to her ears.

She shut off the lamp on the bedside table, sank down on the rug beside Ray's bed, and leaned against his mattress. She breathed in the warm, musty smell of teenage dirty laundry, cage shavings, the air plug freshener that needed to be changed, and under it all the faint unpleasant scent that seemed to emit from the hole in Ray's ceiling.

She glanced in that direction, even though she couldn't see it in the dark. She sniffed the air again. *What* is *that smell?* But just when she thought she was close to identifying it, it seemed to fade in with the other smells, undetectable.

Papa Wessel will figure it out.

Straightening her legs out in front of her, she felt the ache in her muscles. Being on her feet for hours serving, lifting boxes and carrying trays, was hell on her body. She never felt it while she was working, the pace was too fast, no time to notice, but the next day—*hoo boy*—she hurt. Back, arms, legs, feet. Little muscles in her neck and hands she didn't even know she had. She rotated her ankles, felt the tight muscles in her calves protest.

She studied the chairs in the doorway, wondering why Ray had placed them there. Were they there to keep her out? They weren't much of a barrier. That didn't explain the light. He must have been scared last night, she concluded. He did look a little spooked when she got home, his eyes red-rimmed like he'd been crying.

The curtain to his bedroom was ripped down, piled by the door with the rod. She'd picked up the mess, folded the drape, laid it and the rod across a living room chair for when she had time to put it back up.

"Did something happen at school?" she had asked mildly, assuming he'd been frustrated about something. Being new at school. Not having a door.

"No." His eyes on the lock he was picking.

Alane didn't push it, not wanting to restate her reason for the lack of doors, which, she acknowledged, wasn't sufficient for him anymore. Brad felt the same in the end.

Being closed in makes me feel unsafe, she'd told her ex early in their relationship. It used to be enough. He'd affectionately laughed it off as *one of her things*. All of her *things* were why he'd fallen out of love with her. Ray hadn't known any better as a little boy. Now her *things* were bugging him too. She wondered if Ray rummaging through her stuff was his way of getting back at her: Well, there's nothing to keep me out is there?

Ray probably thought Brad had it all together. Was living his best life. The car business, he'd said, had picked up. He was doing all right for himself. Enjoying his new bachelorhood. When Ray went over there, she got the feeling it was like a boys' weekend, all guy things all the time. Pizza for breakfast, lock picking, hiking trips, and R-rated movies. No nagging about dirty dishes, shoes in the house, or laundry; because Ray brought his dirty laundry home from Brad's, didn't he?

She'd mentioned to Brad when he came to pick Ray up last weekend that she was feeling a little stressed but regretted it as soon as it had come out of her mouth.

"If you aren't feeling like you can handle it Alane," he said, "he can stay with me for a while. I'll get him to school."

"We're fine," she said tightly.

Sitting here in Ray's room, gaze fixed on the inky black hallway, she could see how that open doorway might be scary. How anything might be lurking out there. She draped the edge of Ray's blanket over her shoulders.

Her little brother, Philip, had been scared of the dark and suffered from nightmares until he was a teenager. Night terrors, their mom called them. Alane would wake from a sound sleep to hear his small voice screaming her name from his room across from hers, their doors open. Some nights she'd go to him; other nights she'd put her pillow over her head to muffle his pitiful cries and go back to sleep. She winced with guilt. *Where the hell was their mother*?

In her room with the pillow over her head too.

Alane was eleven and Philip was nine, and that was the year the Palmetto Boy dreams started. Alane was never sure if this Palmetto

Boy of Philip's was an imaginary friend, because he sometimes spoke of having conversations with it, or if it was a ghost, or a monster, but the way he talked about it, she could remember almost believing in it herself. One night, Philip's horrible screams brought her to his bed. He sobbed in her arms, the kind of violent crying only kids do, where they hiccup for an hour afterward. When finally he could talk, he told her, "I was on my stomach—I knew it was there, but was too scared—I counted to ten and made myself look..."

He'd described a shadowy figure in the doorway. Deathly still, as Philip was in his bed, paralyzed with fear. The thing stood stiller than any living thing could. It could have been a few seconds or all night. Philip said he didn't know. But suddenly, in a blink, it moved. Ducking into their parents' room. "It was just a bad dream," she promised Philip.

But one night, Alane awoke in the dark, heart already racing, and sat up in bed. An eerie, muffled moan came from behind her parents' closed door. She tried to call Philip, but her throat felt like it was being strangled. There was no light in her bedroom, just shades of gray and black, and she strained to look at each shape that might suddenly come alive... and move. The sound came again. Anguished, unearthly. A low howl in the dark that made her lungs seize. The courage it must have taken for little Alane to creep to her parents' door on shaky legs and open it a crack.

Soft light from the bathroom inside illuminated the bedroom and her parents on the bed. Carl, her father, was doubled over in his boxers, hand to his cheek. Alane's mother rubbed his back. A tortured, animal moan fell from his lips. Nothing had ever frightened Alane more.

"It's okay," her mother whispered to her. "Just a toothache. Go back to bed."

Funny how childhood experiences lose their mystery with the safety of time and distance. Sometimes becoming clear all at once. Like sexual innuendos in song lyrics that suddenly make sense. Oh! So *that's* what that means! Sometimes taking years, decades, to come into focus. Because looking back on that night, Carl Jannell had suffered because there wasn't money for things like fillings. That was the true horror. For years, she'd felt sympathy for him. For the injustices at work he claimed each time he was fired. For the bad luck that constantly dogged him.

But that was before more turns of the lens brought his role into even sharper focus. That was before she learned he'd cash her mother's paycheck—and his, when he earned one—and gamble it away at the horses, the "dogs," Jai-Alai, or whatever betting sport he could find any given night. And the more he lost, the more desperate he was to win it back, until there was nothing left. And the Jannell children went hungry. They went without new shoes. Without phone, electricity, and water. Without dentists.

He'd *deserved* that pain.

The soft tittering of a bird roused Alane from the distasteful memory. The sky outside Ray's window had lightened. No point going back to bed, no matter how tired she still was. She wondered what had woken her up in the first place—if it had been a dream she couldn't remember.

15

WHATISTHISTHING

Ray held the claw in the morning light coming through his window. It was black and slim, hollow, with a sharp tip. He did an internet search for animal claws on his phone. Raccoon, possum, squirrel, coyote, bear. It didn't resemble any of those. What the hell did this come off of? He smelled it at the base where it had broken off. The stump had a faint meaty smell. There were bits of blackened tissue. He made a disgusted face and held it away. He laid it down on his desk next to a ruler, one inch, and took a picture.

He spent the rest of the morning researching, and it almost felt like he'd come to the end of the internet, and maybe he had, when he found *whatisthisthing*. A forum where people posted pictures of stuff, bugs or weird growths on their bodies, some next to a banana for scale, to see if anyone knew what they were. After creating an account with the username dreadlatch, Ray uploaded the photo he'd taken and typed, *I found this claw in my house. What animal is it from*?

Not long after, he heard Papa Wessel messing around in the garage and took the claw down to get the man's opinion.

"Looks like a thorn," Papa said, squinting at the claw in his fingers. "From something like that plant over there." He jerked a thumb at the spiky plant by the apartment steps. "Probably just got tracked in the house."

"I don't know," Ray said, looking skeptically at the saw palmetto, which had tiny needle-like points on its fronds. He opened his mouth to tell Papa Wessel about the thing climbing the curtain, but in the light of day, the incident seemed like something he'd imagined. He and Papa searched everywhere last night. Something that size couldn't just *vanish*.

Papa filled a plastic pail with spackle, mesh, and other supplies. "You ready to patch up that hole?"

They climbed the steps, Ray carrying the ladder again. Mom held the door open for them when Papa knocked. They moved Ray's desk out of the way for the ladder. Then the old man taught Ray how to spatula the gum-like pink paste into and over the hole.

Ray smushed spackle deep into the hole. *Try to eat through* this!

"Looking good," Papa encouraged. "We'll touch up the paint at some point, but this is fine for now."

They took the ladder and supplies back down to the garage, and an hour later, the spackle had dried white. Ray lay on his bed, trying to pick the Masterlock 140 that kept eluding him. With Mom home tonight for once, he felt almost happy, until he inevitably remembered Allie Singer telling Mr. Sowder about the magnesium ribbon. Then, he grew restless, standing up, pacing his room without purpose. Not knowing what to do with his feelings.

He'd never texted Allie back. Anytime he'd started to, he'd deleted it. She hadn't texted him again. He dreaded Tuesday and science class. Would Mr. Sowder say something to him? Would Allie ever talk to him again? Had she told anyone at school about him stealing? The thought made him almost lightheaded with anxiety. Would the police be waiting for him at school? Thoughts, each worse than the next, raced through his mind. Waiting for the inevitable phone call to his mother made him feel like throwing up. He wished Sowder would just get it over with.

He also wished he could bring the claw he'd found to class and look at it with Allie under the microscope. But she'd probably think he was crazy. She'd spread it around school that he was imagining monsters now.

That night, as dinner cooked, he showed Mom his new trick of unlocking the training lock blindfolded. She timed him and he beat his time by a few seconds.

She shook her head. "Well, I never expected your talent to be in lock picking, but you're really good at this."

His chest puffed out. She asked him to show her how, and they played with the trainer for a while. She didn't unlock it, but she did get one of the pins open. Then they ate on trays in front of the TV.

As night fell, his thoughts turned once more to the thing on the curtain whose claw he'd found. He longed to have that sharp machete locked in Papa Wessel's cabinet. *You already broke the locksport code*, that voice inside Ray said. *You're an official thief now*. But no way would Papa not notice the weapon was gone. Instead, Ray swiped one of his mom's big butcher knives from the kitchen block and slipped it between his mattress and box spring. The knife was dull, but it was something. If that... *thing*... came back and tried to attack him, Ray would be ready.

Lying in bed, Ray remembered his post on *whatisthisthing*. He opened the site on his phone, saw there were comments, and excitedly clicked on them. But they were mostly from randos: *Bro, it's from an alien*, Ray read with a small eye roll.

Could be a rhinoceros beetle horn, someone else posted, the most reasonable answer so far.

looks like something I pulled out of my ass. This one made him snicker.

The last comment was from a dude named Cecil with the title "Premier Creature Hunter" (another eye roll from Ray) in his profile.

That's not a claw. DM me.

16

THE SKILL OF DELINQUENTS

Alane stood at the window of the front door Sunday morning, sipping coffee. The sky was bright blue, a few fluffy white clouds in the distance. You wouldn't think a category-2 hurricane was churning out in the Atlantic. The forecast now had Rose hitting somewhere between Key West to Fort Pierce, or 287 miles of coast, which included Hallandale. It didn't look good for the Kenton wedding.

Alane remembered a hurricane from when she was a kid—must have been '81 or '82—that dumped so much rain in such a short time their street flooded. The water came all the way up to within a foot or two of their front steps and had grass floating in it. Their mother wouldn't let them play in it after the storm passed. She said there were worms in the saturated ground that would burrow into their feet.

Back then, the local news channel printed hurricane tracking maps that were stacked at the grocery store registers for people to take and mark the coordinates as the storms got closer. In a way, she wished they were still tracked that way. It was something to do, instead of just waiting for it to hit. *I should do this with my fifth graders.*

A movement caught her eye, and she saw Mrs. Wessel come out onto the patio in orange Crocs and a housecoat. The elderly woman's hair had the same white, cotton-candy floss texture as the clouds. She shuffled over to a bird feeder hanging on a metal pole and reached shakily up to pull it down. Alane put her cup down, slid on some flip-flops, and hurried down the steps to join her in the yard.

"Let me help you," Alane said, lifting the feeder down. The pole had four hooks, all festooned with feeders.

"Oh, yes! Thank you! I want to bring all of them inside. Bruce is at the hardware store for plywood."

"Where do you want this?" Alane asked, taking down a second feeder shaped like a retro camper.

"In that chest."

Alane laid the feeders carefully on top of outdoor furniture cushions in the chest and then fanned out to pluck up all the little whirligigs, garden sculptures, and planters around the yard. She returned to the patio with a bouquet of sharp-tipped garden stakes topped with frogs, snails, and butterflies that would have made lethal flying projectiles in a hurricane.

Impalement by whimsical garden stake.

"Do you think it will actually hit us?" Alane asked.

"Hard to say," Mrs. Wessel said, clearing terra cotta planters off the waxed cotton covered picnic table. "So many times they look like they're heading right for us. We hunker down, and then they veer off. After Andrew, Bruce and I take all of them seriously."

"We were up north during Andrew," Alane said, standing on tiptoe to bring down a hanging plant from a hook on the patio overhang. "But I used to live in Homestead."

"Ground zero."

Alane nodded. "It's weird to have your childhood town wiped off the map. I heard it looks completely different."

"Must be strange to go there."

"I haven't been back." Alane pulled up the last garden spinner. She looked around. "Is that everything?"

"I think so. Thanks, honey. Having you and Ray here is such a blessing."

Back in the apartment, Alane checked her phone and frowned when she saw a call from an unknown number and a voicemail. She listened to the message, her face registering confusion as it played.

"Mrs. Ranew, this is Charles Sowder, Ray's science teacher. I'm sorry to trouble you on the weekend, but there's something important I need to discuss with you. Please give me a call as soon as possible."

With a feeling of dread, she called the number and a man picked up on the second ring.

"Mr. Sowder? It's Alane Ranew, Ray's mom."

"Thank you for returning my call." He paused. "I'm never happy making a call like this, but... I wanted to let you know that there was an incident at school Friday, and Ray was implicated."

Alane's stomach dropped. She lowered herself into a kitchen chair. "What happened?"

"A pretty dangerous chemical was taken from a cabinet in the science room. The cabinet was locked. I always keep it locked." His voice was insistent.

Oh, Ray. Alane's forehead dropped into her hand.

The teacher continued, "A student came to me Friday afternoon with a pretty serious accusation that Ray had taken the chemical and put it in her locker. I asked her why she thought it was Ray, and from what she said, it sounds like he might have taken it for her because she enjoyed the experiment we did with it earlier in the week. This student and Ray are lab partners."

Alane's chest clenched. He didn't have to say more. Ray had picked the lock and broken into the cabinet. It was her son. Alane's eyes got hot.

The teacher asked, "Has Ray mentioned anything about this?"

"No," Alane said, cheeks burning. "*No*. I had no idea. I'm so sorry."

"Ray seems like a good kid," Sowder said. "He's never been in any trouble as far as I can see in his record. It sounds like he was just trying to show off to this student. I know it's difficult being the new kid in school. Since the chemical was returned, I think I can just speak to him and give him a warning. But there should be consequences."

"Of course," she hurried to say. "I'll speak to him right now."

"I'd love to know how he got into my cabinet," the teacher murmured as if to himself.

Alane braced herself for what she was about to say. "Ray's father started him picking locks as a hobby." She heard the sharpness in the word *father*. "Ray's become really good at it."

Sowder gave a short bark of surprise. "Interesting."

"We've told him multiple times he can't break into people's property." She was getting angry now. "There's a code about it."

"I'd like to speak with him, if that's okay and he's around."

"Sure, I'll get him." Alane walked down the hallway and parted the curtain over Ray's room. She knocked on the top of his box. "Ray. Phone call." She kept her voice neutral as if a part of her was worried he'd bolt.

But he crawled outside. "Is it Dad?"

Alane shook her head, holding out the phone. Did she imagine a slight hesitation before he took it?

Yeah, it was petty, but as she left the bedroom, she felt almost giddy that it wasn't her fault this time. She'd never approved of Brad's *hobby* that he'd passed on to his son. Her ex-husband was a serial dabbler, always into trying new things, buying all the expensive equipment, watching video tutorials, with some fantasy behind it of becoming a champion in something, winning contests, money. But when he didn't turn out to be a prodigy, he'd move on to something else. Abandoning the brand-new gear that collected dust until Alane sold it on eBay.

Except Ray never moved on from the picking. He'd taken to it. The way he played constantly with his locks, lining them up by size or difficulty or shininess—it had only gotten worse since they moved—the locks were like a security blanket. *I'll have to take them away*, she thought, pained, knowing what it would do to him. But this was the consequence, wasn't it? Ray couldn't be allowed to break into people's things. *Teacher's things*! Jesus.

Why couldn't he have been into stamps? Pokémon cards? Comics, like other kids. Instead, he'd become obsessed with this skill of delinquents.

She looked forward to—no, *relished*—telling Brad Ranew this one was on him.

17

MONSTERS A TO Z

"Ray, this is Mr. Sowder."

A sharp spike of adrenaline went through Ray. He couldn't speak.

The teacher must have realized because he went on. "I just spoke to your mom. Do you know what this is about?"

"I think so." A small voice. His feet felt rooted to the floor.

"Did you break into my supply cabinet and steal magnesium ribbon? And then did you place this stolen ribbon in a classmate's locker? Be honest. You'll get in more trouble if you lie."

"Yes," Ray said, feeling weight lift from his shoulders just before the fear of consequences settled heavily down.

"Stealing school property is a serious offense. I have every right to contact the police." Mr. Sowder's voice, always so friendly, now had a distant tone Ray had never heard before, even when the teacher had gotten stern with kids in class.

After a pointed pause, the teacher said, "I haven't contacted the authorities yet."

Ray heard his breath shallow on the phone, afraid to hope.

"Because I know this is a one-off." Mr. Sowder pressed, "Ray, can you tell me why you stole the ribbon?"

Ray backed up to sit on his bed. "I don't know." Truly, he didn't. It had been a split-second decision. He hadn't even stopped to think.

"Did you do this to show off to the other student? You really upset them."

"I know." His hand slipped inside his shorts pocket for the lock there.

"Your mom told me how you got into my cabinet. It's great to have hobbies, but not if they are used for doing wrong. Do you understand that?"

"Yes."

The teacher sighed, and somehow that was worse than anything. "There will be major consequences for this, at home and in school. Your school counselor will be contacting you next week to talk about why you made the choice you did. In the meantime, you need to apologize to the classmate you hurt."

"I will," Ray promised. "I'm so sorry. I'll never do something like that again."

"I know you won't."

The relief of knowing he was on the other side of it now, facing the consequences, not the unknown, flooded him.

After hanging up, Ray waited for his mother to come collect the phone. He sat like a cowering animal, bracing for a blow. Mom had never hit him before, but he wasn't sure if this would push her over the edge.

But her face was unreadable. "Bring me your locks."

The words, though spoken calmly, were like a sledgehammer to his chest.

"Okay." He got the box of locks out of his Bunker.

"All your picks too," she said.

He handed everything over, including the lock in his pocket, without meeting her eyes.

"I don't know when you'll get these back," she said. "Not until I know you can play with them responsibly... and abide by the code."

Feeling numb, Ray watched her carry away his locks then crawled inside his Bunker so she wouldn't see him cry, and he eventually fell asleep.

It was late when he woke up, neck bent at a painful angle from sleeping on the refrigerator box floor. He crawled outside to a dark apartment. Mom had let him sleep through dinner and had gone to bed herself. He checked his phone—2:15 a.m.—and clicked on the bedside lamp. BeBe was eating pellets from her little plastic bowl, making soft crunching sounds.

Hungry too, he went out to the kitchen for a bowl of cereal and sat at the table to eat it, checking the *whatisthisthing* forum. Cecil was still the last to reply to his post. Curious, Ray clicked on the link in Cecil's profile that took him to a site called Centre for Creature Studies, an A-Z list of monsters, facts, and grainy photos or "artist renderings" of each. Bigfoot, the Loch Ness Monster, Jersey Devil were on the list, along with ones he'd never heard of like the Slump-Back of Barne's Farm, the entry of which included a boring, rambling "investigation" in the dark of an abandoned barn, where a strange hunched over humanoid figure had allegedly been sighted and whose "existence remains elusive."

Yeah right, he thought, and was about to exit out, but something made him stop. Leaving his empty bowl on the table, he returned to his room and opened the desk drawer for the claw, now contained in a Ziploc bag. The smell had gotten ranker where it had broken off... whatever it had broken off of. When Ray was little, he'd brought a seashell home from the beach and left it with other shells in his pail in the garage. He didn't realize a hermit crab was in it until the garage stank and Dad found the dead crab sticking out of its shell.

Ray touched the tip of his mysterious claw through the plastic. It seemed sharp enough to break through. Was there venom on it? He yanked his finger back. Cecil hadn't said what the claw was, but he seemed to know. Maybe he'd seen something like this before. Ray put the claw away in the drawer and sent Cecil a DM: *Hi. I posted the picture of the claw I found in my house. What is it?*

To his surprise, a reply came just five minutes later: *I have some suspicions but need more details first.*

Fill out the attached encounter report and send it back to me. I want to know about every incident, everything you remember. It's not a good idea at this stage to tell anyone until we know what we are dealing with, unless you are in danger. Once I get that back, we can come up with a plan to evict the creature from your house.

Creature? Ray made a scoffing noise. Are we calling it that now? He was letting this weirdo get to him. But he'd heard *some*thing scuttling on the other side of the wall. He'd seen it with his own two eyes when it climbed the curtain.

Something *alive* had been there. Something he never wanted to see again.

So, Ray sent *got it* to Cecil even though Mom would totally freak out if she knew he'd contacted a random stranger on the Internet.

A reply shot back:

If this creature is starting to reveal itself to you, we don't have much time.

It's growing bolder.

18

ALANE GETS CAUGHT

"Don't even think about it," Alane warned the car's engine when it sputtered turning into the school parking lot the next morning. *...a hurricane watch has been issued for the Windward Islands—* The radio weather report shut off when she pulled into a spot and cut the engine. Light rain pattered the windshield. Her gaze went to the dead crane fly, still stuck in the vent, probably mummified by now. Why did she always notice it when she wasn't in a position to deal with it?

Alane hadn't slept well last night, her mind racing after Mr. Sowder's call. For the first several years of Ray's life, there was nothing her son did, nothing he experienced, that Alane didn't know about and experience with him. It wasn't until kindergarten, really, that Ray had his own day apart from hers. And every year since, there were fewer of their days together. When Ray was a baby, she'd been so attuned to his every want, feeling, and thought. Funny how he seemed to communicate with her more then, through tears and tantrums, than he did now when he had every word at his disposal.

Ray had been more secretive lately, keeping things from her. And now there was this student, probably a girl, he had stolen for, trying in the wrong way to impress her. Which, when Alane thought about it, was so Ray. He'd always been a shy child; hard to get to know. Moving had only worsened it. Now, he spent most of his time in his box, alone. A wave of guilt hit her, bigger than the last one. They kept coming, the waves, swells as far as the horizon, washing the shore of her heart every minute of every day. An endless battering.

She walked in the door of the building and smelled the warm, doughy smell of pancakes from the cafeteria. She'd never told Ray this, but she'd gotten in trouble at school once. That breakfast smell, wafting from the cafeteria, always brought her back to that morning.

She'd been in fourth grade then, Philip in second. Each morning, as soon as they walked in the door at Naranja Elementary, they'd get a huge whiff of scrambled eggs, toast, and pancakes. It *always* made Alane's stomach rumble. But that particular morning, those warm, bakery scents had made her feel weak with hunger.

There hadn't been breakfast at home. Not for weeks now. Alane hadn't said anything when the milk and cereal ran out. The last time she did, her mother snapped, "I really don't have time for this, Alane. You're just going to need to be patient."

Alane knew not to ask again. Most of the time, Mom wasn't even home when they got up. She'd already left for work. Dad was still in bed, out of work again. It wasn't a good idea to wake him up.

That morning, Philip had been slow to wake up and was listless on the bus. "My stomach hurts," he had whispered to her, kids streaming around them in the hallway.

The day in front of Alane seemed impossibly long. She glanced in the direction of the cafeteria.

"Come on," she said, grabbing Philip's hand.

The air inside the cavernous room smelled like warm syrup. About fifty kids were sitting at tables with plastic trays of food.

"What are we doing?" Philip's face was pinched with worry. No one had ever told them not to eat school breakfast. But no one had said it was all right either.

"Just get a tray," Alane whispered.

They took the plastic trays of food the cafeteria lady gave them and pushed them along on the tray rail to the register. Although the air was cold, sweat prickled between Alane's shoulder blades. Her heart beat fast when the cashier looked expectantly at her.

"I forgot our money," she said quietly; it was all she could think of. Back then there was a special card you showed, but eleven-year-old Alane didn't know that.

The cashier and the lady behind the glass exchanged a glance, and then the cashier turned back to the children and waved them to the tables, "Go on."

Dizzy with relief, Alane hustled Philip to an empty table with a glance at the clock. Only five minutes. "Hurry up," she urged, opening his milk carton for him.

Philip's face was bright as he ate. Alane poured a plastic container of syrup on her pancakes and shoveled them in her mouth. The syrup was warm and sweet and dribbled from her fork in a long thread, like the oil droplets spiraling down the lamp at grandma's house with the goddess statue inside. She wiped her chin with her wrist and scooped syrup out of the pack with her finger and into her mouth. Children around them talked and laughed. It was strange to be in an almost empty cafeteria. Nobody looked at them. Nobody questioned them being there.

The first bell rang. Philip quickly finished his milk. Trays clattered as the other kids got up. Alane scraped the last of the syrup off the tray and took her empty tray to the metal cart. Sitting in class later, she felt sleepy. Replete.

But the next morning, when she and Philip took their trays with single serve Rice Crispies cereal and milk to the register, Alane's face felt hot. She knew they weren't allowed and had tried to explain to Philip, but he'd started crying as soon as he smelled the food.

The cashier's expression was stiff this time.

Mom shouted at Alane that night. "Your teacher called me at work. She said you two were getting breakfast. That's for kids who are in a special program. That's not us."

"Can we get in the special program?" Alane asked.

"I told you this is temporary. Why can't you just be patient?" Alane couldn't figure out why her mother was so angry.

The rest of the week there was cereal and milk for breakfast at home and money for lunch. But when it ran out again, Alane knew not to say anything. So, she brought books to read during lunch, and sometimes a friend would give her something they didn't like from their tray.

And in the mornings, when Philip cried, she yanked him roughly toward his classroom.

"Shh," she'd snap at him. "You're not going to die."

19

NOT LIABLE FOR INJURY OR DEATH

The librarian's return cart whispered on the carpet in the aisle behind Ray's study carrel, and he waited until she turned the corner before opening Cecil's email on his phone. The school library was nearly empty except for a few students studying during lunch, and Ray who was hiding out here. All last night as anxiety churned his stomach, he'd thought of running away. Going to live with his dad. Anything to avoid school today. Allie Singer had probably told all her friends about the magnesium ribbon. The whole school probably knew. Ray had kept his head down in the halls and during morning classes. He requested a library pass from his history teacher for lunch so he wouldn't have to go to the cafeteria where kids would whisper about him. *That's him. That's the thief.*

Just thinking of facing Mr. Sowder or Allie in science class tomorrow made him want to throw up. Would Allie say anything to him? Would she pretend he didn't exist? He didn't know which was worse.

He pulled up Cecil's email, clicked on the attachment.

CENTRE FOR CREATURE STUDIES

ENCOUNTER REPORT©

Ray glanced to either side of the carrel to make sure no one was close enough to read his screen and tapped his first name and email into the contact form, leaving the rest blank. Mom had drilled into him never to give out his personal info online. He scrolled to the first question.

Describe your first encounter with the creature/entity.

He sighed and scrolled all the way down a lengthy form. *Ugggh.* With another sigh, he scrolled back up and typed what had happened the other night, squirming a little when he had to explain there was nothing but a curtain hanging over his doorway. As he struggled for the words to describe what he'd heard and seen, his "encounter" sounded more and more dumb. The legs he *thought* he'd seen were probably just June bugs ricocheting off the walls and curtain. Hadn't he read on the Centre's website that most of the cases they investigated were easily explained by natural causes?

Ray dragged his cursor over the X to close out the form. Except.... his finger hovered. The fabric of the curtain had folded like a taco shell around whatever was climbing it. June bugs—even a bunch of them—didn't weigh enough to do that. The pokes in the fabric *couldn't* be random bugs flying into the curtain either. They had moved together in pairs.

Don't forget about the claw.

This Cecil person thought it might be something else but had not said what yet.

First things first: the questionnaire.

Do you have any physical evidence of the creature/entity? Describe.

I found a claw. There was a rip in the curtain like it had gotten stuck and pulled off.

Describe any sounds/smells associated with the creature/entity.

A nasty smell in my room coming from a hole in the ceiling.

This was the first he'd mentioned the hole to Cecil, and he wished he'd thought to take a picture before he and Papa Wessel had patched it.

Have you experienced any supernatural occurrences before this (ghost sightings, possession, monster encounters)?

no

Do you have any experiences (weapons training) that could help in capturing/evicting the creature/entity?

lock picking

Ray deleted that.

no

The rest of the questions were about when the encounters started and how he'd found Cecil's website. His eyes skimmed over text blocks of legal jargon.

I *understand the danger might increase before it gets better. The CENTRE FOR CREATURE STUDIES is not liable for any injuries, deaths, or property damage.*

Blah, blah.

Ray typed his name at the bottom of the form and clicked SUBMIT as the end-of-period bell rang.

"Come on in, Ray." Mrs. Carnett waved him into her office. "How are you?"

"Okay." Ray took a seat on the other side of the school counselor's desk. The last time he'd been here was his first day at school. Her desk had been spotless then. Now, it was cluttered with papers, books, and folders.

"So, we both know why you're here," she said. "Do you want to tell me about it?"

Ray stared at his lap, ears so hot he thought they must be glowing. "I took magnesium ribbon from Mr. Sowder's room. I'm really sorry."

"So, not so good choices, huh?" she said. "I understand you're going through a lot with your family right now. That's a lot for you to go through. That's hard on anyone. Do you want to talk about it?"

The knot in his throat swelled. "No." A lie.

"I'm sure you miss your friends from your old school."

He nodded, still not looking at her. He touched his pocket for the lock, remembered it wasn't there, and folded his hands in his lap.

"Sometimes, when we're kids, or even when we are adults, we don't have a choice whether to move, and it sucks. It sucks being the new kid. But stealing isn't a healthy way to make friends. You understand that, right?"

"Yes." He heard students' voices passing outside in the hall.

"It's the school's right to involve the police in this, but the item was returned. And it's my opinion, and Principal Hernandes's opinion, that you made a bad choice and it won't ever happen again. Am I right about that?"

He looked up. "Yes."

Mrs. Carnett smiled gently. "So, I spoke with Principal Hernandes, and I understand you're going to spend three days with Mr. Sowder at lunch, helping with projects in the classroom, and you're going to write letters of apology to him and to Miss Singer. Would you agree that this will set things right?"

He nodded, his shoulders lifting with relief that the conference appeared to be over.

"Okay. You can head back to class now," Mrs. Carnett said. As he was about to rush out the door, she added, "If you ever *do* want to talk, Ray, I'm here."

After a torturous afternoon of classes that seemed to go on forever, Ray stepped off the bus and let himself into the apartment. He was sprawled on the couch with chips watching TV when his phone chimed with a text.

can we go over your paperwork real quick?

Cecil. Ray sat up. The idea that this person now had his phone number made him feel weird. But Cecil might know what that thing on the curtain was.

Ray texted OK.

Cecil: Do you have more pictures of the object you found that you can send me?

Ray: hold on

He ran for the Ziploc in his Bunker, shook the claw out onto the coffee table. A thick, gassy stench billowed out with it. Turning away his nose, Ray snapped several pics and sealed the thing back up in the bag. He texted the images to Cecil. Several minutes passed before a reply came back.

Cecil: You said you found this spine after seeing an entity climb a curtain?

Ray picked up the bag. Now that Cecil said it, it *did* look like a spine.

Yes, he texted. What is it from?

Cecil: could be insectoid. definitely came off something in a soldier caste

Soldier caste? Before Ray could reply, Cecil texted again: whatever it is, it's dangerous. Did you touch it?

Ray's pulse lurched. Yes. I mean its in a bag now. It smells disgusting.

Cecil: Don't touch it again. I'm going to have to do more research. I think the hole in your ceiling is related. Do you have a picture?

Ray: no landlord patched it

Cecil: Too bad.

Texts chimed in fast succession, Ray's eyes getting wider as he followed.

Cecil: Ok then, I will research this more.

It's not a good idea at this stage to tell anyone else until we know what it is. unless you are in danger.

Don't want to panic anyone.

I will be back in touch with a plan to evict the creature from your house.

Expect the encounters to intensify.

Ray stiffened in alarm, texted: wait. what do I do if this thing comes back?

He glanced at the sharp, possibly venom-tipped spine in the plastic bag, fidgeting as he waited for a reply.

call 911. and barricade the door

Ray groaned and collapsed back against the couch cushion.

That would be great if there were any doors here to barricade!

20

BURNED DOWN HER ARCHIVES

Rain drenched Alane's shoulders and soaked her sandals so that they slid around under her feet as she sprinted for her car. Dropping into the driver's seat and slamming the door, she enjoyed the simple pleasure of not moving, of taking the weight off after a long day in the classroom. Rain streamed down the windshield so that the scrubby trees on the other side of the parking lot appeared soft and haloed. She turned the keys in the ignition, and the engine cranked and died. She leaned back against the headrest. Breathed. *Please. I'll take you in this week*, she promised the car. She didn't need a repair bill after just paying the deductible for Ray's urgent care visit. She swiped hair out of her eyes and tried the key again. The motor hesitated, refusing to catch.

"Damn it," she said, hitting the steering wheel.

She stared in front of her, her gaze narrowing on the crane fly wedged in the crack between the windshield and dashboard. The wing broke off in her fingers when she grabbed it. The rest of the fly slipped into the vent. *Perfect*. She flung open the door and shook the wing off her wet fingers and slammed the door. Rubbed her hand on her pants. Tried the car again. This time, it stuttered to life. She released her breath.

The rain had stopped, and the streets were drying in the sun by the time she pulled into the driveway at home. Her shoulders relaxed, and she turned off the motor. The grinding sound of a chainsaw assaulted her ears as she stepped out of the car. Papa Wessel was up on a ladder cutting down limbs, presumably to prevent them from breaking in the hurricane gusts. The ladder wobbled, and she tensed again, but then Papa steadied himself and kept on sawing. Alane shook her head and started up the apartment stairs. One of these days, the man was going to hurt himself.

She changed into sweats, made some popcorn, and ate in bed as the rotating mass of Hurricane Rose filled her phone screen, a tangle of colored lines showing its potential path. Hallendale was one of the targets. She felt impatient for the storm to hit them or blow away, weaken, or whatever. It always took forever, with so much build up, and all the storms she'd prepared for as a child had blown harmlessly over. At least this apartment was high up, no fear of flooding. Papa's chainsaw spit and buzzed outside. She supposed she should help him batten down things but couldn't get herself to move.

The little pantry and all the cupboards were crammed with food. She still felt uneasy, worried they'd run out. It was an uncomfortable feeling, a constant tap on the shoulder. *Um, don't you think you should pick up a few more things to be safe*?

Ray was in his room—he was in there all the time now—and she often had thoughts of playing board games or putting puzzles together with him, or even watching a movie, but never followed through. She didn't seem to have any energy anymore. When she *was* home, all she wanted to do was veg out. She'd been napping more lately; it only seemed to make her more tired.

Ray's latest thing was the lockpicking videos, and he'd bugged her repeatedly for his own channel. But he was so young, and a channel would expose him to all kinds of internet creeps. There was something else that kept her from saying yes. The knowledge that once he got online, he'd never again have full control over his story. When Alane's mother died, along with sorrow, Alane had felt a guilty sense of relief. The person who knew her longest, knew her secrets, her shames, her failures, was gone. Alane's past had been virtually wiped away. Her archives burned down. Only two others knew her past. Philip, but he was far away. And her father, out of her life for years now, whereabouts unknown.

She knew eventually Ray would wear her down. It would start with a channel and next social media. His archive would be fireproof—every selfie or post forever. Alane was glad she'd grown up when she did. She could control what everyone knew about her past. She'd always taken the position that it didn't achieve anything to run down Ray's grandparents' characters. What purpose would it serve to tell Ray about what happened in her childhood? That was over.

Alane's eyes opened in the dark. The clock on her bedside table blinked at 12:00. Must have been a power outage. She almost drifted off again when she heard faint mewling inside the apartment. She bolted up, put her feet on the floor. Rubbed her eyes. Moonlight streamed in through the window, casting a stretched-out rectangle of light on the floor. The mewling came again from right outside her bedroom.

Neck tingling with unease, she crept to her bedroom door to peek around the drape. The apartment hallway telescoped into darkness. Framed photographs covered every inch of wall space, the faces blurred. Yellowed from cigarette smoke. Tinny television voices came from far away. From decades away.

This isn't right, she thought from some deep place inside, but her feet took her down the passage.

The carpet under her bare soles was a heavy pile, matted down. Crunchy in places. She didn't want to think about what had dried there. Her nightgown whispered against her skin, pink with ruffles, threadbare on the elbows.

Reaching the end of the hallway, movement caught her eye. A picture frame trembled. A family photograph. Herself, around seven, in a brown dress and white socks with ankle ruffles. Philip, five, in a baby blue suit. Mom in white. Dad behind them, smiling. The picture crashed to the floor, glass shattering, shards scattering around her feet.

Still, the mewling urged her onward. She tiptoed past the living room. Scuffed furniture. An overstuffed recliner turned away from her facing the TV, an ashtray on the armrest. A figure in jeans and stocking feet, one big toe with a long nail sticking out, bathed in blue screen light. Haze of smoke in the air.

Pressing back against the wall, she slid along it, toward the tiny cries. Now, she stood in front of the laundry room door. Adult Alane's garage apartment didn't *have* a laundry room, but this fact didn't intrude as she pressed an ear to the door. She heard movement inside. Like something dragging itself across the floor.

She pushed the door open and saw a calico cat in a wedge of light. Alane smelled the copper tang of blood.

Squeaky lay on a red-soaked towel, licking a tiny black kitten with a white patch on its nose. There were five kittens, all wet, scrabbling blindly on the floor, heads bobbing jerkily, mewing that tiny, distressed sound. Alane dropped to her knees. Cat litter dug into her skin. *I have to tell Philip*!

She reached to touch the kitten closest to her, all black. Squeaky hissed then seized something bloody in her teeth.

NO! *Don't eat the baby*! Alane stretched out her hands to stop her.

But it wasn't a kitten. Something else had slipped out of Squeaky's body and was still attached to her by a red, slippery-looking rope. The cat gnawed it, growling low in her throat, as if she thought Alane would snatch it from her.

21

EVERY MONSTER HAS A WEAKNESS

The whirring sound of the orbital sander was slightly muffled by the safety earmuff headphones over Ray's ears. His whole arm vibrated with the sander as he ran it over the long bench slat, smoothing off the old stain. It was soothing work, standing up at the worktable, letting his mind rest as he just focused on keeping the sander flat so it wouldn't create deeper patterns in the antique wood. At another table, Papa Wessel was wiping off the nuts and bolts he'd soaked to remove the rust. Heat and sawdust filled Ray's nose, covered with a paper respirator. The old man had also made him wear plastic goggles. "Don't need you getting hurt again." Pursing his lips at Ray's arm and the bandage he knew was underneath his shirt.

Stupid accident was gonna haunt him forever. Ray had followed all the directions right: preheating the oven, waiting until the little red light clicked off, spreading the frozen chicken nuggets in one layer on the cookie sheet. Setting his phone alarm for when they'd be done. The rubbery oven mitts were like cartoon hands. He'd opened the oven door for the cooked nuggets. Heat blasted his face. He rushed to slide the pan out, and the door sprang back and hit his arm above the elbow. He'd dropped the pan, and it clanked back down on the rack, nuggets bouncing onto the bottom of the oven, sizzling and burning.

There was a delay between the oven door hitting him and it hurting, like when a jet flies faster than the speed of sound. A sonic burn. The skin there turned bright red. He hurried to the sink and ran water over his arm like his mother did when he'd sloshed boiling water on his hand once while helping her make macaroni and cheese. Leaning over the sink, he held the red spot under the faucet stream and hissed. His eyes watered.

Mom yelled at him when she came home that night and saw the blister. "Why didn't you *call* me?" She examined his arm, looking more and more alarmed. "This looks pretty bad, bud."

When he and Mom got home from urgent care that night, Papa Wessel was still working in his garage with the door up, overhead light on, something he never did because the June bugs would get in and zoom around the light. Papa spent time every weekend scooping their dead bodies out of the metal mailbox hanging by his front door under the porch light. The box had little swirling holes in it, so you could see if any mail was in there without lifting the lid. Why those bugs went in there, Ray didn't know, but they flew like little rockets around the porch light and maybe accidentally got trapped in there and couldn't figure a way out.

Papa Wessel had met them in the driveway, wiping his hands on a rag. "You okay there, son?"

Ray held out his arm, bulky with a white bandage. "Yeah." No pain; he had been given a pill at the clinic.

Papa Wessel's eyes went to Ray's mom, who was focused on digging in her purse for her phone. "You need anything?" he asked.

"No," she said, clipped. "We're fine."

Papa Wessel nodded.

Maybe Mom still felt like it was her fault and she felt bad. She didn't want Papa Wessel—*anyone*—to know what happened. To *blame* her.

She must have repeated *I'm sorry I shouldn't have left you alone* fifty times in the last hour, but like *Ray* was the one who hadn't made sure the oven door was fully open.

Papa Wessel seemed to get that, because he said to Ray, "I expect you'll be more careful next time. Don't want to be scaring your mother again."

Mom seemed to relax at that. "Thank you," she said in a softer tone, jingling her keys. "I'd better get Ray inside."

That night, Mom had set down New Rules*: no oven when I'm not here. Just the microwave or toaster.*

The sander's vibration made Ray's burn throb just a little, bringing him back to the present. The sander swiped that old, faded, dirty stain off the wood, revealing clean, fresh wood like magic. When he was done with the first slat, Papa Wessel came to stand over his shoulder. He grunted a *looks good* grunt and went back to his hardware. The garage door was open a few feet to let in fresh air, and the steady rain dripped into puddles on the concrete driveway. Papa Wessel had the radio tuned to a classic rock station, though Ray couldn't hear it between the earmuffs and sander noise.

His mother, working again at a catering job, probably wouldn't be too happy if she knew he was using the sander himself. Ever since the accident, she freaked out over every little thing, like when she got upset about him walking home alone from school. He wondered what would happen if he slipped and sanded his hand. Would it take the skin right off? What about the blue veins right under the skin? Would it shave the tops off so he could actually see inside the tubes?

The rain slowed to a sprinkle outside. Ray finished a slat and started on another, the work a distraction from his thoughts. That morning, he'd felt sick to his stomach, worried about what would happen in science class with Allie Singer. But Mr. Sowder had moved everyone to different tables with new lab partners, so now Ray was with a dude named Josh, and Allie was on the other side of the room. Nobody had looked at him funny.

But his stomach had kept churning until lunch when he had to go back to Mr. Sowder's class for detention. The teacher just put him to work straightening the supply cabinet and time passed without any mention of what Ray had done. Sowder's "see you tomorrow" wasn't friendly exactly, but it wasn't mad either. Leaving the science room after, with all the unknowns resolved, was like shedding a thousand pounds of gravity. He almost imagined he felt his ears pop.

When Ray finished sanding the slats, he wrapped the cord around the orbital sander and then lined all the slats on the floor on an old sheet Papa Wessel had laid there. The old man crouched down, not too easily, and ran his wrinkly hand over them.

He made a face like he was impressed. "Nice work," he said, and Ray's shoulders sat a little higher.

They cleaned up, Ray avoiding sweeping behind the garbage bin where a new glue trap was, and both sat down in the camp chairs. Ray made a groaning sound to mimic the old man's.

Next was soda and Oreos. Papa held out a sleeve, and Ray politely took just two. He remembered how when he was little, when he asked for more cookies, Mom would show him the label on snack boxes and say, *sorry, the government says you can only have two.*

Pretty smart of her.

The Oreos were mushy in Ray's mouth from the humidity, the plastic sleeve having been sealed loosely with a clothespin.

"You hear anything else coming from the attic?" Papa Wessel asked.

Ray looked at his soda can, face heating when he remembered running to the Wessels' in the rain like a baby, afraid of noises in the dark. "No," he said. Things had been quiet ever since Papa patched the hole. He changed the subject. "How did you learn to do all this stuff?" He gestured around the garage, at the bench.

"My pop taught me," Papa Wessel said, sitting back, stomach pooching out over his jeans. "We couldn't afford to hire someone for repairs around the house, so he always had some project going on. Man was exacting. You can bet if I didn't do something right, I'd have to do it all over."

"Do you miss him?" Ray shoved a cookie in his mouth.

"I do." Papa Wessel looked at Ray. "You miss your dad?"

Ray chewed thoughtfully, swallowed. "Yeah. It's weird staying with him at his condo. I have my own room, but it doesn't really feel like mine, you know?" He shrugged, feeling ungrateful because Dad had let Ray pick out the furniture and everything.

Papa nodded as if he understood. "Do you feel the same way about here?" He brushed cookie crumbs off his knees into a cupped hand to throw in the bin later.

Ray shrugged. "At first, I did, even though I have all my stuff. But I'm getting used to it now."

"Same will happen the more time you spend at your dad's."

"Yeah."

"I'm not going to say it's all gonna be all right," Papa said, meeting Ray's eyes. "I don't think that's what you want to hear. Because I think you already know sometimes things aren't all right. But other times they are. And those are the times we got to cling to."

Late that night, Ray slowly came awake. It was pitch black. BeBe was quiet. The covers were tight around him, bunched around his face. It was hot. The foot of the bed dipped slightly, and he felt a light touch on his bare ankle through the bedsheets. His lungs seized. Something seemed to skim over the covers, barely touching, light as a cat. Except a cat had four legs and this had… more by the way it tentatively stepped over him. Ray's insides turned to jelly.

The thing moved up the bed. Ray smelled that oily smell from the ceiling. His eyes bugged, and he tried to scream, but nothing came out. It was like his lungs had deflated. Whatever it was stopped moving on top of him, and he felt a movement over his head in the dark, something whipping the air. Was it going to jam a proboscis into him and suck his guts out until he was just a husk? Tears leaked out of his eyes from not blinking. His mouth formed a silent *MOM!* Then, BeBe stirred in her cage, inside her igloo, and the thing on top of him tensed. He felt the whipping things turn toward her in interest, and that broke his paralysis. He threw his arms up to throw it off, not having the breath to make a noise, heart crashing in his chest, and whatever it was took off.

Ray lay panting for a moment then leaped for the lamp switch. He found his voice and screamed, and this time the dark apartment was shattered with sound.

Mom was there in seconds, rubbing her eyes. "What is it baby? What's wrong?" Her eyes squinted in the lamplight, her hair in a sloppy knot.

"There was something in my room. On my bed!" he said, backing up against the headboard. Shaking, staring at the corner of the ceiling but it was still patched.

She sat beside him on the bed, pulled him to her. "I'm here. You're okay. It was a bad dream, that's all. Just a dream."

"NO! It was standing on me!"

"It was probably just a bug." But she looked creeped out now, brushing the bedspread for insects that weren't there.

"It was big!"

Mom got up and knelt down to check under the bed, then looked in the closet. "I don't see anything. Are you sure you didn't just dream it?"

"I don't know." He felt close to tears. "I don't like it here. Why did we even move here?"

Mom looked at him, sad. "You know why, buddy."

"I want to go home."

Mom sat on the edge of the bed and put her hand on his leg. He flinched away.

"I know," she said quietly. "I know this has been hard on you." She gave him a reassuring smile. "But everything's going to be okay. I promise. I won't let anything happen to you."

"I want my locks back."

"I can't do that, Ray."

He looked away. "You can go now. I'm fine."

"I can stay until you fall asleep." She moved as if to hug him, and he leaned away.

"No, I'm good."

After she left, he grabbed his phone and texted Cecil. Are you up? It's important

Ray waited until his eyes grew heavy, but Cecil didn't text back. Eventually, Ray fell asleep with the light on.

Hello? Ray texted Cecil again the next morning before school.

When the Premier Creature Hunter still didn't respond by lunchtime, Ray sent a DM through the *whatisthisthing* website: this is an emergency! Finally, in English class, Ray felt his phone vibrate in his pocket. He raised his hand to go to the bathroom and hid in a stall to read the text:

You're not my only client you know

Ray: I'm sor—

Cecil's next text came before he could finish. I do this all volunteer. if you want full attention, you can Venmo me.

Ray: I'm sorry. The monster

He backspaced.

That thing came back last night

Cecil: tell me everything

Ray sent off a rapid-fire text of what happened the night before and hit send.

Cecil: where are you now

Ray: school

There was a long pause, and Ray grew aware of how long he was taking in the bathroom.

Just when he was about to go back to class, Cecil texted: Let's talk tonight. I have an idea. But we need to move fast.

"Every monster has a weakness," Cecil said with a deep, gravelly voice. "An Achille's heel. Easy example: garlic and holy water repel vampires. A wooden stake through the heart kills them."

Ray sat in his Bunker with his earbuds and laptop. A still headshot of Cecil showed on screen. The man looked Mom's age, maybe a little younger, pale, beard, glasses. Ray's square on the video screen was blacked out to hide his face, but he still felt sweaty with nerves, hoping this guy wasn't a creep.

Cecil went on, "Right now, we don't know what your... entity's weaknesses are, so we have to test for different things, like when you go to the allergy doctor and they prick your arm."

"Sure," Ray said. He'd never been to an allergy doctor.

Cecil said, "From what you've reported, all your encounters have been at night. This makes me think this creature is nocturnal. It could be light sensitive. If we can make your house bright enough, we might make it so uncomfortable it will leave. Bright light might even kill it."

"Oh-*kay*," Ray said, dubious. "I can turn on all the lights in the apartment, but it lives in the attic and there aren't any lights up there."

"Can you get your hands on some kind of lamp or flashlight that's bright enough to reach every corner and set it up there?"

"For how long?" *What if that thing attacks me when I'm up there*? He didn't ask that part. "Not long," Cecil said. "If it's light sensitive it will run immediately. That's why you also have to keep the downstairs all lit up. You don't want it to escape that way. You want it leaving the same way it came in."

"But what way was *that*?" This was getting too complicated. "I don't know how it got in."

"Just leave the nearest window open and that should be fine. Good luck." Cecil signed off.

Ray crawled out of his Bunker and flipped on his lamp, feeling ridiculous. Cecil seemed confident this might work, *if* the Spiny-Thing was afraid of light. Ray moved around the apartment, switching on lights. Porch light, kitchen light, range hood, hallway.

Even the LEDs in his Bunker. Didn't want the thing taking shelter in there. From one end of the apartment to the other, he turned on every light there was.

This is so stupid.

Now for the attic light. Ray recalled that Papa Wessel had a hanging mechanics lamp he used to work on his car. He could ask to borrow it, but what if Papa Wessel asked what it was for? How would he explain that? A dude on the internet said I need one?

He didn't have his pick set to get into the garage. Even if he did have it, he'd sworn to himself not to ever break the lockpicking code again.

He didn't know what he was going to say until Papa Wessel opened the door and the lie slipped out, "Could I please borrow your mechanic's light and an extension cord for a science project? I'll bring it right back."

"Sure," Papa Wessel said. He shuffled out in flattened suede moccasins with the garage door key and let them in. If he noticed the light glaring out of every single window upstairs, he didn't say anything. The mechanic's light in its red plastic cage was hanging on the peg board. "You know where the extension cord is."

Papa Wessel had several in different lengths neatly coiled up in a plastic bin. Ray took the long orange one. "Thanks." He glanced at the ladder. "Could I borrow the ladder, too?"

The old man squinted at him. "What kind of project you working on?"

"It has to do with light and shadow," Ray said smoothly. He felt a tinge of conscience. Or should have. Actually, his conscience wasn't putting up a fight.

The old man nodded. "Leave the ladder upstairs if your mom don't mind. Need to get up there and lay those traps in the attic." He handed Ray the key. "Lock up after you put everything back."

It took two trips to haul everything upstairs, carrying it into his mother's room. With the lights on, he felt confident, powerful. The light was a force field. A laser that could blow the Spiny-Thing to ash. He set up the ladder, plugged in the cord, and carried the light up the ladder without tangling the line in his legs. He slid the panel over. He didn't hear anything, no Spiny-Thing skittering backwards or into the shadows. That could be good or bad. Hopefully, the light would be bright enough. He clicked on the light and held it up like a shield before taking another step up to look inside the crawl space. The light lit up most of the space. No creature went scurrying away. He saw beams like slightly angled ribs over his head and pink insulation with silver backing that reminded him of fish skin. His pulse raced as he scanned the light over the attic. Nothing.

The floor was just beams with insulation between. If he climbed up and stood on that insulation, would his foot bust through the ceiling? That made him feel better. Nothing big and heavy could be up here unless it was smart enough to walk just on the boards.

There wasn't a hook for him to hang the light on, so he turned it off and left it there, climbed down the ladder, and came back in a few minutes with his phone tripod. He made the legs as long as they'd go, wedged it up there as best he could, and hung the light on it. He turned on the power. The light swung, casting shadows on the exposed roof beams. Ray thought he saw something dash away out of the corner of his eye. The light didn't quite penetrate the farthest reaches of the crawl space. He aimed the light over, tipping over the tripod, and got the full glare in his eyes. He saw black spots. He imagined the Spiny-Thing, something like a spider, scrabbling toward him, and he held the mechanic's light in front of him, eyes squeezed shut, like a shield.

Gradually, his vision came back. He cracked an eye. The attic was empty.

Come on. Finish this.

He secured the light on the tripod. The heat was intense coming from the exposed bulb. This thing better not start a fire. That was probably Cecil's next suggestion—burn the place down.

Back in the kitchen, Ray made a baloney sandwich and took it and a glass of milk to the couch to watch television, which is where his mother found him when she came home early an hour later.

"Every light in this house is on!" she said, swiping off the inside door light. "What are you doing?"

"Science project," he said, jumping off the couch. "I'll turn them off."

"Is Mr. Sowder going to pay my electric bill?" she called after him.

Ray sprinted to her room before she could see the mechanic's light set up. He almost bumped into her in the hallway as he was coming out of her room, juggling the mechanic's light and extension cord. "Papa said to leave the ladder for him to put traps in the attic." She crossed her arms. He inched around her, the end of the cord dragging behind him.

"I don't know how much more of this I can take, buddy." She sighed heavily.

22

HOT DOGS AND SYMPATHY

Alane sat on the side of the bed and rubbed her toes. Tonight's job was one of the worst. Ridiculous tip, no leftovers. Creepy guy trying to pick her up.

While cleaning up in the banquet hall kitchen, Edie and the others still cleaning tables outside, Alane had poured a swallow of wine in a coffee cup and tossed it back. The idea of cooking anything when she got home was overwhelming, so she'd stopped at a convenience store. Left the engine running.

Nobody's going to steal this piece of shit, she had thought. *I'll just grab a couple of hot dogs for dinner.*

A *ding* had sounded as Alane pushed in through the glass door. A long light overhead flickered on the scuffed floor as she walked past a man in a tank top checking out at the counter. The place had that familiar scent of cleaning solution and coffee. No case of hot dogs spinning on hot rollers by the counter. Just gum, lighters. Cigarette racks. She walked through the store and catching her reflection in the coolers of soda and beer as she walked by, glass doors fogged with condensation.

The store was smaller inside than it seemed like from the outside. Older, worn. More of a mini grocery. At the back, she found only shelves of bread and potato chips. No fountain drink machines. No hot food.

I'll get Ray a candy bar.

A little girl, around eight, and a younger boy in shorts stood in the candy aisle, scoping what was there. *The customer's kids*, she concluded. The man was still at the counter, talking low to the male clerk. Maybe buying lottery tickets.

Alane remembered going to the 7-11 with Philip when they were kids for Fun Dip, Necco Wafers, and Now and Laters whenever they had money. Now and Laters were her favorite because they lasted the longest.

The little girl's eyes followed Alane almost greedily as she chose a bag of M&Ms for Ray. Alane smiled at her and the child looked away. The girl whispered to the boy, "Come on," and pulled him away.

Alane frowned. There was something familiar about this girl. Was she an Edgewater student? The girl had a world-weary, sharp look to her. The children walked to the magazine rack at the front window. Did anyone even read magazines anymore? The children's faces appeared pale and ghostly backlit in the dark window. A funny feeling started to clot in Alane's stomach. *Just get the candy*, she told herself.

She walked to the counter. The bell hadn't *dinged* once since she'd come in. The customer was still talking to the clerk, a loaf of bread and a pack of bologna on the counter between them.

The clerk looked at the man with narrowed, disapproving eyes. The customer shifted restlessly, sweat dampening the back of his shirt, a defeated slope to his shoulders. Kept looking over at his kids. There was something calculated in it. And now Alane, rooted to the grubby floor with her bag of M&Ms, saw everything. The clerk's eyes shifted to the children who were gazing at boxed donuts on an end cap, and he seemed to deflate. He bagged up the bread and lunch meat and slid a pack of Camels over to the customer with a matchbook on top.

Alane watched the girl's face. Saw the flush of mortification. The downturned eyes. The curled-in shoulders. The longing to disappear. Alane saw herself at the same age with Philip. Her father at the counter. "Help us out, man," he'd told the clerk. "Just this time. I'll pay you back." He'd thrown pointed glances at her and Philip. *Used* them.

Ding. Alane's gaze shot toward the door. A young woman walked in. When Alane glanced back at the counter, the children were beside the man, giving him the candy they'd selected. The hot food case Alane had been looking for was beside her on the counter, throwing off heat. Hot dogs spun lazily on the metal rollers.

"You got something?" the father asked cheerfully. He opened his wallet and counted out bills. "Thanks," he told the clerk, slipping the Camels into his pants pocket.

Alane stood disoriented, confused, watching the dad and his kids leave.

Ding.

"Next in line," the clerk said, startling her.

She must have walked out without the M&Ms. They weren't with her when she got home. She'd come home without anything for Ray to find every light on and a ladder in her closet.

When Alane slipped into bed that night, she surrendered to sleep with almost euphoric pleasure. She dreamt of the kittens again. They wiggled around on the towel, eyes still squeezed shut. Squeaky wasn't there. Maybe she was somewhere else in the house or roaming outside like she did. Alane was able to hold the tiny black one with the little white speck on his nose. She and Philip had named him Spitter and had just about convinced Mom to let them keep it.

The kitten's sharp claws dug into her palm as it squirmed to get down, and Alane squeezed her fingers tighter to keep the little thing from falling, the kitten mewling and squirming. Soft fur in her hands. *Shhh. Don't be scared*. She brought the little ball of fur to her chest. But the kitten scratched, panicked, and she squeezed harder. Trying to let it know she wouldn't hurt it. Feeling the claws pierce her skin. Sharper than she expected. Like needles. *No, stop. That hurts*. She felt her grip on the kitten slip. The ground was a long way down. The kitten tiny, so fragile. If it fell, its bones would break.

But the kitten kept struggling, so violently Alane nearly dropped it again. *Mom*! She called out for help. But her mouth hadn't moved. *MOM*!

Alane's eyes flew open, and the laundry room was gone. Shadows of the couch, the coffee table. Her own living room surrounded her. Her back against the wall, knees to her chest. Ray was crouched beside her. His fingers gripped her wrists, hard.

"Mom! Let *GO*!"

Her son's face was stark white in the dark above her. She stared up at him uncomprehendingly. Let go of what? She was half in and out of the dream. Some of it still lingered. She could feel the prick of claws in her hands.

"You're hurting her!" Ray pulled on her arm.

Something wiggled in Alane's cupped hands, scratched at her. The kitten! She looked down, saw a white mouse caged in her fingers, BeBe's little pink nails scrabbling.

Oh my god.

She put the animal into Ray's waiting hands.

"I'm so sorry." Her voice pleaded, confused. She didn't remember taking BeBe out of her cage. Couldn't remember leaving her bed.

He cradled the mouse to his chest. "You could have killed her!"

"No—" She shook her head, the realization of what she'd done crashing down. "Is she okay?"

"No, she's not okay! She's scared." He stormed off to his room.

What's wrong with me? Alane covered her face with her hands. *Why did I* do *that?*

You were protecting her, a voice inside said.

You were keeping her safe.

23

FOOLPROOF

Ray lay in bed with the desk lamp on and the knife from the kitchen wrapped in a hand towel beside him. He wasn't sure if he was protecting himself and BeBe from the Spiny-Thing or his own *mother*.

She could have squeezed BeBe to death!

Ever since they'd moved here, Mom had been acting weird. Okay, she had the right to be mad at him for stealing the magnesium ribbon. But she seemed stressed and mad all the time now. Maybe if she hadn't split up with Dad it would be different. It would be for *Ray*, that's for sure. Right now, he'd be in his bed in his old house, attending his old school in the morning with all his friends. He fell asleep wondering if they thought about him anymore.

He woke the next morning when he felt the bed dip down. For a second, he thought the Spiny-Thing was back and struck out with his fists, but it was just Mom sitting on the mattress with gauze and bandages.

"Sorry. Didn't mean to scare you," she said. "I need to change your dressing before I leave for work."

Eying her warily, Ray pushed himself up and held out his arm. Her face showed that she saw his distrust. After a slight hesitation, she began to remove the dressing. "I feel terrible about last night," she said. "I think you deserve an explanation."

Ray said nothing, hissing in a breath as she gently peeled the gauze stuck to his wound. The burn was shiny red in the middle, shredded skin raised around it like a red mountain range around a crater on Mars.

Mom glanced at BeBe's cage and made a face like she was in pain. "Is she okay?"

Ray looked. His pet was curled up in her igloo. "I think so."

As soon as Ray had put her in her cage last night, she'd gone right to her food bowl. But Ray wasn't going to tell Mom that and let her off easily. After last night's weirdness and the glue trap, Ray didn't think BeBe would ever trust him, let alone ride in his pocket.

He wondered if BeBe really was safe here with them.

Mom finished putting on a new bandage, wrapping it loosely, and sat cross-legged on the bed.

"I haven't told you much about my childhood." She rubbed her face. "I haven't because... well, I don't know what good hearing those stories would be."

Ray leaned forward. This was new. "I want to hear them."

"It's more me not wanting to *tell* them. Does that make sense?" She smiled hopefully.

A lift of his shoulder. "I guess."

"My father—your grandpa—had this thing about bringing home strays, even though we couldn't afford to take care of them. One of the cats had babies. I got attached to a little black one." Mom's eyes got far away. "I think I was dreaming of him last night. I think I thought BeBe was him."

"What happened to him?"

She sighed, seeming to search for words. "Sometimes my dad would make promises he couldn't keep. I didn't get to keep him."

"It's okay, Mom," Ray said. "You don't have to worry about BeBe. She's fine."

Mom smiled at him, her eyes watery. Sighed. "This storm has me stressed out. I haven't been myself. How about as soon as it passes, we do something fun? What do you think?"

"That sounds cool."

"All right." She reached down by her feet and picked up Ray's padlock box. "I'm going to give your locks back. I'm still disappointed that you stole from school, but I think you've learned your lesson."

Ray's stomach buzzed with joy that he tried to hide. "I won't *ever* do anything like that again."

"I know you won't." She gave him the box.

When she left, Ray took each lock out and arranged them on the bed. He picked the #5 in under a minute, pumping the air when the shackle popped open. *OH YEAH*!

Later, on the bus to school, his phone buzzed with a text from Cecil.

Update?

I think it might be gone, Ray texted back. He hadn't heard any noises from the attic last night.

Good. We need to be sure. I want to try and trap it.

I don't think that's a good idea. Sweat broke out across Ray's upper back just thinking about it.

Look. I'll be straight with you. I want a picture of this thing on my website. I'll give you naming rights.

NO, Ray texted. We should leave it alone.

Don't you want confirmation it's gone? Blinking dots, then: the trap is full proof

Foolproof you mean? Ray texted, then deleted. Wasn't this guy supposed to be a professional?

I'll send instructions, Cecil texted.

Ray shoved his phone in his front pocket and exhaled up at the bus ceiling. Okay, *yes*, he would love to know the Spiny-Thing was gone. But what if Cecil's trap just pissed it off? What if it came back while Ray was asleep to suck out all his fluids?

And what if Ray actually *caught* it?

What then?

24

ORGAN FAILURE

The wheeled recycling bin from outside stood in the hallway when Alane let herself into the apartment after work.

What now?

"Ray!" she called, dumping her bag on the kitchen table.

The bin was empty except for a two-by-four covered in spiderwebs and dirt, like it had been pried up out of the ground. The lid hung open, and she caught a whiff of sour milk. At least it wasn't the garbage can, otherwise the whole place would have reeked. *Where were all the bags of recycling that had been inside*?

"Ray," she called again, sharper. "Why is this in the house?"

A muffled "science project" came from his box. She stuck her head around the curtain door.

Another science project? "Come out and talk to me, please."

She wondered if all these projects were part of Ray's punishment. More a punishment for *her*, really, considering there was now a damn recycling bin inside her apartment.

Hearing her son in his box, rustling around, she walked into his room, glanced at BeBe's cage, and winced. Ray had modified the lid with a padlock.

Her gaze skipped away when Ray crawled out. "What is this science project that you need a giant recycling bin in the house? Is this for class?"

"Yes. We have to design a futuristic waste management system," he said, fiddling with a lock in his pocket.

"You couldn't do this outside?"

"It's raining. And I'm not supposed to be in the garage without Papa Wessel."

She blew out a breath, gestured at the hall. "How long is it going to be out there?"

"Just tonight," he promised.

"All right," she said. "But I want all of it out of here tomorrow and the floor swept."

"Okay."

"I'm going to take a shower. Why don't you set the table for dinner?"

Alane stepped into her room and flicked on the lamp. She put her hand on the back of her neck and massaged the aching muscles there. Times like this, she missed having a partner. With Brad now, she felt like she had to sound capable and on top of everything, because if he ever got wind she was out of her depth or overwhelmed, he'd use it as a wedge to prove Ray would be better off with him.

She groaned when she found the ladder still in her closet. "Ray, did Papa say when he was coming to set the traps?" she shouted but didn't receive an answer.

Later, after a dinner of grilled cheese and soup, and during a break in the weather, she sat outside on the stair landing with a glass of wine and went through the mail, sorting the fast-food menus, department store circulars, and credit card promotional deals she didn't open because it was too tempting to apply. Ever since she'd split from Brad, it felt like she received more of these offers, but maybe that was because she was the only one sorting the mail now.

She stretched out her legs and rolled her head on her neck. If Ray had his Bunker for privacy, this was hers. The wood underneath was slightly damp from all the rain, but the night was clear. She could see the stars. The air smelled fresh and slightly of the ocean, though they were miles from the beach. A light burned from the Wessels' front porch, but their other windows were dark. Sitting here, she almost felt like she was in her twenties again, free and living in her own place. She felt giddy, actually, now that she and Brad had actually split, the decision to divorce behind her. Her phone buzzed beside her, and she looked at the screen. Lisa, from the catering company. Call me when you get the chance.

Alane put the phone face down beside her. She didn't want to think about taking on more work at the catering company, even though she needed to. Her phone buzzed again; she groaned and then peeked at the home screen.

Edie: Did you hear?

Alane felt her stomach plummet. The Kenton wedding. *Did it get postponed*? She called Lisa who picked right up.

"Yeah," Lisa confirmed. "Wedding's off. The family's trying to reschedule. Everybody's canceling their events because of the damn storm."

Shit. "Okay. Thanks for letting me know." Alane banged her phone down on the step after ending the call.

Okay, she told herself as her legs started to bounce on the stairs. *Okay*.

Her savings were nearly depleted, and now she'd have no extra income from the wedding to get her through. And wasn't that how it started? With a string of bad luck. A doctor's bill and a car repair, then you lose your transportation and your job because you can't get to work, and you get behind on your rent. She'd heard it described as a domino effect. One crisis leading to another until the toppling can't be stopped. But to her, it felt more like a body, organs failing one by one. Brad, having grown up in an upper middle-class family, never worried, even during the recession when car sales tanked. He didn't know, like she did, how it could start with just one thing.

How everyone is just a few crashing organs away from total system failure.

25

PAPA'S RULE

When Ray came home from school the next day, Papa Wessel was sitting in his old, faded web strap chair on his back porch with a beer. "Son, I'd like a word."

There wasn't anything sharp in Papa's voice, but Ray immediately tensed. He walked over.

Papa took a sip of beer. "Some tools and such been missing from the workshop. Wondered if you might know anything 'bout that?"

Even though it took less than a second for Ray to answer, his brain sifted through a million options from outright denial to confession, and everything in between. Denying it was the most attractive option, because if he admitted he broke into the workshop and picked the lock, and Papa told Mom, she'd take his locks away forever. His stomach twisted with guilt, Papa looking at him like he knew the truth already.

"I'm sorry," Ray blurted. "There's something in the apartment, and I needed a weapon."

Papa's wrinkly brow furrowed so much that his eyes almost disappeared. "You still scared from the other night? We went through the place top to bottom."

"It's not gone. It comes at night." He shuddered remembering the Spiny-Thing on top of him in bed.

"Son, I promise you, there's nothing in that apartment that can hurt you. We can't have you messing around in the workshop. There's dangerous chemicals and tools in there. That's why I keep it locked. How did you even get in there?"

Ray shifted and looked away. "My dad taught me how to pick locks. It's a hobby. We have a rule about not picking locks without permission, but I didn't know what else to do."

Papa squinted up at Ray and repeated, "You picked the lock on the door."

"I'm sorry," Ray said. "I know I should have asked, but I was afraid you wouldn't believe me."

"You told your mom about you being afraid?" Papa drank his beer.

"No. I didn't want her to worry."

Papa grunted. "I understand you want to protect your mom. I can respect that. But I don't abide thieves, you understand?"

Ray felt the hot prick of tears.

Papa stood up with effort. "Come with me." He led Ray into the garage and flicked on the overhead light. He opened a drawer. "My pop said every man ought to have a pocketknife." He held Ray's eyes and handed him a folded-up blade. "You know how to use it?"

Ray nodded. The metal was smooth and heavy in his fingers.

Papa ushered him outside again and shut the door. He kept his hand on the knob. "I don't want you in here again without me. That's *Papa's* rule." He looked at Ray from under his eyebrows.

"Yes, sir."

"All right then. Why don't you show me how you picked this lock."

Ray felt weird with Papa watching, so the metal pick was slippery in his fingers, but finally, the lock turned. Then Papa wanted to try, so

Ray stepped back and gave Papa directions. But after fifteen minutes of fiddling, Papa gave up. He shoved his hands in his pockets and eyed that doorknob with a look that said, *this ain't over.*

Ray charged up the apartment steps afterwards. Papa might not have fully forgiven him, but it wasn't awkward anymore. Inside, he crept up on the recycling bin trap. Nothing. He hadn't expected the Spiny-Thing to come out during the day anyway. He had to lie to Mom again when she got home, explaining he hadn't gotten all the data he'd need for his experiment.

She looked at him with narrowed eyes and said, "One more day, that's it."

Late that night, Ray was jolted awake by a loud clattering in the hallway. Pressing his back against the headboard, he grabbed his phone to text Cecil.

The trap went off! What do I do?

"Ray!" Mom's voice came from her room, and he almost screamed. "What the hell was that?"

Ray fished the pocketknife out from under his pillow, opened it, and held the point at the open doorway.

Dot, dot, dot appeared on the phone screen, then, do you have a weapon?

He squinted at the knife blade in the dark. The very small blade. Yes.

Do you hear anything moving?

No.

OK. go look but be ready to defend yourself.

"Ray?" He heard Mom's bed squeak as she got up.

Wait!

Ray swallowed but he didn't seem to have any spit. Heart pounding fast, he slid out of bed as quietly as he could and crept over to the drape.

He lit the flashlight on his phone and yanked the drape aside at the same time. The board was on the ground. He shined the light in the bin and breathed out when he saw it was empty.

"The board fell," he said to his mom, appearing at her doorway. "Sorry. I'll clean it all up tomorrow."

Mom sighed heavily and went back to bed.

Back in his room, he texted: There's nothing in the trap. something destroyed it.

it's smart. Interesting.

Interesting? Ray looked all around, pulse spiking.

We're going to have to try something else, Cecil texted. Let's talk tomorrow.

It took a long time for Ray to sleep again. The next morning dawned bright. His bleary eyes tracked to the ceiling over his desk.

The hole was back.

26

UP AND DIES

Alane's car seemed to miss a gear, losing power then jerking ahead strangely, as she drove home from school the next day. Her fingers tensed around the steering wheel. *No, no, no*!

She rocked back and forth as if she could physically propel the vehicle forward. How twisted that the car would decide to fall apart now when she wasn't with Brad. The entire time she had been married to him, there'd been an endless revolving door of cars. This one she'd had for over a year now, and even though Brad hadn't thought much of this model of compact in boring white—*transportation appliance*, he'd called it, being more into sports cars—it had gotten her around and been reliable. But it had over 100,000 miles now, and as the mileage kept spinning up, it had become a source of anxiety.

Now, as she sat at a light, wipers swishing away a sprinkle of rain, she could feel the motor starting to shake abnormally. The light turned green, and she pressed her foot on the gas. The engine sputtered. She could have powered the motor on her racing heartbeat. She'd just barely turned into a church parking lot when the engine died. She shut off the key, sat back, and breathed. *I don't need this right now*. She felt the hot sting of frustrated tears. It had been a long day; she just wanted to go home.

She tried the key again, but now the car didn't even start, just clicked in a way that made her think the battery was dead. It was a hassle, but a new battery wouldn't break the bank. She texted Ray.

The car broke down. I'm getting a tow now and will call you in a little while. I'm fine.

OK, shot back instantly.

She called insurance, listened to elevator music for ten minutes on hold, and arranged for assistance. Hopefully, she could just get a jump so she could make it to the auto parts store for a battery. They'd install it for free. She relaxed back in the seat, staring out the windshield at the cars passing by on the road. Her gaze dropped to the dashboard vent. She leaned forward. Was that another bug? *Why do they keep getting in there*?

It looked like the tip of a pine needle or a coarse straight black hair sticking out. She blew at it, and it seemed to withdraw slowly, as if attached to something alive down in there. That was silly. It was gone with the dead crane fly, and the insect parts, crumbs, and decayed leaves that were probably down there too. There must be some kind of filtering system, she thought, keeping all that from flying out when the defroster came on.

If stuff's too big to fit through the vent, how does it even get in there?

But she didn't have time to think about it further because a woman from the church came out to ask if there was a problem. Alane explained she'd broken down, and not long after that a tow truck pulled up. The operator tried to jump the battery first, but it wouldn't hold a charge.

"I bet it's your alternator," he said. "It's only good for around 100K miles. There's no warning; it just up and dies."

She rode with him to a garage a few miles away, sick to her stomach with worry about how much this was going to cost. The benefit of living with Brad was he generally dealt with the cars because there was a shop on site of the dealership. They'd never paid for repairs, and if a car was turning into a money pit, they'd trade it for something else.

Car repairs were like computer repairs to her and not knowing what could be wrong made her feel helpless and edgy. It wasn't like she could actually double-check the repairs were fair. She knew nothing about cars, and this intimidated her and sort of pissed her off about the unfairness of it, and being at the mercy of people who knew you didn't know anything.

She opened the window for air, and rain dripped inside, wetting her arm. The sky was gray, the hurricane cloud bands coming in. What if she and Ray had to evacuate in this car and it wouldn't start? Or the defroster didn't work? She'd have to remember to bring a towel. Kids these days didn't know the anxiety and fear of breaking down. It seemed like her parents' cars were always breaking down or running on fumes, or the hood was held down with a piece of rusty chain. This was before safety inspections. She remembered her father having to warm up the car before it would run properly. It made her feel like she should show Ray how to change a tire, though she'd make damn sure she'd keep up the roadside assistance so he never had to. Hopefully, by the time he got his license, they'd be in a better place and own a newer car.

Waiting in the garage lobby that was really more of a tire showroom, Alane debated whether to call Brad. *No, I'm an adult. This is my problem*. There had been a slight eye raise from the guy who'd checked her in when she gave him her name, but he didn't say anything. All he had to do was look at the frame around the license plate to see where the car had come from. *Just Like Ranew*. She made a mental note to remove it when she got home.

It was the alternator, the repair estimate about what she was expecting, which was more than she could honestly afford. But she told herself it was still less than making car payments.

"Will you check the defrost vent too?" she asked the mechanic. "There seems to be some debris in there, and I'm afraid to use it."

Two hours later, she handed over her credit card, holding her breath until it was approved; no more on that card now. The defroster, the mechanic told her, had worked fine for him.

She walked into the apartment exhausted and hungry. Ray, bless him, had laid out sandwich stuff for their dinner, and they ate in front of the television. She put the car and the repair out of her mind as well as she could, even though worries kept creeping in. She felt her control over this new life, over Ray, her little family, slipping, one finger losing its grip at a time.

You're fine. They had food. She had a job. And this place. *It's all okay.*

27

DOUBLE WHAMMY

The next day at school passed uneventfully with Ray spending his second day of lunch detention with Mr. Sowder making sure equipment was ready for the next day's lab activity. He got a text from Cecil while he was on the bus home: let's talk at 7.

Ray crawled into his Bunker just before then, put his earbuds in his ears, and waited. It got hot in there with all the lights on, and he felt sweaty. The phone rang, startling him. It was a video call this time, and he expected to see the same headshot of the professor-looking guy pop up. Instead, a Black girl about his age with a cloud of curly hair and glasses appeared on screen. He squinted at her. Checked the name and number.

"Uh... I think I'm maybe supposed to talk to... your *dad...?*" he said.

The girl stared pointedly back at him.

Ray's mouth opened. *No way. This whole tim*e? "Um... you're younger than I expected." he managed.

"You thought I was a boomer, didn't you?" It was weird hearing a man's voice coming out of her mouth. "I use 'Cecil' to get around the age restrictions and so I won't have old dudes creeping on me."

"Is that a voice changer?"

"Yeah, hang on." The phone jostled around dizzyingly, then her face appeared again. "Okay. That good?"

A girl's voice now. "Cool," he said, impressed. A new thought occurred to him. "How did you know *I* wasn't a creepy old dude?"

Her look said *duh*. "I'm an *investigator*. I could tell from your voice. Plus, you said you were in school the other day."

"Okay," he said, his mind still processing that the Premier Creature Hunter was a girl the whole time. "What's your real name?"

"Cecil's good." A computer screen reflected in her glasses. "Okay. Let's assess where we are. The Light Tactic failed. Standard trap didn't work. It's definitely acting more aggressive," she said as if to herself.

"Maybe we should leave it alone," Ray offered. "Maybe it will go away on its own." He didn't want to piss it off; what if it crawled on him again and this time *did* drain out all his fluids?

"It sounds like it's got a good thing going on there. It's not going to leave willingly." Cecil's eyes flicked back and forth as she read something on her computer. "Just to warn you: these things usually get worse before they get better."

"Worse?" he cried.

She looked over the rim of her glasses at him. "If it really wanted to hurt you, Ray, it would have by now." She glanced back at her screen. "I think we try freezing it out next. Make it *really* uncomfortable."

"How am I supposed to freeze it out? I don't know if you investigated this, but I live in Florida."

"You have A/C, don't you?"

"Yeah, I have A/C, but my mom's not going to let me turn it on full blast. She was mad I turned on all the lights."

"This is life or death, Ray. You decide."

"Come on! You just said if it wanted to hurt us, it already would have."

"I don't know what it's going to do!" Cecil's dark eyes flashed at him behind the glasses. "Maybe it's harmless. Maybe it's just curious. Or maybe it's sizing you up. I'm troubleshooting here. You don't have to take my advice." She shrugged one shoulder. "What do I know? I'm just a monster expert."

Ray regarded her. "How many monsters have you actually helped people kick out of their houses?"

Cecil's mouth flattened. "That's confidential. But a lot."

Sure, Ray thought. But she clearly knew more than *he* did about these things. "Okay, fine, what about the hole?"

"Leave it. The thing needs a way out. In fact, I think you should leave your window open a bit so it can escape that way."

"Okay." A/C blasting and window open. That made sense. He stifled an eye roll.

"I'm wondering...," she muttered. "I'm thinking maybe we should also give it a double whammy. In case we're dealing with something darker."

"Darker? What do you mean?"

"This creature of yours behaves in a mischievous, almost taunting way that makes me think it has a higher intelligence. Demonic maybe."

Ray's eyes rounded. "What?"

"My instinct says not a demon." Cecil tapped out something on the out-of-sight computer. "Still... can you get hold of some holy water or a crucifix? Put it up in the attic?"

"Seriously?"

"Yeah. Let's hit it with full barrels."

Ray seemed to remember there was a crucifix on a beaded necklace in his mom's jewelry box. "You really think a crucifix will do anything?"

Cecil sighed with infinite patience. "Dude. You have a *monster* in your house. If *that's* real, why isn't a crucifix's power? Open your mind. Otherwise, you're just wasting my time. I have plenty of clients who listen to my advice. *Paid* clients."

"Okay, okay. I'll do it."

"Tonight. Because you're running out of time."

"Tonight. Okay."

"Good luck." Cecil hung up.

28

25413

When Alane pulled into the driveway next to Papa Wessel's impeccably kept pickup truck the next afternoon, his wife was standing at the side entrance of the garage, peeking in the workshop window.

"I was looking for Papa." Mrs. Wessel smiled as Alane approached.

"Do you need help with something?" Alane was not tall, but she towered over the elderly woman, who always seemed older and frailer than Papa, even though Alane knew they were around the same age.

Mrs. Wessel waved away her offer. "No. He's around somewhere."

Probably up in my apartment without my permission, Alane thought nastily, and instantly felt bad. "If I see him, I'll tell him you're looking for him."

Upstairs, the lights were off except in Ray's room, and she relaxed.

"I'm home," she called, unloading her purse and work bag on the kitchen table.

"Hi, Mom," Ray answered back.

She skimmed through the mail Ray'd left on the table. Nothing but bills and junk.

"How was school?" she asked as she went past his room to hers to change.

"Okay."

Considering he'd been serving lunch detention with Mr. Sowder this week, *okay* didn't sound so bad.

The ladder was still in the center of her closet, under the closed attic panel.

"Ray!" she yelled. "RAY!" No answer. He probably had his earbuds in.

That's it! She folded the ladder with a sound of screeching metal and wrestled it down the hall. Leaned it by the front door.

Later, sitting across the table from Ray during Office Hours, she asked him, "Did you get all your science projects done?" Her tone suggested the answer she wanted was *yes*.

He looked up from his open laptop with confusion that quickly cleared. "Oh. Yeah. I may have to do one more thing."

"No." She shook her head. "No more experiments in the house."

"I just have one left." Ray's gaze dropped to his screen in a way that struck Alane as evasive. "Something to do with cold."

"Ray." She forced him to look at her. "I'm serious. No more ladders or garbage cans. No more going into my room when I'm not home. Do you understand?"

"Yes," he said, hunching his shoulders.

As he returned to his homework, Alane pulled up a free credit report site on her phone. She stared at the screen for a moment, debating, and then clicked the *request your free credit report* button.

The whole way home from the garage, Alane had argued with herself about opening another credit card. But she had no emergency parachute left.

I just want to know what I'm starting with, she told herself.

She filled out the online form, followed the steps, and a report popped up on screen.

Alane quickly scanned the results, brow furrowing when she saw what appeared to be three open accounts with high balances for bankcards she did not have, all marked delinquent.

Are these Brad's? She felt a flare of anger, got up, took her phone into the bedroom, and dialed him.

"Did you open credit cards in my name?" she demanded when he picked up. "I just looked at my credit report and there's stuff on here I don't know what it is."

"No," he said, sounding as confused as she was. "Can you send a screenshot?"

She snapped images of her report and texted them. "It says I owe money, but I never opened these cards." She paced the room, jittery with anger, with nowhere to direct it, as Brad seemed genuinely surprised.

Finally, he said, "I don't know, Alane. They aren't mine. If you don't remember getting these cards, you need to open a dispute."

"I think I'd remember if I applied for a credit card!"

"I'm just telling you that you should probably freeze your credit."

Alane sank down on the side of the bed. "How?" She heard the tears in her voice, hated that he heard it.

"This happens all the time to people," he said in his calming, insufferably mollifying tone. "It will get resolved; you won't have to pay."

Alane ended the call with a grudging *thanks for your help* and then got up to pace restlessly around the room. She returned to the kitchen table with Ray and opened her phone again, searching through her report, feeling overwhelmed with a suffocating compulsion to FIX THIS RIGHT NOW.

Because, if her credit was bad, she wouldn't be able to open a new card even if she wanted to. What would happen to her and Ray if there were another emergency like today with the car? She remembered the spam calls she'd been getting lately. *Is this related*? she thought. An uncomfortable pressure settled in her chest.

29

NOCTURNAL CHEWING

Ray lay in bed that night with the pocketknife Papa had given him under his pillow, staring at the ceiling over his head where he thought the necklace might be. He'd gone in Mom's closet right after school to fish out the string of plastic black beads with a crucifix from her old jewelry box. The necklace had a tiny see-through charm with some clear liquid in there that he hoped might be holy water. He didn't want to think about how much trouble he'd get in if Mom found out he'd taken more of her stuff. Or thrown it into the attic.

I'm protecting us, he told himself now, shivering when he remembered sneaking into her closet after school that day to find the panel wide open. Like a yawning black portal to nothingness. He'd stood in the doorway for what felt like forever, frozen. Terrified. Listening with every cell in his body. But there was no sound.

Somehow, he broke through his paralysis to quietly dig through his mother's old carton for the jewelry box, ears straining for any noise from above, but only hearing the pounding of his own heart. Then, crucifix necklace in hand, he held his breath, crept up the ladder, and without looking over the edge of the opening, flung the necklace as hard as he could in the direction of where his room was. He heard the plastic beads clatter together as the necklace flew through the air but didn't wait to hear it hit the ground. He closed the panel, scrambled down the ladder, and banged out the front door of the apartment before starting to breathe again. He watched through the window for movement. The Spiny-Thing coming. But the apartment was still.

Maybe the crucifix scared it away?

Still, he tossed and turned in bed, unable to find a comfortable position, trying to figure out how to pull off the second part of Cecil's Double Whammy, the A/C blast. Mom didn't have any catering jobs scheduled because of the storm, and he couldn't figure out a believable reason to give her for making the apartment freezing cold.

Hours later, he slowly came awake to the sound of gnawing.

"BeBe," he whisper-shouted. "Stop!" Like she'd actually listen.

Did mice chew on stuff all night? But then realization dawned that the sound wasn't coming from BeBe's cage. It was coming from over his head. From the corner. From the hole.

His skin went cold. The sound was like fingernails being scraped rapidly over wood. He sat up, heart beating fast. Reaching for his phone, he switched on the flashlight. The beam shook as he pointed it in the corner of the room, then up to the ceiling. His shoulders relaxed a little when he saw the hole wasn't any bigger. But the gnawing went on, on the other side.

He texted Cecil. It's starting again the chewing it's trying to get into my room

To his immense relief, thinking dots immediately showed up on his screen. turn on your lights

He threw the phone down and scrambled to turn on his lamp, then leapt back into bed, feeling like his insides were sloshing around. He didn't know if he was just imagining it, but the sound felt closer, louder, like any second now he'd see something poking out of the hole, something glistening and curved to a razor-sharp point.

I did it. He typed.

Any change?

NO!!!!!!!

Now he heard footsteps in the hall. He almost screamed when the curtain parted, but it was Mom.

She rubbed her eyes. "What is that?"

"You hear it?" he said. "It's in the attic."

"I thought it might be tree limbs." Ignoring Ray's gasped "Mom, don't!" she stepped under the hole where the sound was coming from. "I thought Papa Wessel patched that."

Ray's phone vibrated. Hey what's happening

Mom's awake, Ray furiously texted. She heard it too

"Ray!" Alane snapped. "Put your phone down. Who are you texting at this hour?"

"Nobody."

"Okay. I'm going to go look and see if I can see anything."

Ray's heart jumped. "No!" He scrambled out of bed after her. "What if it's an animal? It could have rabies!"

He followed her into her room, and she turned on the light in her closet. The gnawing abruptly stopped. Ray and his mother looked at each other, listening. She seemed more curious than scared, while he felt like his heart was going to explode out of his ribs.

Mom whispered, "I don't hear it anymore."

He looked at her wide-eyed. It was so quiet he heard the fridge humming in the kitchen.

Mom took a step back and softly closed the closet drape. "I think you're right. I don't want to open the hatch and have whatever it is come down here. I'll call animal control in the morning and get someone out." She rubbed Ray's shoulder. "I'm sure it sounds a lot scarier than it actually is."

"Okay," Ray said, wishing he was little so she wouldn't look at him funny if he asked to sleep in her bed tonight.

She smoothed the hair from his forehead. "I promise I'll take care of it tomorrow. Now back to bed."

Back in his room, he checked his phone and saw another text from Cecil. You're scaring me Ray what the hell

I'm sorry. I'm ok. The chewing stopped

What happened

He texted all he could remember in one long, punctuation-less sentence.

Cecil replied, it sounds like the closets the origin site

He felt a surge of panic for his mom's safety. My mom's calling animal control

I thought we established it isn't an animal

I know but it hides. Maybe the animal control guys can find it and kill it. They can throw a poison bomb up there

Cecil took so long to respond Ray thought she might have fallen asleep. Then again, he had no idea where in the world she lived. It could be daytime there. Then a message from her buzzed:

Ray it might be time to tell your mom everything

He shook his head as he typed. She won't believe me

You need to warn her

He felt cold all over. I'll try

Okay. Let me know what she says

Mom was asleep when Ray peeked into her room, so he climbed back into bed leaving the light on and drew the covers over himself. *I'll tell her tomorrow.* He listened for a long time, pocketknife clenched in his hand, but didn't hear anything, and eventually, sleep overtook him once more.

When Ray stepped off the bus the next day, a pest control van was in the driveway. He hurried inside to find his mom outside her closet, a tall man setting up a stepladder inside in a uniform shirt and shorts. The man's name patch said JAVIER.

Mom was saying, "My son and I heard it last night above his bedroom. It sounded like chewing or digging."

"Okay, I'll take a look." Javier reached for a heavy-duty flashlight by his feet. "You'd be surprised at all the animals we find in people's houses. Rats, possums, bats. They can cause a lot of damage. Sometimes they'll die, and it'll stink up the whole place. You don't want that.

"One time—" he looked at Ray with exaggerated, surprised eyes. "I came across a six-foot long boa constrictor *alive* in someone's attic."

"Did you use a dart gun to get it out?" Ray said.

Javier laughed. "Nah. We just used a trap."

Ray frowned, picturing a paper glue trap long enough for a six-foot long snake.

"Ray, let him work in peace," Mom said.

"That's okay, Miss, he's not bothering me."

Javier smiled and held his flashlight out to Ray. "Here, hand this up to me." He climbed up the ladder and moved the ceiling panel aside, then reached down for the flashlight. "Thanks, man. Now hold the ladder steady. Let's see what kind of critter is making all that noise and scaring you and your mama."

Ray wanted to say he wasn't scared, but he just braced his hands against the ladder legs, tensing when Javier clicked on the flashlight and put his head and shoulders up in the attic. Wooden ceiling beams and pink insulation lit up as he panned around.

"Jesus Christ!" Javier scrambled down the ladder so fast he missed a step and fell flat on his back on the closet floor.

30

CRAWL SPACE

Alane sat with Ray in the car in the driveway, rain pattering the windshield. Ray's face was red and tear streaked. She held his hand, looking up at nothing, her own face numb.

The whole time, she thought. *The man was over our heads the whole time*. She shuddered.

How long had Papa been alive up there and they didn't know? Hearing them walking around the apartment below him, but unable to call for help. Could he have been saved if they'd heard? *That gnawing sound*. Was that Papa Wessel scratching for help?

I folded up the ladder. I took it out from under him. Guilt and horror took her breath away. She closed her eyes to block out the picture.

After Javier had discovered the body, God bless him, he'd censored his horror, what he'd seen. He'd kept it together, asking for a private conversation with her, sending a worried glance at Ray, who stood confused. Ray didn't want to go, but she'd made him.

Javier's voice lowered. "There's a guy up there." When she only looked at him blankly, he said, "I think he's dead."

Her first reaction was to laugh; she felt terrible about it now. "What?"

"There's a body up there."

It hit her then. Papa Wessel. It was him up there wasn't it? She'd felt a surge of anger. How many times had she asked him not to come into the apartment when she wasn't home? Stupid old man. She could have done something.

Now she had to tell Ray... what? And Mrs. Wessel. *Oh God.* How was she going to tell Papa's wife that he had been lying over them all night?

"I'll call 911," Javier offered.

"Okay," she managed.

Javier hurried down the hall past Ray, who poked his head into the room around the drape, questions all over his face. He looked very young.

"What's going on?" he asked.

He started for the closet, and she turned him around by his shoulders to propel him out to the living room. "Let's go outside, okay?"

Out in the yard, she'd forgotten that Papa Wessel had taken in all the yard furniture. He'd put the picnic table upside down and piled stuff on it. There was nowhere to sit, so she left Ray on the driveway and ran back upstairs for her keys, and they got in the car out of the steady rain. For a long time, they sat there. Ray didn't ask any more questions, as if he dreaded hearing the answers. She watched Javier in his truck behind her in the side mirror, phone to his ear. It had only been five minutes.

"Ray." She sighed. "This is hard. We found Papa Wessel."

"Where is he?" His face lit up, which finally made Alane's tears come.

Her voice cracked. "Up in the crawl space. The bug man is calling an ambulance."

Ray's face crumpled. "Is he hurt?"

"Yes."

I think he's dead, Javier had said. But Javier wasn't a doctor.

Ray's hand went to the door handle. "We need to help him!"

"No!" Her voice was loud with near panic. She softened her tone. "The ambulance will be here in just a minute, honey. We need to stay out of their way."

"But he's alone." Tears began to stream down his cheeks.

The sound of a siren saved her from answering. "There, see, they're here. They'll take care of him."

Ray scrambled up on his knees to look through the back window. She rubbed his shoulder. A firetruck was the first to arrive, lights strobing against the apartment even in the cloudy daylight. Javier got out of this truck to meet the firefighters and led them to the bottom of the apartment steps.

"Wait in the car, okay, honey?" Alane said.

When she approached the men, Javier was pointing up over his head, saying, "He looked dead."

"Okay," a firefighter said. "You both just wait here, okay? We'll check on him."

God forgive her, but Alane couldn't go back to the car and face any more of Ray's questions. But he looked distracted for now, watching the firetruck and an ambulance and police car which had just pulled up. She waited with Javier at the bottom of the steps in silence. She could have asked him what he'd seen up there, what the dead man looked like, but she didn't want to know. For a moment, she allowed herself to think that maybe it was an animal Javier had seen, and that's what had been making the gnawing noise last night. Oh god, maybe something had been gnawing on Papa Wessel! A sudden wave of nausea made her reach out for the wall for balance.

"Are you okay?" Javier said, reaching for her arm. "Maybe you should sit down."

"No. I'm fine."

Now Mrs. Wessel came to her front door, having seen the red and blue flashing lights. Alane watched as understanding slowly dawned on the woman's face. Mrs. Wessel took one step out and stopped, hand still on the doorknob as if fearful of letting go.

It took everything Alane had to go to her.

Mrs. Wessel looked at Alane pleadingly. "What's going on?"

"I don't know," Alane said, truthfully. "The pest control man thinks he saw somebody lying down in the attic."

The woman's face was slack with puzzlement. "In the attic?"

"They're checking now."

They can tell her if it's him, she thought.

Alane's gaze went to Ray in the car. He was sitting now, staring straight ahead at their apartment, thin shoulders moving so she knew he was fiddling with a lock. Soothing himself with the action.

Papa Wessel had been like a grandpa to him; a far better grandfather than Carl Jannell had ever been.

This was going to crush him.

31

PUT YOUR TOOLS AWAY CLEAN

Ray had seen this on TV before, on crime shows, grim-faced paramedics wheeling the dead person on a gurney all zipped up in a black bag. It didn't seem real, and he wasn't able yet to think of Papa Wessel inside the bag. His mind wouldn't go there. His tears had dried up now, and his face felt crusty and tight. He looked away, squeezed the #5 lock in his fist, as the paramedics lifted the gurney into the ambulance. His pick set was still upstairs so he couldn't open it, so he just rubbed his thumb over the warm metal.

The sound of glass tapping made him look up. Javier outside his window. "You okay kid? I'm going to get going."

Ray nodded.

He watched the man lift his hand in farewell to the female police officer in a blue rain slicker with the hood up, standing at the bottom of the apartment stairwell. As the pest control van rolled out, two more police cars pulled in. Cops gathered by the bottom of the stairs and started up.

Ray wanted to warn them about the thing in the attic. The thing that had killed Papa Wessel. They all filed into the apartment with their guns still in their holsters. Ray waited for the shots. Time passed, his mother gently waving for him to come inside Mrs. Wessel's house, but he shook his head. He could not go in there. Could not look at Papa Wessel's recliner, the old man's worn moccasins by the door.

There was no gunfire. No flashes of light behind the darkened windows. No cops running for their lives down the steps. Instead, they stomped down in the rain in their boots. They went as a group to Mrs. Wessel's door and spoke to the women. Mrs. Wessel, already so little, seemed to collapse in on her herself. Then the cops got in their cars and drove away.

Mom came to the car and opened Ray's door. "I need to take Mrs. Wessel to the hospital," she said. Her face looked strained. "I don't want to leave you here by yourself."

"I'll be okay," he said, realizing a second later that *leave you here by yourself* meant up there, in the apartment, where Papa Wessel had been murdered. But Mom didn't seem to have heard him anyway.

"I have to go get my purse," she said.

Her words shot a bolt of terror through him. He grabbed her wrist. "No, don't go in there!"

She knelt down beside the car, looked up at him, and put her hand over his where it was on her wrist. "Nothing's going to happen to me, okay. Papa Wessel was old. He had a heart attack. That's what the paramedics said."

Ray shook his head. *They're wrong. They don't know what's up there.*

Mom pulled away gently. "Can I get something for you while I'm up there?"

"BeBe," he said. "I want BeBe and my lock box."

"Okay. I'll get them."

He wasn't sure he breathed until she came out a few minutes later with BeBe's entire cage and his lock box balanced on top. Mrs. Wessel came outside in a raincoat with a plastic cover over her hair, holding a tissue to her face. He moved to the backseat of the car so she could sit in front. Mrs. Wessel was very pale with red blotches all over her face. Her eyes were bloodshot. Alane got in, and they backed out of the driveway, the apartment over Papa Wessel's garage growing further and further away like it was at the end of a long tunnel.

BeBe huddled in her igloo on the seat next to Ray. He cradled his lockbox in his lap, watching the landscape flash by through his window. Everything looked different, sharper, more unreal.

"I'm going to need to call the funeral home," Mrs. Wessel said, sniffling. "I don't know how this all is going to work."

"They'll know. They'll walk you through."

Ray waited in the hospital lobby while his mother went with Mrs. Wessel to identify the body. He left his locks in the box. He didn't want anyone in the waiting room to see him picking them. The women returned in an hour. Mrs. Wessel looked dazed and had to be propped up by Ray's mother.

She kept pressing a wadded tissue to her mouth. "I just can't believe it."

"I'm so sorry," Mom said.

Ray felt like a ghost, invisibly following after them.

"You go on up with BeBe," Alane told Ray when they pulled into the driveway, matter-of-factly, as if she knew he was scared of going back into the apartment himself. "I'll be up as soon as I get Mrs. Wessel settled."

The police hadn't blocked off the stairs to the apartment with yellow crime scene tape. Ray paused halfway up, then turned around and went back down. He stood in front of Papa Wessel's garage door for a second, then, making a decision, he put the mouse cage down, and quickly picked the lock, watching over his shoulder for Mom.

Inside, it was dim and cool, the concrete sweating; he could almost feel the mist coming off it, the chill. He felt Papa's absence here even more than he did in the big house or the apartment. This was Papa's domain, and everything about it was infused with the old man's essence. Everything was orderly, clean. *Always clean up your workspace. Always put your tools away clean, son*, he'd preach during every project they'd worked on together. The park bench Papa was building for his wife was still in pieces on the floor. Ray felt tears coming and blinked them away.

I'll finish it for her, he swore silently to Papa.

He went over to the locked cabinet where Papa stored the dangerous stuff: sharp tools, poison. The glue traps. Crouching in front of it, Ray jiggled a pick in the lock until it clicked open. He grabbed the gleaming machete, then, leaving the cabinet door open a crack in case he needed something else, he hurried out of the workshop, locking the door behind him.

He was so focused on sneaking the machete up to his room that he didn't even think about being scared until he put BeBe's cage down and saw the hole in the ceiling. His grip tightened around the blade handle as he looked up. It hadn't gotten any bigger, but it looked aged somehow, the stain around browned and faded. He pictured Papa Wessel lying right above him, scratching for help.

Papa must have gone up there again to check on the noise Ray had heard. It was Ray's fault he was dead. Ray's leg bones seemed to liquefy; he crumpled heavily to the floor.

When his phone vibrated in his pocket a few minutes later and he saw who it was, hot rage shot through him.

"I thought you were the monster expert!" he shouted at Cecil before she started talking. "You said you could help me!"

"What happened?" Cecil asked. "What's wrong?"

"The monster killed Papa Wessel in the attic! Right over my room." Now the tears came.

"Who's Papa—?"

"We shouldn't have tried to trap it. It made everything worse."

"Ray, I'm sorry. You're my first client, okay? I didn't—"

"Sorry? This isn't some kind of game Cecil, whatever your name is."

"I never thought it was!"

He wiped his tears angrily on his sleeve. "I don't want any more of your help. Don't ever contact me again." He hung up and threw the phone aside.

After a minute, he stood and opened BeBe's cage, cradled the mouse in his hands, and brought her to his cheek. Her fur was silky soft. Her whiskers brushed his skin. He climbed into his Bunker with her and pulled the blanket around them.

32

25413 SW 127TH PLACE

Rain pounded on the Wessel's covered porch as Alane gathered her resolve and dialed her brother, Philip. Part of her hoped her call would go right to voice mail so that she could avoid this conversation. Philip was younger than her by just eighteen months, a big man, with salt and pepper hair. He lived on the other side of Florida. She hadn't seen him in, what, four years now? You'd think they would have been close, going through what they did as kids. And they had been, at times. But when you're surviving, it's really a special human who doesn't just look out for yourself. For a time there, she and Philip were feral children, raising themselves. She wished she could have been the type of person to overcome a bad childhood and create something good from it, like those kids you hear about who establish their own nonprofit or invent something to make the world better. The bar was so low, though, that the fact that she didn't beat her kid had broken the cycle. She was already a better human than Carl Jannell was.

As the phone rang, she imagined Philip staring at her name on the screen and bracing himself to answer. But he picked up on the third ring. "Hey, Alane."

"Hey," she answered.

He must have caught the nervousness in her voice. "You doing okay?"

"Yeah. Just getting ready for the storm. You?" She started pacing back and forth across the concrete slab.

"Got the yard cleaned up. Looks like it won't be too bad. Are you outside? It's hard to hear you."

"Yeah, sorry. The rain's started."

"Be careful with this storm, okay? Don't take any chances. You remember Andrew. If it looks really bad, our door's always open."

"We'll be careful." She took a breath and let it out. "Philip. Can I ask you something?"

Guarded. "Sure. What's up?"

"Do you remember Palmetto Boy?"

The pause was so long, she wondered if the call had been dropped. "I remember."

"I... I think he's back."

Another pause. "Alane." His tone was tight. "That was just a made-up thing. Are you all right? I know the separation must be really hard on you and Ray."

"It's not the separation." A gust of wind blew a mist of rain on her face. "Things... haven't felt right. I've been having nightmares again. Hearing things in the apartment. Our landlord...." She sucked back a sob. "Papa Wessel died last night from a sudden heart attack."

"Jesus, Alane. I'm sorry. That would mess anybody up. But he was old, wasn't he? Palmetto Boy was just a monster we made up to explain all the fucked-up shit that was going on. It wasn't real."

She stopped pacing. "What about the Little Professor calculator?" Philip didn't reply. She pressed her ear to her phone, heard his breathing on the other end. "What about the party line? Did we both imagine that?"

"I believed in a lot of things when I was a kid. Santa, the Tooth Fairy." He lowered his voice, as if his wife or kids were around. "Doesn't mean it was real. Look, I don't want to talk about this. There's nothing happy to remember about that time."

Surprisingly, this hurt. Alane had fond memories of selling lemonade, jumping skateboards over makeshift ramps, chasing down the ice cream truck, and playing Star Wars. She got her first love note while living there. One day, she and Philip organized a bike race inspired by the Indy 500. Though nobody actually finished all five-hundred laps around the block, they'd spent hours in the attempt.

She asked him, "Have you been back to the house?"

"No. Why would I? Mom's dead. I've moved on. You need to move on too."

"I know. But Ray. He's been affected by whatever this is. He's acting out. Being secretive." She hated how desperate she sounded. Even though she was the older sister, she felt stupid, vulnerable, and hysterical.

"What does that have to do with Palm—with anything from when we were kids? Ray's a good kid. A breakup is hard on children. You're not helping with this Palmetto Boy shit." His voice had gotten an angry edge.

This was the Philip she remembered when he was a teen, not the young boy plagued with night terrors that summer long ago. Maybe they'd used up all the solidarity then. This man knew more about her than anyone. He knew her secrets, and she knew his. Maybe that's why they kept so many miles between them.

She breathed out. Ran her fingers through her hair. Closed her eyes. "You're right. It's probably just the stress of everything messing with my head. I let my imagination get away from me."

Philip's voice softened. "I know it's been hard, Sis. But you need to forget about all that stuff that happened. You have a good life and a good kid, and that stuff can't touch you anymore. You need to get inside out of the rain, and if that hurricane starts looking really bad, you know you can come here."

"Thanks, Philip."

"Anytime, Sis."

After she hung up, she huddled against the side of the house to keep dry from the blowing rain and opened her phone browser. Hesitated a moment before she typed *25413 SW 127th Place* into the search box. In the instant it took to pull up Google street view, she wondered if it was even real, that house. But there it was.

A sensation like fine hairs on bare skin crawled across her back. The thumbnail image was so different from what she remembered except for the bricks framing the front windows. They'd been white when the Jannell's lived there but had been painted brown since. Most of the front lawn had been paved over to create a horseshoe driveway, a feature you'd see at a manor house, not in a neighborhood of modest single-story houses with sunbaked flat roofs, stucco walls, and humble facades. She zoomed in.

She remembered sitting on that concrete stoop out front.

Remembered that door.

Fingers shaking, she panned back out. Blinds covered the living room window. Alane remembered playing for hours in the room behind that window, after the furniture had been sold. Acres of carpet for her and Philip to spread out their Fisher Price houses to make a whole town, or to create a ranch for her model horses.

The palm trees around the yard were mature, but she really couldn't say what trees had been there when she was a child, or even if there'd been trees at all.

Using her fingertips to maneuver around to the street view, she recognized very little of it now, and yet there were shadows of familiarity in the lines of the sidewalks and rusty chain link fences, like faces she knew from long ago that had changed over time.

She whirled back around to the front of the house and almost dropped the phone when she saw a figure in her parent's bedroom window, a shadow she swore she hadn't seen a moment ago. She held her breath, zooming in once more, heart pounding, and the figure became the reflection of one of the palms.

Alane laughed uneasily to herself. *You're being stupid. It's a house.*

She closed the site and hurried to the Wessel's front door in heavy rain to check on the grieving woman inside.

33

CUTTING AND SLASHING

As afternoon waned and rain gusted outside, Ray flicked on the overhead lights in his Bunker and released BeBe to scamper around. By now, she knew where he kept the treats. Smart girl. He scattered a few pieces on the cardboard floor, listening to her delicate munching. When his stomach growled, he realized he had not eaten in hours. He gently picked up the mouse, climbed out of the box on his elbows and knees, and returned her to her cage, fastening the lid lock. He turned on the hallway light before stepping out of his room and went to the apartment door to look out the glass window. Mom was still over with Mrs. Wessel. He fixed a bowl of cereal and took it to the couch, propping his phone on a pillow to watch lockpicking videos. Right now, in this moment, he could pretend Papa was okay, and that everything was the same. One day, Ray would have his own channel with a million subscribers and sponsors that sent him free stuff. He'd do giveaways.

A rattling noise came from his bedroom. He paused the video and turned to listen, muscles tightening. The noise came again. It sounded like BeBe banging around in her cage. She'd never been that loud before. It sounded like she was turning all of her toys over. All his protective instincts went on alert. Something was wrong. He quietly slid his cereal bowl onto the coffee table, feeling fear rising in his chest. Stupid, he'd left Papa's machete in his bedroom. He debated running out the front door for Mom. What would happen to BeBe if he left her? His eyes burned with hot tears.

Please just leave us alone.

Ray slipped to the kitchen for the sharpest knife he could find, a long, serrated bread knife with two points on the end. Heart racing, he tiptoed down the hallway to his room, swallowed hard, and used the tip of the knife to open the side of the drape so he could look in. A rancid, oily smell assaulted his nostrils and he almost gagged. His gaze went to BeBe's cage. The mouse was scratching violently at the clear plastic in a corner. *What—*?

A faint movement drew Ray's eye. His Bunker *shuddered*. Like someone, or something, was moving around inside. There was a scuttling sound like tiny sharp claws on cardboard. Ray felt his bowels loosen. He backed away, trembling, knife slack in his hand. The Spiny-Thing was in his box. The thing that killed Papa Wessel.

whatdoIdowhatdoIdowhatdoIdo

Get help, he screamed inside. Then, *what if it gets away and hurts Mom*? It would be his fault. Just like it'd been with Papa.

This is your chance. Cecil's voice spoke in his head. KILL *it.*

Ray's chest heaved. *It's never going to go away unless you do.*

He crept to the doorway, exhaled silently through his nose, and hefted the knife. Exploded through the drape. He launched himself at the Bunker, which pancaked under his weight.

"Leave us alone!" he screamed, stabbing the cardboard, cutting and slashing until the knife blade sunk into the floor. He ripped the flattened Bunker to pieces. "I HATE YOU! I HATE YOU!"

Nothing fought back. Nothing tried to escape.

Nothing was there.

34

OOZED FROM THE CREVICES

Alane set a mug of hot tea on the table beside Mrs. Wessel and tucked a blanket around the elderly woman in her chair.

"I'm going to check on Ray, okay?" Alane said. "I'll be back in a few minutes to wait with you until Caitlin gets here."

The woman's eyes filled with tears. "You've been so kind. Thank you, dear."

"Of course, anything." Alane smiled. She got the cordless phone from the kitchen and put it in Mrs. Wessel's hand in case her daughter called. Caitlin was driving through the storm from North Carolina to get to her mother.

Exhaustion dragged at Alane as she ran to the apartment hunched over in the pouring rain. At the bottom of the steps, she found a soggy pile of ripped cardboard that she thought at first was the remains of another of Ray's "science experiments," but then she noticed letters in marker written on pieces of it. Ray's Bunker! She picked up a large, mushy piece to move it out of the way and her blood went cold when she saw jagged cuts in it.

She raced up the stairs holding the piece of cardboard, flung open the door. "Ray?"

The TV sounded like it was on its highest volume setting. Her son was balled up in the corner of the couch, arms wrapped around his knees. His tear-filled eyes stared off in the distance.

"Ray." She went down on her knees in front of him and grabbed his hands. They were ice cold. "What's wrong, baby? What happened?"

They both knew what happened, of course. Papa Wessel had happened.

"I'm sorry." She gathered Ray in her arms. "I shouldn't have left you alone up here." She stroked his back. "I saw your box, Ray. What happened?" Rain beat against the window.

Mentioning the box seemed to jolt Ray out of his fog. He pulled away. "The thing that killed Papa Wessel was in my Bunker! I tried to kill it."

"What thing, Ray? Papa had a heart attack. That's what the doctors said probably happened."

"It's my fault he's dead." Tears spilled down his face.

"No!" She hugged him fiercely. "Don't *ever* think that. It's not your fault. It's terrible, but he just had a heart attack. It could have happened anywhere."

Her gaze lifted to the ceiling. When would she ever not think of Papa's body up there?

Ray squirmed out of her arms as if he felt like he did not deserve comfort. "He wouldn't have gone up there if it wasn't for me. I kept hearing the Spiny-Thing up there. I asked him to check."

Spiny-Thing? She looked at him. "Ray, what are you talking about?"

"I was trying to make it leave. But nothing worked. And now it hurt Papa."

She sat back, dread coming over her. "Ray. What did you see? Talk to me." The living room lamp flickered. The wind outside was getting worse.

"I haven't seen it. But it comes into my room at night. It watches me. I think it wants to hurt me."

"Ray." Alane's voice was firm. "It's an animal. That's all." She couldn't tell if she was trying to reassure him or herself.

Ray cried harder. "I don't want you to die. We need to leave."

A shiver ran down Alane's spine. "We can't leave, Ray. Not tonight. The hurricane. Mrs. Wessel. We can't leave her alone."

Ray buried his face in her chest. He seemed so young and small.

"I know." She sighed, held him closer. "I know. I don't think I can stay here anymore either. I would just feel sad. We'll start looking for a new place to live tomorrow, after the storm passes. Okay?"

He nodded against her.

After a moment, she pulled away. "I need to go back to the big house. Mrs. Wessel needs us right now, and I think we should stay with her during the storm." She made him look at her. "Okay?"

"Okay."

Alane stood up and gave him a reassuring smile. "Why don't you go get your stuff. Pajamas, pillow. BeBe, if you want."

Alane went to her room and began shoving things into an overnight bag. *Let's just get through the storm*, she told herself. *Then we'll figure out what to do. Where to go.*

A thump on the other side of the apartment startled her. Shouldering her bag, she walked to the living room and looked around. Something scrabbled over her head in the attic crawl space.

Ray's *Spiny-Thing.*

Don't be ridiculous. It's the wind.

She walked down the hallway, the thing seeming to follow her movements, stopping when she did at Ray's bedroom doorway. "Ray," she said, voice controlled. "Let's go, bud."

Ray looked at her, wide-eyed, and she did a double take when she saw he had a machete. "I'm scared."

"It's okay. Get your things." She would ask about the machete later.

The thing in the ceiling took off then, low and soft, yet giving the impression of size, scurrying toward Alane's bedroom.

Alane hissed at Ray. "Run. To Mrs. Wessel's."

She waited until he slammed out of the apartment to go to her bedroom. She listened at the curtain for more movement and heard something dry and leathery rustle in the space above her closet. It almost seemed to be holding still, listening to *her*. Lightning flashed outside followed by a crack of thunder.

With a deep breath, she yanked the curtain aside. A thick stench filled her nostrils, and she clapped a hand over her nose and mouth. She remembered the smell now. How it hung in the air of her childhood home like a haze. Oozed from the crevices. Clung to her skin no matter how much she washed. Sour bile rose in her throat.

Racing for the front door, she heard the ceiling panel in her closet split and crash open, hangers rattling. The curtain over her doorway billowed, and something light and swift careened down the hallway and up the side of the wall, closing the distance between them.

35

WE GAVE IT A NAME

Ray bounced up and down on his toes as he watched out the kitchen window holding Papa's machete. Finally, Mom's shadow appeared in the apartment door window. She burst out and down the steps, banging the door behind her. Light inside the apartment darkened suddenly, like a shadow over a lamp, and brightened again. Ray ran for the front door and held it open for his mother against the gusty wind. Rain sprayed his face.

"Inside," she gasped, wild-eyed, hair plastered to her head, shirt stuck to her skin. She slammed the door and locked it. Leaned against it, breathing hard.

"Did you see it?" Ray whispered, aware of Mrs. Wessel watching from the couch, her wrinkled face alarmed.

"No." Mom's eyes flicked to the machete in his hand. "Put that away," she hissed. She kept her back braced against the door as if to keep something out. "And go get a towel."

"In the closet." Mrs. Wessel waved Ray in the direction of the hall and started to rise. "I'll make some hot tea."

"No, please, don't get up," Mom insisted in her brisk everything's-fine voice.

But everything was not fine. Everything was not fine at all.

Ray put the machete on the kitchen counter before rummaging in the hall closet. He grabbed a faded beige towel that smelled faintly of mildew and ran it back to his mother who wiped her face and toed off her wet shoes.

"I'll put the kettle on," Mom said, with a forced smile for Mrs. Wessel. "It's getting windy out there."

Ray followed Mom into the dark kitchen. She walked over to the same window where Ray had been standing. She touched her fingers to the machete handle, then gazed at the apartment through the rain, her body trembling, an expression on her face Ray had never seen before.

"Mom?" Ray whispered. "What happened?"

She didn't answer right away, just stared ahead as if she hadn't heard. Then, with a weary sigh, she tore her gaze from the window. She pulled him close and kissed the crown of his head.

"Nothing," she said, her eyes faraway again. "Everything's fine now."

She stepped away to put the teakettle on the stove. Ray took her place at the window and looked out. The apartment was barely visible in the rain. Nothing stirred in the distant glow of the window. Lightning flashed, followed by a low rumble of thunder.

"Maybe we should call Dad?" Ray suggested.

"No," she fired back, then softened her tone. "No. Ray, we're fine. We'll stay here with Mrs. Wessel until the storm's over, or until her daughter comes, and then we'll figure out what to do." She rubbed her eyes as the kettle steamed. "I need to think. Why don't you go ask Mrs. Wessel what she wants in her tea?"

Later, Ray sat on the floor while the women sipped their tea, leaning against the end of the couch next to his mom's legs, BeBe's cage tucked against him. The mouse hadn't poked more than her nose out of her igloo since they'd gotten here, not even for the treat Ray had dropped inside.

The living room was cast in blue light from the TV. They watched the weather coverage as Hurricane Rose's compact rain bands began to lash the coast, the broadcast switching from Key Largo to Miami to Boca Raton. Plywood sheets over the front window rattled. Papa hadn't finished covering the other windows before he'd died.

If there were such things as ghosts who stayed on earth because of unfinished business, Papa must be hovering around.

Ray tried not to look at Papa's empty recliner, because when he did, a zippered-up body bag flashed in his mind, and he got a tight feeling in his chest that made it hard to breathe.

Restless, Ray got up to watch the storm through the kitchen window. Rain gusted sideways, and the windowpane glass shuddered. The saw palmettos by the apartment steps swayed. The street pole lights flickered with the wind. Obscured by the heavy downpour, the apartment appeared like a lookout tower in the dark.

The Spiny-Thing was still in there. Had it retreated to its attic lair? Or was it lurking just inside the door, waiting for Ray and his mom to come back?

I hope the hurricane rips the roof off and carries you away! Ray blasted his fury at the monster, wishing the power of his thoughts could kill it.

I hope you get impaled on a tree and DIE!

So many times tonight, Ray had wanted to text Cecil to tell her what happened. But Cecil wasn't a real monster hunter. She wasn't even a real Cecil. All her dumb tactics, the traps, the lights, the crucifix, had failed.

I failed, Ray thought.

Papa was not the only person to leave a job unfinished.

Ray dragged a sleeve over his face when Mom walked in the kitchen. "Hey," he said.

"Hey." She opened the refrigerator. "You shouldn't stand by the window. Something could shatter it. Help me make dinner."

"I'm not hungry." He took the head of lettuce she handed him.

"You need to eat something." She took cheese and bread from the refrigerator and put it on the counter. "It's going to be a long night."

Ray watched the knife tremble in her hand as she spread mayonnaise on bread. "Mom—"

"Just help me with the sandwiches, okay, bud?"

"What did you see?"

Mom's fingers clenched the knife handle. "Nothing."

"That's not true!"

She breathed in, stared down at the knife. "I know you're upset about Papa, Ray. I am too." Now she looked at him. "We're both in shock. When something terrible like this happens, a person's mind can imagine all kinds of scary things."

"I didn't imagine anything." How he wished he could talk to Cecil. She was the only one that believed him.

"I saw a lot of strange things when I was a kid," his mother said, opening the package of cheese. "I've told you things were hard for Philip and me growing up. My father, your grandfather, never took responsibility for his part in that. Instead, he told us it was 'bad luck' or an evil presence in the house we lived in.

"He had Mom believing it too. She insisted for years he never was the same after we moved in. That the house was 'no good' and poisoned him so he couldn't get along with people or keep a job." Her voice grew clipped, angry. "They blamed an evil spirit rather than themselves. Philip and I were just kids. We believed all that talk. We believed it so much we thought there really was a monster living in the house that made weird things happen."

"What things?" Ray asked.

"Oh, I don't know." She picked up the knife again and sliced a tomato a little too forcefully. "Philip had a Little Professor Calculator he played math games on, and he told me someone called Palmetto Boy wrote him messages on it. It wasn't even possible to spell words on that toy. The buttons only had numbers. But one day... I thought I saw words there.

"So, we decided Palmetto Boy was the evil thing in the house that Mom and Dad talked about. We gave it a name... gave it life in a way." Her brow creased in what looked like pain. "It was like some kind of shared family delusion."

"What words did you see?" Ray whispered.

She chuffed a laugh, as if she could not believe how silly she'd been. "I don't remember. But I scared myself pretty bad." She put slices of cheese on the sandwiches. "The point is, our brains can make us believe things that aren't real."

"Mom... that thing in our apartment... could it be Palmetto Boy?"

Mom cut him an exasperated look. "I just told you, Ray, we made it up."

"I never want to go back in there," Ray said.

Mom nodded. He wasn't sure if that meant she didn't want to go back to the apartment either, or if she was fine with him going to live with his father, but after that, they didn't say anything more.

Ray helped her finish the sandwiches as the light over their heads flickered and rain scratched the glass like invisible, liquid claws.

36

BOOGEYMAN

Alane switched on her phone flashlight, and the Wessel's tiny bathroom filled with light. The power had finally gone out a few minutes ago. She was surprised it had stayed on as long as it had. Gale-force winds howled outside, rain sounding like a barrage of rocks spraying the house.

Alane turned on the faucet, splashing cold water on her face. She glared at her ghostly reflection in the glass.

Why the hell had she told Ray about Palmetto Boy? Put that shit in his head. *That thing in our apartment... could it be Palmetto Boy*? he'd asked.

Jesus.

She dried her face roughly with a faded hand towel.

Didn't you wonder the same thing the other day though? The thought wormed its way in. *About Palmetto Boy being back. You even called Philip.*

Yes, and he understandably thought it was all in her head. There wasn't anything supernatural or evil to blame for Ray's burn, or the car breaking down, or Papa dying, or anything else.

But what about the letters she saw on the school calculator, A... L... A... appearing one by one? Did she imagine that?

Enough. Alane slung the hand towel back on the rod. She wasn't eleven years old anymore. If things were falling apart in her life, it was because of her choices, or just rotten luck, not because of some boogeyman.

By the time Mrs. Wessel's daughter, Caitlin, pulled into the driveway, flooding the living room with the glare of the headlights, the power had been out a few hours. The three people taking shelter in the Wessel's living room dozed on and off with a couple of candles burning, waiting for Caitlin's arrival. Alane got up to open the door, the wind almost whipping it back on its hinges.

"Whoa! It's getting bad out there," Caitlin said, bring a mini squall of rain inside with her. "Everyone okay?"

"Oh, yes." Mrs. Wessel's voice sounded feeble in the dark, croaky with sleep. "I've had Alane and Ray with me. You really didn't have to drive up here in this weather."

"It only just got bad." Caitlin threw Alane a grateful look. "I'm going to use the bathroom and dry off. Be right back."

The big house didn't seem that big anymore with Caitlin there, and when she returned to the living room to kneel beside her mother and take her hand, and they talked quietly together and cried, Alane felt like an intruder, a voyeur to their grief. After checking Ray was still asleep on the couch, covered with a crocheted blanket, she withdrew to the kitchen. There, she sat in the dark, trying to figure out what to do.

After the storm was over, she and Ray would have to go. But where? Not the apartment. The thought surprised her. The decision had somehow already been made, even though she had not consciously made it. It just didn't seem right to stay after Papa. Honestly, the idea of living where he died creeped her out. She couldn't do that to Ray.

But where would they go? Alane's mother was dead. Her father was... somewhere. She had no idea, and even if she could track him down, he was the last person she'd ask for help. No way was she crawling to Brad.

That meant she'd have to find a new place to live. Quick. *I can't even open a credit card!* Tears threatened. Now she and her kid were really in trouble. Desperate. She'd seen it coming.

The organs failing.

What am I going to do?

Alane almost jumped out of her skin when the phone buzzed with a text from Philip. You up?

Yes, she tapped back.

Her phone vibrated with an incoming call from him. She answered in a hushed voice. "Hey."

"Just a head's up, you probably want to check your financial accounts," Philip said. "I just found out Carl opened credit cards in my name. The bastard."

"What?" Having expected her brother to be calling for an update on the storm, it took her a second to understand what he was saying. Then, it all became clear. She dropped her forehead in her hand and moaned. "Oh God. He got me too. I saw it on my credit report and didn't realize. How could he do this?"

Philip gave a laugh carved from decades of resentment. "How could he keep on screwing up our lives you mean? I'm pressing charges. I'm done with this shit. I've worked too hard to let him fuck up my life again."

"Do you know where he is?"

"No. The last time I spoke to him was three years ago, when he came crawling around asking for a loan. Looks like he's using 127th Place for an address, but I checked and it's empty. The bank foreclosed on the last owner. That house really is cursed." The phone went silent for a second. Then he said, "I need you to do this with me."

Alane rubbed her forehead. The thought of taking her derelict father to court, seeing him again, made her chest flutter with anxiety. "I don't know."

"We have to do this together, Alane. He won't ever stop. He can't keep doing this to us."

"Okay," she said, her voice hollow and small.

"Get through the storm," Philip said. "I'll call you tomorrow and we'll handle it together. We'll make a plan."

After hanging up, Alane stared at the phone in her hand, then paced in circles around the kitchen.

My own father.

No. She stopped, then walked on. He doesn't deserve to be called that.

Carl had made her childhood something painful that had to be overcome, and years later, he was yanking her back, wrecking her life, betraying her. Betraying Ray. Using them.

What kind of parent does that? Alane could never use her own child like that, no matter how desperate she was. She swiped furiously at her eyes, hating that he could still make her cry.

The phone vibrated with a call again, and she answered it without thinking.

Beep. Alane's blood turned to ice.

"Alane." A voice, faint and crackly.

Beep.

"Come."

Beep.

"Home."

Alane threw the phone, and it skittered across the floor. The screen went dark. Then lit up again with another call from the Jannell's old number, cut off by the phone company decades ago for delinquent payment. She pressed her shaking fingers against her eyes and gathered herself. *Please stop*!

It's Carl. He's making me crazy.

Alane took several deep breaths and marched over to the phone, picked it up, and switched it off. She crept into the living room to retrieve her purse and car keys.

She should wait. A hurricane was raging outside. But she was so angry. She didn't know what to do with that anger. What kind of man steals from his own children? He must have her social security number, all her personal information. How long had he been doing this? And not just to her, Philip too. Was he using her dead mom's information too?

Ray's?

Her teeth ground together. Why couldn't he leave them alone? She'd told herself all these years, blood didn't matter. There was no law saying you had to have ties with your family. Not if they hurt you. It had been easy to walk away. To avoid calling until it dwindled to just his birthday, Christmas, Father's Day—Jesus, what a charade—and then to nothing. It wasn't as if he'd reached out to her. He'd never even met Ray. Brad had supported her not seeing him, cutting him out of her life. Yet part of her had felt sorry for her father all these years. Because he was a damaged human being. Selfish. Destructive. Unhappy. It had to be miserable to be that way.

Philip had said Carl was not at the old house. That the place was empty. But what if their father was there, living there as a squatter? Alane shoved her phone into her bag. She would be damned if Carl Jannell was going to affect her life. Hurt her or Ray. This was her life.

It was a bad idea, going out in the storm. But she was going to end this tonight.

Because that monster of Carl Jannell's? That thing that Alane and Philip had named Palmetto Boy, given life to all those years ago?

It was back.

You want me to come home? Alane started for the front door.

I'm coming.

37

TURN AROUND AND GO HOME

"Where are we going?" Ray asked from the car's passenger seat.

"There's something I need to do. And I *really* needed you to stay with Mrs. Wessel." Mom's fingers looked like they were about to snap the steering wheel.

Ray had thrown a DEFCON-One fit when she'd tried to leave without him. Probably the only reason she let him come was he was embarrassing her in front of Mrs. Wessel and her daughter. The daughter had looked at Mom as if she had lost her mind, going out into the storm. Ray had left BeBe behind, figuring she'd be safer there.

It was pitch-dark outside. Rain lashed down, wind gusts spinning it sideways, sparkling when the headlight beams hit it. Wiper blades on full blast. Ray felt a sinful thrill, being out in the storm, in danger. He was with his mother, but he felt like they were breaking the law. There wasn't anyone else on the road. Now and then, a branch or broken palm frond skittered across the road in front of them. The stop signs shook back and forth on their posts.

Mom had the radio on low. The storm had made landfall in Miami. Ray heard fragments of the broadcast over the rain. *Stay inside... tide rising... 90 mph wind gusts.*

The car was stuffy and hot. The windshield fogged. His mother pushed the defrost button, holding her hand over the dash vent. "Damn it!"

"What's wrong?" he asked.

"The defroster's not working. The shop was supposed to fix it. Grab some of those napkins in the glove box for me."

He handed her a wad of thin fast-food napkins that only seemed to smear the condensation around.

Ray sat back, content to just ride. Away from the apartment and from the Spiny-Thing. From Papa's recliner. Away from all the questions there were no answers for. Where would they live? How would they get their stuff? Would he have to go live with Dad now?

His phone vibrated with a text and he glanced down. Hey

For some reason, that single word from Cecil made him feel more like crying than anything.

Hey he texted back.

Blinking dots. How are you?

ok

Breathing deep, he texted everything that had happened since they'd last spoken, aware of the curious glances his mother threw at him.

We're out in the hurricane, he finished. He held the phone at a slight angle so mom couldn't see. Mom won't tell me where we're going

There's a hurricane? Where?

Florida where I live. Where do you live? He expected her not to answer. To say something about staying professional, not getting personal. This was business.

Maryland.

His heart sank. A universe away.

Mom turned onto U.S. 1 South. At least now, Ray knew what direction they were going in. The road looked like it was being pounded by ocean waves.

He texted Cecil: what else do you like to do besides help people get rid of monsters?

Five long minutes passed without a word, then thinking dots.

I like to draw

My dad's an artist and he is the one who got me into it

Send pics, Ray texted.

More minutes passed before an image appeared of a long-limbed, emaciated creature with a Venus flytrap for a mouth. More drawings followed. A slug covered in hair. A humped dog-like thing with tentacles instead of feet. A cloaked being with five glowing eyes.

These are amazing.

A blushing emoji popped up on screen.

You should put them up on your website, Ray texted.

Nah. they're just practice.

Ray bit his lip. I have a hobby too

What

I pick locks

No shit

I got into it from my dad too.

Is he a burglar?

Ray smiled. No, he's ... just a dad.

His smile faded. My mom doesn't like me to. I got into trouble a couple of weeks ago for doing it.

What did you do?

He let out a breath, quietly, so his mom wouldn't notice. It was dumb. I broke into the science teacher's closet and took something.

Bruh. why?

He hesitated, imagining Cecil waiting, eyes behind her glasses fixed to her screen. What did it matter if Cecil knew? She was in Maryland.

I got it for a friend. *Not that Allie's a friend anymore*, he thought.

He texted the whole story, and more, including attacking his Bunker because he thought the Spiny-Thing was inside.

You know you're really brave Ray, Cecil texted.

This time Ray sent the blushing emoji.

I can't believe you tried to kill it. that's bad ass

Ray frowned. Do you think the monster is Palmetto Boy?

Maybe. it could have tracked your mom down

Ray shivered. Mom looked at him with concern.

I'm scared, he texted before he could think better of it.

Your mom's there. And me

Ray read through blurred vision. He sent a smiley face.

text me updates ok

ok

Ray laid his phone face down on his leg and leaned back.

"Who was that," Mom asked.

"Just a friend."

Mom sighed softly through her nose. "God. I don't know what we're doing out here, Ray. I'm sorry."

A gust blew the car so hard it seemed to rock. "Where are we going?" he asked her again.

"Homestead. Where I used to live." She took a breath as if it were hard to say the words. "I found out a little while ago—Uncle Philip told me—that my dad... your grandfather... did something... really wrong." She swiped the fogged windshield again, clearing a portal to see through. "I'm going to drive by the old house where I used to live in case he's there. He's probably not. I just want to check, and then we'll turn around and go back."

They drove on, the weak glow of their headlights reflecting off the dark night and the sparkly rain so that it looked to Ray like they were flying through outer space. Like they'd jumped to light speed, into another universe.

38

PRICKLED AND CRAWLED

Alane wiped the fogged window with the wet wad of napkins again, clearing a hole to see through. Put her hand over the defrost vent again. Nothing. Something light as a cobweb brushed the tip of her finger, and she yanked back her arm. The pine needle, hair, whatever it was was back, sticking out of the vent.

Great. The shop was supposed to clean all that debris out and fix the defroster. Now, she'd have to take the car in again. For something that should have been taken care of the first time.

"I have to go to the bathroom," Ray said. "Can we stop somewhere?"

Where? she thought. Visibility was terrible in the pouring rain. Power was out up and down US-1, gas stations and fast-food restaurants dark. Boarded up. "Can you hold it?"

He visibly squirmed. "No."

"I'll stop at the first place I see," she promised.

What were they even doing out here? What kind of mother brings her child out into a hurricane? She had almost turned the car around a dozen times, each time, an angry voice inside her roared NO! Now they were just thirty minutes away from the house, and she got the feeling she couldn't turn back now even if she wanted to. The storm wind seemed behind them, driving them on. For the most part, Ray had been quiet. He hadn't asked many questions even though he must have hundreds of them. She should not have let him talk her into coming with her, but she had to admit she was glad he was with her.

Through the smudges in the windshield, Alane saw the outline of a large building ahead. A hotel, one of those suite type complexes with a lobby and covered portico. She turned into the parking lot. The hotel's sign and windows were dark. But when she pulled under the canopy—the rain pounding the car roof stopped abruptly—she thought she saw a faint light through the lobby's double doors.

"See if the door's open," she told Ray, who was already climbing out of the car. She watched as he tried the door. It opened, and he held a thumb's up. She rolled down the passenger window. "Try to grab some extra paper towels if you can." When he didn't come back in a minute, she figured he'd found a bathroom.

The wipers squeaked against the windshield, and she cut them off. She turned the defroster on full blast again, testing it. The motor inside whirred, but no air came out. She flicked on her phone's flashlight and aimed it at the dash. The piece of... it looked like a hair... sticking out of the vent was thick and black, slightly curled. She pinched it with her fingers, pulled, but met resistance, like there was a mat of hair below, knotted to a single strand. When she took her fingers away, they felt tacky.

A loud blast of hot, moist air hit her, and she screamed and turned away her face as she was sprayed with fine fragments of dust, dirt, or crushed leaves. She swiped her mouth, felt grit in her mouth and eyes. Shit! She fumbled to turn off the vent, then spit what felt like blueberry stems into her hand. Not blueberry stems. Legs.

She realized with dawning horror that the fragments covering her were tiny insect parts. She screamed and convulsed against the locked seatbelt, frantically brushing at the legs, wings, antenna, heads that covered her skin and clothes. Spiked parts clung on to her clothes, breaking into more pieces.

"Mom!"

Alane jerked her head around and saw Ray with the passenger door open with a stack of paper towels. He was leaning down, an alarmed look on his face, as if he'd been calling "Mom" for a while. She looked down at herself. There was nothing on her clothes. She held out her hands. Rubbed her face. All clean.

Shuddering uncontrollably, Alane unbuckled her seat belt. "I actually have to pee now," she told Ray. "Be right back. Don't get in the car."

Ignoring his questioning look, she hurried into the hotel. A camping style lantern glowed on the counter in the lobby, but the room was empty. Alane's body trembled as if from the inside. Her skin prickled and crawled. She burst into the dark bathroom, moving by feel in the darkness. She turned the water on full blast, filled her mouth, rinsed and spit, again and again. She put her head in the sink, fingers in her mouth, feeling between her teeth for anything stuck there. Splashed water on her face, on the back of her neck, down her shirt. Her fingers searched her face, her hair, her cheeks scratched and bleeding from where she'd raked her face.

Okay, okay, okay.

Alane couldn't stop shaking. Slapping at her clothes. Spitting into the basin.

Couldn't stop crying.

39

BUG HIDEY-HOLE

Rain fell in a torrent as they turned onto a side road, headlight beams glancing off of a weathered wooden sign that read *Princetonian Homes*.

"This is it," Mom said. "My old neighborhood."

Ray peered out the window at empty pine fields and a tennis court, then streets of plain, one-story houses with dark windows. Light poles gleamed sliver. Palm trees jerked and swayed.

The car crept forward as Mom strained to read the house numbers, easing to a stop in front of what looked like a big red and white striped circus tent like the one that had completely covered Papa Wessel's neighbor's house when it had been bug bombed. Papa had explained the process, how a whole house is sealed up and pumped with poison gas to get every crevice and bug hidey-hole.

Mom's face scrunched. "I *think* this is right?"

She peered uncertainly at the houses on either side before shifting into park at the curb, cutting the engine. The car rocked slightly from a wind gust and rain pattered the windshield.

"I don't think anybody's in there," Ray said, gazing at the tent-covered house through the rain.

"Stay here," Mom said.

"Where are you going?"

"I just want to check something."

She opened the car door and sprinted with her shoulders hunched to the front of the house. Ray could make out a sign posted there. After a minute, she ran back, climbed inside. The air from outside was cooler than he expected. Mom was soaked and a little winded.

"The sign's old," she said. "It says it was supposed to be safe to go in two weeks ago." She reached behind the seat for her purse and grabbed her phone.

"You can't go in there," Ray said, alarmed. "There's fumes."

"The fumes are gone. See the tube there? It's used to release the gas. They just haven't taken the tent down yet. Probably because of the storm."

Ray's gaze followed the yellow, ribbed gas release tube on the corner of the house, which was the size and look of a water park covered tube slide.

"Let's just go," Ray said. "Let's go back to the hotel."

She checked her phone for messages. "Ray, I know this doesn't make sense to you, it doesn't make sense to me. But I'm here now, and I just need to make sure he isn't here."

If he's in there, he's dead, Ray thought.

She shoved her phone in her front jeans pocket. "I'm going to peek in a window real quick. Be right back."

"I'm coming with you." Ray grabbed his backpack.

"No. I let you ride with me. You're staying in the car."

"I've got a headlamp." He took it out of his backpack, put it on, and looked at her as if to say, *see, you need me*. Even though, yeah, she had a cell phone flashlight.

She sighed heavily. "Okay. But I don't want to hear it when you get wet. All we're doing is looking in a window."

Ray shrugged on his pack. Before stepping out, Mom said, "Keep your headlamp off until we're around back. We don't want the neighbors calling the cops. Hopefully, they're smarter than us and taking shelter in their closets right now."

On the count of three, Ray flung open the car door and sprinted across the yard. Almost instantly, his hair flattened against his head with rain. Cold seeped through his T-shirt. He followed Mom around the side of the house, through high grass and spongy ground to the back. A seam ran the entire height of the tent, held taut by metal clamps. Mom swung open a rusty chain link gate. The windows of the house next door were dark.

The tent was loose and flapping in the wind over the back door, like someone had recently been inside. The clamps had been removed halfway, leaving a split. Ray ducked in under cover behind his mother, immediately feeling the rain lessen on his body. It was darker here and smelled strongly of warm vinyl. Ray flicked on his headlamp, which glanced off of a sign: *Notice/Aviso* in red, with a date and time when it was safe for re-entry. Over two weeks ago.

Mom squeezed between the stucco and tent vinyl, cupped her hands around her eyes to peer into a window.

"It's too dark," she said. She tried shining her cell phone flashlight inside. "I can't see anything."

Ray felt his phone buzz in his front pocket, knowing it was Cecil. Didn't answer. Instead, as his mother tried another position at the window, he pulled out his pick set and went to work on the door. He dried his fingers off when they slipped off the tensioner tool.

His mother sighed. "I guess you're right. Nobody's here."

Snick.

Ray felt rather than heard it. The rain hitting the vinyl over their heads was thunderous, like a waterfall hitting an umbrella.

He turned the doorknob and swung the back door open into a room void of all light.

40

PESTILENCE SOAKED

"Ray! Close the door!" Alane whisper-shouted, even though nobody could have heard her over the howling wind and rain. Against her better judgment, she joined her son at the threshold to peer inside when he lit it up with his headlamp. Wind snapped the fumigation tent over them like a ship's sail. There was the sound of papers being blown around.

Ray's headlamp beamed over scuffed linoleum floor, revealing two clean squares outlined in dirt and exposed pipes where appliances had been. There was a wire shelf above, caked in detergent and piles of store ads and mail. Papers fluttered to the ground, blown by the wind that gusted in.

"This is the laundry room." Alane spoke in a raised voice to be heard over the storm. She held up her cell phone flashlight, sniffed, and got a faint whiff of chemicals and mostly stale, moldy air. She stepped inside, holding Ray back with an arm, but he ducked under it. *We shouldn't be in here.*

As rain gusted in, she fought the wind to pull the door closed, but once it shut, it was as if woolen, mittened hands closed over her ears, muting everything but her shallow breathing and the soft, distant sound of the storm. She looked around again. The room was bare except for the water heater.

"We used to keep the litter box in here," she said in a hushed voice, shining her cell phone flashlight around. "We had a cat named Squeaky who ripped the drywall up." She laughed softly. "One day, Philip and I painted over it with some leftover paint. We thought we were helping. But it dried a completely different shade, so there were all these off-white streaks on the wall. Our mother was *not* happy."

There was a light switch beside the door, and she flicked it on. Nothing. "Looks like the power's out or it was turned off." The tent snapped outside, gravelly debris pelting the exterior wall from the wind, like someone sandblasting in bursts.

"I don't think anyone's lived here for a while," Ray said, panning his headlight beam over bare, dirty walls, a domed ceiling light with the remains of dead bugs within, the closed door leading to the kitchen. "Were there doors when you lived here?"

Alane's throat closed; it was hard to speak. "Yes."

Taking a deep breath, she put her hand on the knob. A strange, eerie noise like wind shrilling through a corrugated metal pipe sounded through the house. Something clattered overhead. Alane jumped when she felt Ray's hand on her arm.

"Mom." He pulled at her. "I... I think maybe we should go." A minute ago, he'd wanted to see inside. Now, he sounded scared.

Her fingers came away from the knob tacky with some kind of substance. She shined her light on it; black and greasy. "Okay." She nodded, wiping it on her pants. "Okay, we'll go."

Go where *though*?

The hotel. We'll ride out the storm there.

As she turned, her foot scuffed a paper on the floor. Ray's headlamp beam shined down on a white envelope. Something in the arrangement of letters behind the little plastic window on the front made Alane pick it up. Her skin prickled.

The letter was addressed to her at this address.

He's here! Alane's head snapped up.

Carl. He was here! Or *had been* here. Or he was just using the address. That was the likely scenario. Still. She walked to the interior door holding the envelope. She heard Ray say "Mom!" but she was already opening the door to the kitchen.

Her cellphone light illuminated the kitchen. Every cabinet door and drawer hung wide open, like a poltergeist had gone berserk. The fumigation company must have opened everything for the poison to fumigate. Alane doubted any toxin, no matter how potent, could kill the pestilence soaked into every particle of this house.

She panned her flashlight across the grimy laminate countertop, strewn with take-out menus and fast-food containers. The window she had tried to look through a few minutes ago was fogged with grime. She couldn't see out from the tent covering the outside, which gave her a claustrophobic feeling. The sink faucet and hardware were missing. Inside the drawers, in the corners, were discarded egg casings, little piles of what looked like coffee grounds.

Roach shit.

Alane wondered if the generation of roaches they had tried to eradicate this time had origins in the infestation that had begun decades ago with her family. It started with a Friskies cat food box borrowed off the neighbors. Neighbors poorer than them, Carl liked to point out.

She remembered vividly her mother opening the box and dropping it with a horrified gasp. Roaches exploded out of the box when it hit the floor, darting in all directions, vanishing in seconds into tiny crevices Alane didn't even know were there. It wasn't a week later that bugs were everywhere. Clustering behind the appliances, laying egg sacs in the silverware drawer. *Massing*. Alane shuddered.

"Gross," Ray whispered, shining his headlamp over upside down roach corpses littering the floor.

"Don't touch anything," Alane whispered. Sweat trickled down the back of her neck between her shoulder blades. She felt dirty just being in this house.

Ray's headlamp beam spun. "What's that?"

"What?" She froze, instantly alert. It was probably the storm. But then she worried somebody had seen Ray's headlamp. Was it the cops? She listened, not hearing anything at first. Then, a tiny, almost imperceptible squeak. Very faint. Coming from somewhere in the house. Her throat went dry. It came again. Plaintive. Distressed. She grabbed Ray's backpack strap when he brushed by her.

"Don't," she whispered, razer edge of fear in her voice.

"There's an animal in here," he said.

"No! Nothing could be alive! The gas."

Ray escaped her grip, and she hurried after him. First, into the empty dining room. Small, with yellowed walls, nail holes, and a broken sliding glass door boarded up with plywood. As she looked around, Alane pictured the old table and mismatched chairs. Her grandmother's cut crystal candlesticks that, one day, vanished without her mother—without *anyone*—saying a word. Those candlesticks, which had once been so cherished by her mother, were sketched on her mind like tracing paper that when lifted, left behind only faint indentations. All the carpet in here had been pulled up, revealing naked, stained particle board. She and Ray entered a larger front room, where a police officer had once stood after a break-in and asked Alane's mother if they'd just moved in because there was nothing in the room. There was nothing now but a step ladder. Staples and carpet padding scraps scattered around. More food wrappers. Bare front windows. The fumigation tent billowed and snapped against the glass.

"It's coming from outside," Alane whispered, even though she knew no kitten could be alive out in that storm. Because that's what it was. A kitten.

Alane had heard that cry before.

41

BANG

"The family room's through there," Ray's mother whispered to him.

The soles of Ray's sneakers stuck to some tacky substance on the bare wood as he crept after her into an empty room. Two windows, a small half-bath, exposed pipes. No toilet or sink. He checked everywhere. No kitten either. His mother stood at the window to shine her flashlight down between the tent and house wall.

"Anything?" Ray said, coming up to her. His headlamp beam flickered. He tapped the lens with his fingertips, and it brightened.

"No." She held up her phone to light the room. "Must have been the wind." She didn't sound convinced.

The vinyl tenting smacked against the window, and they both jumped.

"Jesus." Mom's hand flew to her chest. "Let's check the other rooms and get out of here."

As they turned to go back into the living room, Ray's phone vibrated in his pocket. When he pulled it out of his pocket, the lit phone screen provided a foggy glow that made him think of submersible headlights deep in the Mariana Trench.

Cecil: where are you

His fingers flew across the buttons. In the house. There's nothing here.

OMG

"Ray!" Mom snapped over the howling wind, making him jump again. "What are you doing?"

"Just answering a text." He slid his phone back in his rear pocket.

"Now?" She gestured impatiently. "Come on."

This house should *not* have been creepy. It wasn't a rundown old mansion or cabin in the woods. It was a regular old, boring house in the suburbs. But Ray did *not* like the look of that pitch-black hallway on the other side of the living room that looked like the opening to a creaky staircase descending into a cellar of horrors. Houses in Florida didn't even have cellars! Unless whoever lived here had carved one into the coral rock below. Ray pictured tunnels with white porous walls and rusty dungeon bars. Scuttling crabs.

Bones.

Something scraped overhead, and they both looked up at the same time.

"What if the storm rips off the roof while we're in here?" Ray said.

"We're safer inside than out." Mom shined her cell light in the direction of the hallway and called, "Hello?"

Her voice, like the light from her phone, seemed to fade out before ever reaching the black-hole-looking hallway. Something about the angle of the hallway walls seemed wrong to Ray. He couldn't tell if the walls were slanted, or if *he* was. The walls didn't even look like walls. They looked flimsy, like cardboard. Like they might suddenly fold in on themselves. The ceiling bubbled down like water pooled up there, and some kind of yellowy substance with a dull shine and black specks covered the floor.

Had the storm caused this? There didn't seem to be any damage to the walls out in the living room or any water coming in. Then Ray smelled it—cloyingly sweet, bitter, caustic—it burned his nose. He grabbed his mom's sleeve.

"Wait!" But no sound came out... or his voice was sucked into that black hallway the way his mother's *hello* had been.

Mom shrugged off his grip and stepped closer like she was in a daze. She lit the hallway with her cell phone light. The hallway seemed to stretch for more than was possible for the house's size before narrowing to a glinting pinprick. He saw her stiffen.

Things lay far inside. Shadowed, oddly flattened-out forms with long and slender limbs. Weird, contorted appendages that looked like the snapped frames of giant wings or spider legs. Ray froze, held his breath, but the figures lay deathly still.

"Do you see that?" his mother said over a gust of rain thrashing the side of the house and roof above.

Ray's pulse pounded in his ears as her light glanced over a work boot on its side. Another boot, upright, a person's foot still in it, ankle broken at an unnatural angle, bone sticking up out of the skin. Like the person fell but their boot stayed stuck to the ground. The top of the sock was black with blood and the hem of the person's jeans.

Dungarees, Papa would call them.

Ray whimpered, backed away.

"Oh, God," his mother said.

"Please let's go!" Ray's voice was the high, frightened sound of a child. "Now. I want to go."

His mother pulled him against her, said, "It's just pictures, baby, that's all." She squeezed him tight. He felt her shaking all over.

Pictures?

But his mother kept talking. "I'm so sorry. I never should have brought you here."

Ray swallowed and braved a look at the hallway over his mother's shoulder. Blinked and looked again. His headlight beam flickered, lit up normal walls. Scuffed drywall. No bodies stuck inside.

No glue.

Was he seeing things? Where were the bodies?! Now, there were just dozens of frames in different sizes covering both walls of the hallway like an art gallery. Ray stepped away from his mother, and he could tell she didn't want to let him go. Part of him didn't want to let her go either, but he had to see for himself if the pictures were real. Because why would there be pictures here when the rest of the house was empty? No one lived here anymore.

This time, he reached around to unzip the main compartment of his backpack for the machete. The wooden grip felt solid in his hands. He held it up in front of him as he stepped cautiously toward the hallway opening. His mother followed close behind, holding the loop of his backpack like she used to when he was little

He stopped short of the threshold, even though the floor looked like a regular floor now, not sticky and crusted with mutant bug parts.

Or dead people.

His mother spoke in his ear. "Do you see them?"

Was that why she'd let him move towards the hallway again, to make sure she wasn't seeing things that weren't there? Were fumigation chemicals still in the air making them hallucinate? He covered his nose with his arm.

"I see them," he said in a muffled voice. "There's a bunch of pictures."

He heard a soft moan from behind and wasn't sure if it was her or the wind. Ray's light hit the first picture, a black and white portrait of a young woman in an old-fashioned looking dress. When he panned his light over it, the woman's eyes didn't follow him. Her features didn't morph into a zombie or skeleton like decorations sold at Halloween. She looked normal and so did all the other family pictures he could see from his vantage point. Because no way was he going in there.

"These shouldn't be here," his mother said, so quietly he almost didn't hear her over the storm.

His light fell on a photograph with a familiar face. He'd seen this picture before but couldn't remember when. Mom showed it to him once. A grainy color picture of her as a kid wearing frilly socks, standing beside a bike.

Why is her picture here?

A shiver went through him, even though the house was hot and stuffy. His headlamp beam flickered again, so rapidly it made the frame look like it was vibrating. He smacked the headlamp lens again, impatiently. The light blinked back on, weaker, but the frame kept shaking.

Ray's mother yanked back so hard on his backpack he stumbled, but not before he saw bugs scatter from under the frame. Roaches. Like the dead ones he'd seen in the kitchen. Only alive. The picture shook on the wall and dropped to the ground with a crash, glass shattering across the floor. Roaches, hundreds of them, big ones too, exploded like a starburst over the wall, surged together and streamed like one organism to hide under the next frame, which shook violently before it, too, fell. BANG!

Glass shattered on the floor. Bugs multiplied by the thousands as they darted from picture to picture, squeezing their mass underneath until the heavy frames crashed, one by one, to the floor with a cascade of breaking glass. The floor sparkled with shards.

A blast of sour warmth hit Ray in the face, like the rotted air trapped inside an old refrigerator. A stench that made him gag. He'd smelled it before, from the hole in his bedroom, only this was more pungent, thicker, almost perceptible in the air. Ray pressed his arm tighter over his nose. Held the useless machete in front of him.

The insects surged over the opposite wall now, back toward Ray and his mother, their bodies forming a writhing shadow spreading over walls, ceiling, and floor, moving as one, releasing what looked like brown pills all over the floor that burst open with more roaches. Some big ones flew above it all, directionless, pinging off the walls. Frames smashed on the ground.

BANG! BANG! BANG!

"Get back," his mother screamed, pulling Ray away. It felt as though he'd stood frozen there for hours, but it had been less than a minute.

They ran as millions of roaches clambered over each other in rolling waves behind them. If Ray fell, would they swallow his body? Devour him alive? His heart felt like it would rupture from his chest.

Reaching the front door, Mom fumbled to unlock the deadbolt, fingers slipping off the metal. Behind them came a sound like dusty leaves rustling, the chittering of countless mouths.

"Hurry, hurry, hurry!" Ray screamed, though, if he weren't so panicked, he would know from watching lots of horror movies this never helps.

The lock turned and Mom shoved the door open only for it to bounce back, blocked by the fumigation tent. Ray's headlamp went dark, and he pounded the lens.

Dead.

42

LOOK WHAT YOU DID

It's not real!

None of this is real!

Alane's fingers slipped off the metal deadbolt lock. The roaches were coming, skittering in a boiling, glistening mass behind her and Ray. She smelled them. Felt the sticky, fetid stink of them cloaking her skin, her hair. She remembered when she was eleven, roaches bursting from the cat food box, scattering around her feet. The insects had multiplied in the shadowed places in the house, colonized every nook and cranny, until there were no nooks and crannies left. Nobody realized how bad the infestation was until one day, playing tag with Philip, he bumped into the wall and knocked a picture down, revealing a cluster of them. A picture that had been taken at a JC Penney portrait center and had yellowed over time from cigarette smoke. A picture that should not be here. In this house.

A tiny part of her brain still capable of rational thought tried to explain it away. Carl had put them up.

But her disaster of a father wasn't here skulking in the nooks and crannies with the bugs. He hadn't been here since the family had moved out—been *kicked* out—decades ago. He'd just used the address—used *her*—for his credit card schemes. Poisoning this place again. Luring her back to this rotten shell of a house.

The lock kept catching on something so it wouldn't turn. How could she have brought Ray here? To everything she wanted to forget. To everything she had tried to protect him from. She banged her shoulder against the front door in desperation to get out. The noise from the insects grew louder. Ray screamed.

They were going to die here.

Not like this, she prayed. *Not like this.*

The lock slid open.

Alane thrust open the door. Fresh air hit her face. The late afternoon sky was clear. The house under construction across the street stared at her with black empty window-eyes.

Alane was so mad. She'd come home after school with Philip, and he'd taken off like he always did to play with his friends down the street, leaving her alone again to straighten the house before Mom came home from work. Why was he always running off leaving her to do everything! It wasn't fair!

"PHILIP!" Her hands tightened into fists.

Tired from school, stomach pinched from hunger, having to step over kittens meowing for food, she had stormed out of the house after seeing the toys he had left on the floor. The fury inside her swelled. Ballooned until it felt too big for her body. She stepped onto the stoop.

"PHILIP!" Her enraged voice carried down the street.

She slammed the door behind her hard. The door bounced back. There was no BANG. No

sound at all as it sprang almost gently back on its hinges.

That was the dreadful part. How quietly it happened.

A tiny kitten, the black one, their favorite, had run after her. Had slipped outside just as the door was closing. The door she'd slammed purposefully, wanting it to splinter, crash, even explode into pieces. The kitten's body slid limply onto the concrete stoop.

Even in this moment, the full impact of what she'd just done could not be entirely absorbed. Even then, her child's brain was erasing the images—like a little broom and dustbin sweeping everything up. I don't want you to see this.

While another voice inside said, look what you did.

Time jumped ahead. She was in her bedroom now with the kitten on her bed, had no memory of picking him up, carrying him there. He lay still on the pink coverlet. He had released his bowels. She knelt on the floor, screaming raggedly, voice gone. She hadn't stopped screaming. Philip would tell her later her screams could be heard all the way down the block. A neighbor came and gently wrapped the kitten in newspaper. Alane never saw the person's face, just their hands. The kitten's paw stuck up from the newspaper. There was a color picture on the paper of islands outlined in bright pink. The work of an artist named Cristo, she'd find out later.

Look what you did.

"Mom!" a voice shouted. But Mom wasn't home, wouldn't be until seven. Had her mother comforted her or was she angry after she got home? She must *have consoled her. But all Alane could remember was her saying, "I guess you won't be slamming any more doors."*

Alane never had.

"MOM!"

Alane's head slowly cleared. She found herself kneeling on the hard floor, and she looked around in the dark. She saw Ray's terrified face in the glow of his phone flashlight.

"Mom!" he shouted.

"Here," she said, picking up her phone off the floor with the flashlight still on. "Are you okay?" The tent flapped outside the window.

"You left me!" he yelled over the howling wind; it sounded right over their heads. "You opened the door, but the tent was there, and we couldn't get out and then the roaches scattered and disappeared and you left me."

Standing unsteadily, Alane realized they were in her childhood bedroom. She swayed slightly as the frightening events of the last hour flooded back. Oh my god. "Baby, I'm so sorry," she hugged him to her. "I didn't mean to leave you. I don't know what happened."

It wasn't true. She remembered everything now. How she'd blamed Palmetto Boy for the kitten's death because it was easier than living with what she had done. How she'd convinced herself, and then her little brother, that an imaginary monster was responsible for everything bad that happened in this house.

She hugged Ray tighter.

I was just a kid. A fucking kid.

Ray twisted away. "We have to GO!"

Alane sucked in a breath and glanced around at the empty bedroom. *Okay. Okay.*

"Listen to me." She made Ray look at her. "We're going to get out of here. We're going back to the laundry room. Give me the machete." A violent gust of wind shook the house, and the fumigation tent smacked the bedroom window so hard Alane was surprised it didn't shatter. She gripped the blade. "Stay behind me."

As they crept toward the open doorway, she felt Ray's hands clutch the back of her shirt. At the threshold, she looked over her shoulder at her old bedroom. Could traumatic events leave psychic imprints on a place, like an echo replaying itself over and over? Had the people who'd lived here after her family seen or felt strange things? Did they see shadows in the dark? Did they hear doors slamming on their own?

If this house wasn't haunted before we moved in, it is now, because of us.

Because of me.

Alane led Ray into the hall, expecting to step on glass from the broken family pictures. But the floor was clear, the walls bare. They tiptoed down the hall in a bubble of light from Alane's phone. The edge of the hallway could have dropped off into an abyss for all she could tell, it was so dark beyond her flashlight beam. There was maybe the impression of walls. The house creaked and groaned from the battering wind.

Alane froze. Something had shifted in the dark ahead, something that slipped back into the shadows so smoothly she couldn't be sure she'd actually seen it.

"Shhh," she said to Ray, even though he could not have heard her over the wind. She pointed her light ahead of them, illuminating a wedge of living room floor, the stepladder.

Again. The faintest movement, outside the flashlight's glow. An animal taking shelter from the storm, she told herself. Flat to the ground. Something more afraid of them than they were of it.

Except.

A chill ran down Alane's spine.

It's not afraid.

She put out a hand to shield Ray. The thing that had chased them out of their apartment was here.

Followed them somehow.

Palmetto Boy.

43

SPLINTERED

"Go back, go back!" Ray's mother yelled, pushing him ahead of her.

Glass shattered. Ray's ears popped as the bedroom door they had just exited slammed with deafening force.

"What's going on?" he shouted, his voice drowned out by the shrieking wind behind the closed door. The window must have blown out, the vinyl acting like a stopper and creating a vacuum. Ray dashed to the next door a few steps away, maybe a bathroom, phone vibrating in his hand from Cecil texting or him shaking. The knob turned, but the door wouldn't budge. Locked or jammed.

Mom shoved him again. "Keep going!"

Go where?! They were almost to the end of the hallway. There were two closed doors left across from each other. Mom's cell phone flashlight beam bounced up and down as she ran after him. Ray's heart pounded in his ears. Every shadow looked like it was alive, ready to spring. He tried the door on the right, threw his shoulder against it, while Mom banged with her fist. Jammed too. Ray glanced behind his mother. A big shadow moved along the wall. Darted erratically. He saw the impression of legs, segmented appendages whipping the air. Heard a clicking sound, like bones on strings in gale force winds.

Palmetto Boy. Ray's insides seemed to dissolve to liquid. He squeezed his eyes shut. If he didn't look, maybe it would disappear like the bugs had. *Go away, please go away.*

Mom grabbed him and pushed him inside a bedroom on the other side. Shut and locked the door behind them. No deadbolt to protect them, just a button Ray could pop in seconds with the end of a paperclip. She braced against the door, breathing hard and motioned to an open closet. "Quick! In there!"

The bedroom wasn't much bigger than the other one, but the distance to the closet seemed as far as the length of a school gymnasium. The floor was bare plywood, the air dusty. Loose metal nails rolled underfoot, making his steps unsteady. There were two windows, unbroken, covered in tenting like the rest. He flashed his phone light around the small walk-in. Empty, no rods even. Mom appeared and slammed the door. She shone her light around at an attic panel like the one in their apartment. Ray shrank back. *Uh-uh. Nope.*

A heavy thud shook the bedroom door outside. More thuds, in rapid succession, as if the creature were throwing its body against it. Ray's and his mother's eyes met. She put the machete down, stood under the attic panel, and linked her fingers together for a foothold.

Come on, she signaled with her chin.

He shook his head, flattened against the wall. No way was he going up there. Not after what happened to Papa Wessel. Palmetto Boy probably lived up there.

But a new sound came from outside in the hall now. A harsh scraping, like when Papa Wessel stripped paint from a board.

Chewing. The monster was chewing its way in!

Ray dropped his backpack onto the floor and shoved his phone in his pocket. He put a sneaker in Mom's hands so she could hoist him up. He felt her arms shaking. He put his palms against the thin wooden panel to lift it, felt resistance, and pushed harder. The panel sailed out of his hands into the attic. Rain pelted his face. Wind flattened his hair against his skull.

"There's a hole in the roof," he yelled down, hanging to the frame with both hands. Something bounced off his cheek, something squashy and papery like a wasp's nest and was carried off by the wind. Mom dropped him down. Rain cascaded into the closet. They looked at each other, out of breath, as the chewing on the bedroom door outside intensified.

Mom yelled to be heard: "I'm going to cut through the tent with the machete. Stay here. Do *not* move."

"No!" He reached to stop her.

"I'll be right back." Her eyes glinted in the darkness. "I promise. Now keep back."

She picked the machete up off the floor, and with a last look at him, she left and shut the closet door behind her.

Ray retreated to a corner and sat down, hands over his ears, rain and wind blowing in from the attic. What if she didn't come back? What if the monster got in? The wall he was sitting against shook from the battering wind, Palmetto Boy's relentless chewing just one more noise in the clamor of sideways rain, sudden gusts, and the crashes of flying debris striking the house.

I thought fumigation was supposed to kill everything in here!

The roaches though, a voice inside countered.

Those weren't real!

His phone buzzed, and he dug it from his pocket. Texts from Cecil, each one more panicky than the last.

Ray answer!

I'm here, he typed. The letters blurred from sudden tears. We're trapped in the house. My mom—

He couldn't finish. He called Cecil instead, and she answered after the first ring.

"Ray! Where are you?"

He hunched over the phone, straining to hear her voice. "In the house! In a closet!" He rushed to fill her in, talking so fast she kept yelling at him. *Slow down, wait, I can't hear you.*

"My mom's out there!" he said. "I don't know what to do."

"Ray. Listen to me." Cecil's voice shouted in his ear. "I need you to calm down. Tell me about the creature. What did you observe?"

"Observe! I don't know." His voice caught on a sob.

"It's important Ray. Think!"

He dragged in a breath. "Okay, it... it had a bunch of legs... it made a weird sound."

"Weird how?"

"I don't know! Weird."

"Did you actually *see* it? Talk to me."

"It was too dark. It kept away from the light."

Silence.

"Cecil?" Ray cried.

"I'm here. Listen. I was right. It doesn't like the light. It's afraid of it, or light hurts it. I was right."

"I can't turn on the lights, there's no power."

"You have your phone?"

"It's not bright enough."

"Make it brighter in settings. You need to be—"

The phone went dead. "Cecil!" he screamed. "CECIL!" He called her back and got an *all circuits* are busy message.

He stared at the dark screen for a second then quickly opened his phone settings; he saw where Cecil said he could make the flashlight stronger. The beam brightened a tiny degree. *This isn't going to work.*

The phone vibrated with a text: Remember how you went after this thing before with the knife

Be ready with the light if it gets in

Ray blew out a breath and ripped off his headlamp. Switched OFF/ON. OFF/ON. Banged the lens on one knee. Nothing. He rummaged for a lock pick in his backpack to pry open the battery compartment, rain dripping into his eyes. His heart pounded. Outside, wind and rain thrashed the house. He popped out the batteries. Replaced them in a different order—a trick Papa Wessel taught him to "get that last little charge out of them"—and closed the cover. A sudden glare of light blinded him a second before his eyes adjusted.

He got shakily to his feet and held the phone up like a shield. Closed his eyes before turning the closet doorknob. Five... four... three...

The knob shuddered once under his fingers, the door and floor reverberating, as if the very foundation of the house had taken a blow. A crash came from outside in the bedroom.

Ray heard his mother scream.

44

YOUR MONSTER

After Alane had shut her son inside the closet, she swept her phone light around the empty room and at the door. At that, the chewing intensified, as if Palmetto Boy knew she was there. As if it could *smell* her.

We need to get out!

Rushing to the window, she kicked something. Trash, probably left by a worker. Something about the shape, the way it was tightly twisted, seemed familiar. *Looks like a unicorn horn*. Stupid to think that right now, but it came with a wispy memory of herself as a girl, wringing a paper lunch bag into just this shape. She picked up the bag without thinking. Wind slammed the tent into the window and rattled the glass.

The paper was light and brittle in her fingers, like it might crumble to dust. There was something loose inside. Her chest fluttered with an emotion that had nothing to do with fear.

Trembling, she wedged the machete under her arm and juggled her phone to untwist and shake the bag open over her palm. A ring dropped into her hand. Glinted.

Grandma's ring.

How?

Tears sprung to her eyes. Once so big she could only wear it on her thumb, the ring fit snuggly on her middle finger. She held it to the light, a watery blur of gold in her eyes, and let out an astonished laugh of pure joy. This seemed to agitate the monster; it chewed with an almost crazed savagery.

Startled back to her present frightening reality, Alane ran to the window with the machete, shoving her phone in a pocket to unlock and push the window up. Humid, vinyl-smelling air rushed in. She stabbed the tent fabric, sawing at the thick fibrous material.

It was all coming back now, the day she had arrived home with Philip after school to find the house broken into, their toys strewn across the living room floor. She'd gone to her room, opened the green velvet box, and felt lightheaded with relief when Grandma's ring was there.

Alane didn't have the words then to understand why she'd slipped it into her pocket and told her mother it was stolen. But a cruel part of her wanted to see her mother's eyes when she heard. Because her mother *knew*. She knew her own husband likely had taken it. She had thought it safer with Alane than with her. Because what father could steal from his own child?

I want you to have it. Put it somewhere safe.

After school the next day, when Philip was at a friend's, Alane had twisted the ring inside a paper lunch bag until it was coiled like a shriveled-up brown unicorn horn and dragged a chair into her parents' closet. She stood on tiptoes to slide the attic panel and hide the ring up there. Right over Carl Jannell's head. Where it would remain all these years. Safe. Forgotten even by her, her mind constructing a false memory, a sort of failsafe lock of her own making, so she would only ever remember finding the empty ring box.

The bag must have blown out of the attic when Ray opened the panel.

A splintering noise came behind her. She swung her light at the door. A black talon poked through a ragged gash and began clawing at the wood to widen the hole.

Terrified, Alane dropped the phone to slash at the tent vinyl. The room darkened, just a faint smudge of light under the phone where it had landed face up. It was taking her too long to cut through the tough material. *Come on, come on*! She caught a tantalizing glimpse of houses across the street through the slit in the vinyl and felt cool rain on her face. She would never cut the hole big enough in time!

"RAY!" she screamed, uncertain if she was calling him or just howling her anguish. All the defenses and rituals she had performed to keep her child safe... taking down doors, stockpiling food.... none of it had made any difference. She had done everything to erase her past. *Nothing Happened, Nothing Happened, NH, NH*. Yet here it was, chewing its way in to get to her.

They were going to die here. She would never be free of this place.

Grandmother's ring pinched her skin as she chopped desperately with the machete. She still could not believe she'd found it, was so proud of eleven-year-old Alane for hiding it. Brave girl! She'd done what she had to do to control her own story, lied as shamelessly as her father did to protect her most prized possession. Invented a monster to blame for the breakdown of her family—for what happened to the kitten. Convinced her little brother Palmetto Boy was real until she even came to believe it herself. In doing so, she had protected the child she was and the woman she would grow to be.

In many ways, Alane felt more afraid as an adult and mother than she'd ever felt as a kid, even living here.

This is your monster. Alane slashed at the shredded vinyl, sweat and tears dripping down her face. *You brought it here. Brought it to Ray.*

The bedroom door behind her exploded into splinters. She screamed and cowered by the window as Palmetto Boy glided into the room in the way of creatures with too many legs. A low shape in the dark, the meager light from her phone gave it vague form. Skeletal limbs with saw-toothed edges, the suggestion of outspread claws, a sloped back with a leathery sheen.

It smelled of dirty crevices; clothes left too long in the washer. Neglect.

Alane got to her feet, making a fist around her grandmother's ring, and raised the machete. The blade felt like it would leap out of her hand from shaking. "Go away!" she yelled.

The creature halted and lifted its back in the air in a menacing, almost insectoid stance. A bony, chittering sound came from it that Alane sensed more than heard over the roar of the storm. Eel-like feelers lashed and rippled above.

Was this nightmare from her eleven-year-old imagination? A grotesque amalgamation of every Florida bug that had given her a full body shudder, every scary shadow at night, every alien creature she had seen on TV? This King of Creepy-Crawlies?

Alane jumped back when a section of ceiling collapsed, narrowly missing her. Rain drove in. The attic beams holding the damaged roof creaked and groaned under the onslaught of the wind. She had to get Ray out of here.

We're not dying in this fucking house!

"GET BACK!" She pointed the blade at Palmetto Boy.

She couldn't tell if the monster was slyly advancing or if she was imagining it. She slid along the wall with wet hair in her face, trying to lead it from the closet. The creature turned with her, tracking her movements. *That's right, that's right.* At least its attention would be on her so Ray could escape.

She was pulling in a breath to shout for Ray to run for it when the closet door banged open. Ray's headlamp lit the room making her squint.

"Ray!" She moved between her son and Palmetto Boy. "Stay back!"

But the creature had already retreated into the dark hallway.

"It's afraid of the light," Ray shouted. "Use your phone!"

"How do you know that?" she shouted back when she could catch her breath. She grabbed her phone off the floor with the flashlight still on and met Ray at the doorway, lighting up a section of the hallway. "You were supposed to stay in the closet!"

The hall, what they could see in the glow, was empty, but when Ray took a step, she grabbed his shoulder. "No! It's still out there."

"It won't come near us, not if we stay in the light."

Alane didn't have time to argue with him. A surge of wind blasted the house, sounding like an oncoming train. Rain strafed the exterior walls in whistling gusts. Something snapped above, attic beams cracking under the strain. Alane threw her hands over her head as more ceiling came down. Her ears filled with the deafening sound of howling wind, breaking glass, and twisting metal. "The roof is going!"

She ran after Ray in a crouch, holding her phone light up. "The laundry room!"

Their light beams bounced and overlapped like chaotic Venn diagrams down the hallway. Just beyond the edge of light, she could see the shadow of Palmetto Boy hovering. It scurried up a dark section of wall. Over their heads. The thing was trying to get behind them where it was dark and unprotected.

"Ray, watch out!" Alane spun with the machete, sweeping her light behind them. Nothing. It was as if the thing had vanished. Gasping, she barked, "Run to the laundry room. Go!"

"Mom!"

"GO!"

She kept her light on her son until he was out of sight around the corner, then turned in circles, brandishing her machete and light. "Where are you?" Did it get around her to go after Ray?

Swirling rain reflected in the beam of light from her phone. She thought she saw movement, a glimmer in the dark. Like dulled armor. Palmetto Boy circling her.

"Come on!" She felt almost euphoric with rage. "What are you waiting for?"

It's afraid of the light. Ray's words came back to her.

She had to end this now, or Ray would never be safe. She had created this thing; it was up to her to un-create it. *What are you doing?* she asked herself as she swiped her shaking phone screen, hovering her thumb over the flashlight icon. *You are out of your damn mind.* She drew in a shaky breath and tapped the light OFF.

The hallway plunged into darkness. Crashing sounds of the house being ripped to pieces were amplified in the dark. She prayed Ray had gotten out, run to the neighbor's. He was a smart kid.

Come on. Come on. I'm dead if I don't go now.

Something slammed her from behind, knocking her down. The phone flew out of her hand. The machete skittered across the floor. Did the ceiling collapse? Then she smelled it. A gassy, fusty smell. Damp rot. Infestation. Something beat the air over her head. *Oh God.* She kicked out, foot glancing off something alive behind her. Scrabbling for the machete, she waited to feel claws rake the flesh of her back. Branch-like legs with pointed ends planted themselves on either side of her head. Not legs exactly, some kind of extremities, like leather stretched over long bones. They looked fragile, as if a hard kick would snap them, and were fringed with lethally sharp spines, like serrated knives.

She felt the lightest brush against her hair and jerked away. Something cold and rubbery stroked her skull, the curve of her face. Another tapered appendage curled delicately under her chin. Warm, foul-smelling liquid dripped on her cheek. She heard a kind of alien chirping sound; pictured bristly mouthparts rubbing over her head. She scrambled on elbows and knees for the machete. Stretched for it, touched it with the tips of her fingers. Caught a glance behind her of features that should not have existed at that large of a scale: segmented abdomen, elongated stinger.

The machete grip escaped her grasping fingers. *Please, please.* She felt the creature lower over her, unearthly chirping growing louder in her ears. Could almost picture the stinger curving to strike.

Light suddenly encircled her. Palmetto Boy recoiled, and Alane got her fingers around the machete handle. In one movement, she twisted at the waist, with her arm and blade outstretched, and sliced at the air above her. A severed appendage landed beside her with a meaty thud, spewing black fluid and writhing. Palmetto Boy made a shrill distressed noise. Even in the light from Ray's headlamp, Alane's brain struggled to comprehend the monstrous creature before her, raising itself to strike—or flee, she couldn't tell which.

It wasn't going to escape again. Past thinking, she ran at it, lifting the machete with both hands over her head and swung down as hard as she could. Watery black liquid sprayed her face and clothes as the blade sunk into what she thought was its head. Distorted, almost blurred, the monster's features seemed unformed, as if the little girl who had imagined it into being had not completely visualized a face beyond grippers for a mouth and rows of fangs. Eyes. Eyes Alane wished she hadn't looked into just now.

Milky blue, human, hungry.

Palmetto Boy was *starving*.

"Kill it!" Ray's voice broke through Alane's shock. The creature was hurt. Confused. Its remaining tentacle-thing flailed in the air.

Alane lopped it off with a broad swing, and screaming her rage, stabbed and hacked until Palmetto Boy was on the ground, sticky black blood spreading around it. Until Ray had to pull her away to make her stop. She stood over the dead creature, chest heaving, machete limp in her hand.

"We have to go!" Ray said, yanking her after him, past the motionless and bloodied body.

Alane had forgotten all about the storm, which had sheared off a portion of the roof and living room ceiling, leaving a large hole open to the air, so that she and Ray had to sprint through torrential rain and wind to the kitchen. Ray tore open the door to the laundry room. Thank God, it was still under cover.

The pair huddled in the corner, heads down, as the back door bowed with the pressure of the wind and the walls shook.

"It's okay, baby." Alane rocked her son in her arms. "It's going to be okay."

45

LATEST INVESTIGATION, WITH PROOF

TWO MONTHS LATER

Ray stared at the garage apartment as his mother pulled into the Wessels' driveway.

"Are you sure you want to do this?" she asked, a worried look on her face.

"Yeah." Ray nodded.

"Okay." She nodded back. "I'll be back at four and bring dinner."

"Cool."

Ray closed the car door, shouldering his backpack, and waved as she pulled out of the drive.

Mrs. Wessel had left the door to the garage unlocked for him, and he stepped inside. First, with a look over his shoulder in case Mrs. Wessel was at the door, he crouched to pick open the locked cabinet, slid the machete out of his backpack, and replaced it on the shelf inside. His gaze fell on the glue traps. After a brief hesitation, he grabbed the whole box, zipped it up in his backpack, and locked the cabinet again. Ray thought that Papa might not be mad if he threw the glue traps away. Because wherever Papa was now, he must know how cruel they were and could see into Ray's heart and understand.

The bench slats and armrests lay where Ray and Papa had arranged them, on an old sheet on the floor, ready for assembly. Ray hit the garage door button, and the door creaked open, letting in light and fresh air. He turned on Papa's radio, leaving it on the last station Papa had tuned it to—classic rock—and took down the tools he needed from the pegboard. The burn bandage was gone now, just a long brownish scar on his arm. Doctor said it would fade in time.

After Papa's death, Ray had made a promise to himself to come back and finish the bench for Mrs. Wessel. So, now he began to carefully assemble the frame, losing track of time as he bolted the pieces together. He almost felt Papa there guiding him. A quiet presence, watching him work, offering an occasional grunt of approval. He liked this Papa. Not the one who haunted his dreams; the one lying above him in the attic with a look of horror frozen on his face. Ray threaded a heavy screw through a slat hole and tightened the bolt, wiping his forehead on his sleeve.

Papa's was the first funeral Ray had ever been to. It had made him feel all kinds of ways: sad, of course; curious; haunted by what his old friend looked like inside the gleaming wood casket, something Papa could have made himself. Maybe he had. Mom had said later that he'd looked peaceful and "gentlemanly" in his suit after she'd gone to the visitation. Strange to call it that, a visit to see a body. Just the idea of seeing Papa dead had made him tremble all over. Now he regretted a little not going. Papa wouldn't have thought that was brave, but maybe he wouldn't have minded. Mom had understood when Ray said he didn't want to go, said, gently, "Papa wouldn't have wanted you to think he was scary."

Ray had gone to the graveside service. The sky was bright blue, like Hurricane Rose had scrubbed all the dirt away, leaving it clean and clear. The grave was under a tree, away from the road. Most of the people attending were old, all standing in a protective cluster around Mrs. Wessel, who looked pale and frail. Next to Ray, his mother cried silently, wiping her eyes with a balled-up tissue. At the Wessel house after, she'd helped lay out platters of food for the small reception as people took turns talking in quiet tones to Mrs. Wessel on her couch. There seemed to be a force field around Papa's recliner. No one sat in it or even seemed to want to look at it. Ray had drifted outside, stared up at the darkened apartment, feeling hot and itchy in his nice shirt and tie, which his mother had bought the day before and didn't have time to wash, so it still had the creases where it had been folded in the package.

Mrs. Wessel came into the garage around lunch with a peanut butter and jelly sandwich, a banana, a few generic sodas, and ice for the old metal cooler. Ray was drinking one and sitting on the completed bench, which was only a *little* wobbly, when Mom pulled up a little after four.

"Wow, great job!" she said, as she always said for any little thing he did since he was, like, a baby.

Together, they carried the bench to the patio, Mrs. Wessel directing where exactly to place it. Then Mrs. Wessel sat on it, eyes brimming.

"It's beautiful, Ray. Papa would be proud."

Ray looked down, blinking.

After that, they ate KFC on the little patio table, and Mrs. Wessel told a story about Papa Wessel renovating a bathroom after they were married. Papa got his measurements wrong, and the bathroom door hit the toilet so nobody could use it. "He had to start all over again," Mrs. Wessel remembered, laughing with tears rolling down her cheeks.

The story made Ray think of what Papa Wessel had said once about his father, about how he would make Papa as a boy do things over if they weren't done right the first time. How Papa had become *exacting*, like his dad.

After everything that happened the night of the storm, Ray and his mom ended up staying with Mrs. Wessel at her insistence in the big house until Mom rented a new apartment with money Uncle Philip sent. Philip and Mom had talked several times over the phone since that night of the hurricane. She cried a lot during these conversations, but they were "good tears" she'd told Ray so he wouldn't worry. Mom had explained to Ray that she and Uncle Philip had pressed charges against their father for stealing their identities.

"I'd always wanted you to have a neutral feeling toward your grandfather," she had told Ray in the car coming home the night of the storm, "not that he even deserved that. But if you couldn't have a decent grandfather in your life, at least you could have the idea of one that wasn't harmful."

After they finished dinner, Mom helped clean up, and told Mrs. Wessel, "I'll be by later in the week." She'd made a routine of shopping for a few things for Mrs. Wessel and checking on her every Thursday afternoon since her daughter had gone back home. Sometimes, Ray went with her. One day, Mrs. Wessel asked him to haul black trash bags up to the apartment. He'd felt funny climbing the stairs to the old apartment. It was locked, but Mrs. Wessel had given him the key. More trash bags and some boxes sat right by the door, as if they'd been shoved inside quickly. Feeling like he was peeking into something he shouldn't, he opened one of the bags. His throat tightened when he saw the golf shirts and dungarees that had belonged to Papa. His daughter must have cleared some things out of the house so they wouldn't make Mrs. Wessel sad.

After retying the bag, Ray high-stepped over the boxes. The rest of the apartment was empty and already smelled musty and damp.

The drapes were still over the doors but swept aside. He stood in the doorway to his room, his gaze going immediately to the ceiling corner. The hole was no larger, the ragged marks around it dry. There was nothing alive up there anymore.

He didn't know what Mrs. Wessel would be doing with the apartment now. It seemed weird to rent it to anyone after what had happened to her husband. He shoved that thought out of his head before it could take a turn to his nightmare imaginings. His mother's old room was lit with a wedge of sunlight. The closet was empty, the ceiling panel in place. He stared up at it for a moment then left.

The morning after the hurricane moved off, Ray and his mother had opened the laundry room door of her childhood home to a strange, apocalyptic landscape outside. The sky was tinged with green, yet it seemed glaringly bright because the trees for as far as they could see had been flattened, stripped of leaves. They had stepped out cautiously, teetering on pits of soggy, broken drywall and downed chain link fence, shoes crunching on broken glass. Ray had felt Alane's hand heavy on his shoulder and didn't know if she was using him as a support or giving him comfort. Ray looked up to see what was left of the house. Shredded vinyl tenting, like a tattered, abandoned big top circus tent gently flapping in the breeze that smelled fresh and clean. Most of the roof had been torn away except over the kitchen and—luckily for them—the laundry room. They would learn later that the storm had spawned tornadoes, which destroyed some homes while leaving others almost completely untouched.

Ray felt relief that the house was leveled. Whatever evil lived there was now gone. Other than some plant debris stuck on the car with rainwater, it seemed undamaged. The street was littered with palm fronds, limbs, and wood scraps. He opened the car passenger door, glancing behind him at the house. He could see the full destruction. Alane stared for a long time at the collapsed facade.

"Okay, I'm ready," she'd said.

Their new apartment was in an older complex a few miles from Alane's school. This place had doors, and for now, it seemed Ray's mom was fine with keeping them up.

School was getting better. He was slowly making some friends. As always happens, the next drama overtook his theft of the magnesium ribbon, and though he would always feel awkward around Allie, no one ever mentioned him stealing to his face, so he didn't think she ever told anyone, and he would always think she was cool for that.

With Ray's help, Cecil had made a special page on her website for Palmetto Boy. Ray honestly doubted it would show up to terrify anyone else. It was Mom's and Uncle Philip's monster. But Ray worked with Cecil on her investigation summary "with PROOF." Ray tried hard to describe Palmetto Boy for her—the shadowy impression of it, the whipping appendages, the glitchy way it moved. She'd really wanted to know what it looked like dead, what he'd seen after his mother had killed it. Cecil wasn't too happy with his, "I didn't see anything; it was too dark." It was too dark because when Mom had taken his hand and told him, "Close your eyes, baby," he'd closed them and followed her like a trusting little kid and didn't open his eyes again until they were back in the laundry room.

From what descriptions he *had* given her, Cecil had sketched a rendering of Palmetto Boy that was pretty sick. A sort of alien cave cricket with fangs dripping venom. It looked nothing like Ray remembered, though he couldn't say exactly why. Anyway, Ray had buried those memories of what he'd seen—or *thought* he'd seen—in a box locked with a hundred unpickable padlocks.

Cecil had invited Ray to join her as a full partner in her monster slaying business, but Ray had had enough of monsters.

I'll be your consultant, he'd texted her.

Oh ho! She'd texted back with a smiley face emoji.

Sometimes, Ray woke up in cold sweat at night, not really remembering what had caused his heart to beat thunderously, just the feeling that there had been something hungry and monstrous pursuing him.

One day, not long after they'd moved in and his mother was out of the apartment, he'd dragged a step stool into the hallway under the attic panel, and climbed up it to carefully slide the panel to the side, closing his eyes to keep dust out of them.

Tottering on the stool, breath caught in his throat, he raised his shaking flashlight and panned it around. Just bare wood beams and pink insulation.

But just there, a spot where the insulation had been disturbed, heaped up, like it had been burrowed into. He reached for a wrinkled paper lunch bag rolled into a cylinder, opened it carefully, and pulled out an old velvet ring box, Great-Grandmother's ring glinting inside.

Author's Note

Palmetto Boy was inspired by my childhood living with a compulsive gambler and the food insecurity my family experienced.

Families can be in financial crisis for all kinds of reasons: physical or mental illness, addiction, job loss, neglect, abuse. We don't know what a child might be going through at home. Providing free nutritious meals at school for all students regardless of income is such a simple way to support every child. Several states have made lunches free for all public school students, and I'm hopeful more will follow their lead.

A percentage of proceeds I receive from the sale of this book will be donated to local and national organizations working to end childhood hunger and to eliminate school lunch debt.

For gambling addiction help, go to https://www.Ncpgambling.org

24-Hour Helpline: 1-800-522-4700 or 1-800-GAMBLER

Acknowledgements

Lifelong dreams can sometimes take a good part of a life to come true. I'm 58, and this is my debut novel.

Massive thanks to Timber Ghost Press and Sylvia Langille for taking a chance on this story and helping make the dream of seeing my work in print a reality. I'm so grateful to Beverly Bernard for her thoughtful, skillful editing, and to Greg Chapman for designing a cover that feels so right for this story. Thank you!

To my agent, Tricia Skinner, you've believed in me every step of the way. I'm so grateful for your support, encouragement, and friendship.

Nick Bruner and John Stipa, your feedback on early drafts was invaluable. Thank you!

A special thanks to Ted Loht for revealing the chemicals that might be locked away in a middle school science classroom and to Allie Loht for sharing her insight as a school counselor. Any mistakes are entirely my own.

To Melinda "Mindy" Prause, my bestie from elementary school. I've never forgotten how you shared your lunch with me when I didn't have any. Thank you, my friend.

I'm forever grateful to my friends and family who have cheered me on and believed in me from the beginning. Love also to my dog, Scout, who kept me company as I wrote.

Steve, Nick and Henry, you are my everything. I love you.

ABOUT THE AUTHOR

D. A. Jobe's short fiction appears in *Found 2: More Stories of Found Footage Horror*, *Monstrous Futures: A Sci-Fi Horror Anthology*, and *Bodies Full of Burning: An Anthology of Menopause-themed Horror*. *Palmetto Boy* is her debut novel.

Website: dajobeauthor.wordpress.com

Bluesky: @d-a-jobe.bsky.social

A Note from Timber Ghost Press

If you enjoyed *Palmetto Boy*, please consider leaving a review on Amazon or Goodreads. Reviews help the authors and the press.

If you go to www.timberghostpress.com you can sign up for our newsletter so you can stay up-to-date on all our upcoming titles, plus you'll get informed of new horror flash fiction and poetry featured on our site monthly.

Take care and thanks for reading *Palmetto Boy!*

-Timber Ghost Press

www.ingramcontent.com/pod-product-compliance
Lightning Source LLC
LaVergne TN
LVHW020708110826
845149LV00012B/2153
9798992576733